HAUNTING PERFORMANCES FROM BEYOND THE GRAVE . . .

As the house lights dim and the first ghostly notes of the overture cast their spell over an audience held captive by chilling dramas that will live on long after the final curtain call, it's time to take your seat in this theater of the horrific. Among the acts on tonight's playbill are:

"The Phantom of the Soap Opera"—It began with seemingly harmless pranks on the set of one of the top New York soap operas, but harmless soon became harmful when the Phantom wrote a new script entitled *Revenge!*

"Dark Muse"—When he played the music it worked its magic on all who heard it. But when he sought the mysterious composer who had given him this gift of beauty it led him to horror beyond imagining. . . .

"Comfort the Lonely Light"—The ring had been a gift he could not refuse, but he never would have accepted it had he known the evil that would haunt him from the moment he put it on. . . .

PHANTOMS

Other blood-freezing DAW Horror Anthologies:

VAMPS *Edited by Martin H. Greenberg and Charles G. Waugh.* Terrifying tales of those irresistible ladies of the night—vampires!

HOUSE SHUDDERS *Edited by Martin H. Greenberg and Charles G. Waugh.* Fiendish chillers about haunted houses.

HUNGER FOR HORROR *Edited by Robert Adams, Martin H. Greenberg and Pamela Crippen Adams.* A devilish stew from the master chefs of horror.

RED JACK *Edited by Martin H. Greenberg, Charles G. Waugh and Frank D. McSherry, Jr.* The 100th anniversary collection of Jack the Ripper tales.

Phantoms

EDITED BY

MARTIN H. GREENBERG &
ROSALIND M. GREENBERG

DAW BOOKS, INC.
DONALD A. WOLLHEIM, PUBLISHER

Why the Phantom? © 1989 by Isaac Asimov.

The Opera of the Phantom © 1989 by Edward Wellen.

The Phantom of the Soap Opera © 1989 by Henry Slesar.

The Other Phantom © 1989 by Edward D. Hoch.

Dark Muse © 1989 by Daniel Ransom.

Too Hideous to Be Played © 1989 by J. N. Williamson.

The Final Threshold © 1989 by K. Marie Ramsland.

Marian's Song © 1989 by James Kisner.

The Light of Her Smile © 1989 by Karen Haber.

Time-Tracker © 1989 by Barry N. Malzberg.

Dark Angel © 1989 by Gary Alan Ruse.

The Unmasking © 1989 by Steve Rasnic Tem.

The Grotto © 1989 by Thomas Millstead.

Comfort the Lonely Light © 1989 by Gary A. Braunbeck.

DAW Book Collectors No. 778.

First Printing, April, 1989

2   3   4   5   6   7   8   9

Printed in Canada
Cover Printed in U.S.A.

To Gaston Leroux, thanks for the memories. . . .

CONTENTS

WHY THE PHANTOM?

by Isaac Asimov

Gaston Leroux (1868–1927) was a French writer of mystery stories, with a tinge of horror, in the first quarter of the twentieth century. His stories are, however, gone and forgotten now, even though a couple were reprinted, in English translation, in *Weird Tales*.

Except one!

It was Leroux who wrote *The Phantom of the Opera* and there are few who haven't heard of it. It is the tale of a malevolent psychopath named Erik, who dwelt in the subterranean depths of the Paris Opera and who hid his deformed face behind a mask. He was obsessed with love for a beautiful young singer, Christine, and in that love was the possibility of redemption. But, as you might suspect, the beautiful young singer loved a handsome young man and didn't feel it her business to redeem monsters. So the story ends tragically, and not without considerable sympathy for the Phantom.

Those who know the story are not likely to know it from the book, but from the three motion pictures that were made of it. The first, and by far the best, was a silent in 1925 that featured Lon Chaney as the Phantom. Then there was one in 1943 with Claude Rains as the Phantom and a British version in 1962 with Herbert Lom as the Phantom.

The three versions have great differences, but in one respect they are alike, and must be. There is no way of omitting the climactic moment, when the young lady, who is treated with love and kindness in the Phantom's lair, is overcome by curiosity. She approaches stealthily while the Phantom is absorbed in his music, and while the audience's hearts all but stop, for we know she intends to remove the mask. And, in a flashing movement, she does so, and the face of the monster is revealed in all its gruesomeness. I saw the silent Phantom when I was five or six years old and the moment when Chaney's face was revealed burnt itself into my soul so that I still remember the horror of it.

But what does it all mean? In one way, *The Phantom of the Opera* is a ghost story, for the Phantom is an elusive magician, always, till the very end, a step ahead of those who oppose him. He comes and goes unpredictably, as, in the second most effective scene, when he saws through the support of the great chandelier and allows it to fall on the audience. (I have never liked to sit beneath a chandelier since.)

It also has the thrill of a revenge story, for the Phantom (a point made more clearly in some versions than in others) has been mistreated, or has been cast out for his loathsome appearance, and wants revenge on the world. (And who among us has not felt mistreated at times, and unfairly put upon, and has not longed to show them all.)

And it has the pathos of a hopeless love. There are many stories of such loves that wring the heart. In *Nicholas Nickleby* (1838), by Charles Dickens, there was Smike's love for Kate. In *The Hunchback of Notre Dame* (1831), by Victor Hugo, a book which may possibly have influenced Leroux, there was Quasimodo's love for Esmerelda, and so on. Who, of us, especially in our teenage years, has not agonized over a hopeless love?

But then, *The Phantom of the Opera* was also the tale of an innocent singer driven by a figure of horror to surpass herself, to force more of herself into her art—something that failed in the end. This was reminiscent of *Trilby* (1894) by George du Maurier, in which Trilby, who possessed a glorious voice but was tone-deaf, was hypno-

tized by the vile and sinister Svengali. But Svengali died
and at once Trilby's art disappeared.

I can't help but think of the symbolism here. The true
artist is frequently *obsessed* by his or her art, driven to
subordinate all of life to it, forced to occupy every moment with it. Might it not be possible that the power of
the Trilby/Svengali story, or the Christine/Erik story lies
in its splitting of the fused personality that drives the
artist onward, like the fatal red shoes in the motion picture of that name. (To some who know me, this may
sound as though I am bemoaning my own fate, but not
so. I love the driving force that propels me onward and
has never ceased in fifty years.)

The Phantom of the Opera suddenly experienced a rebirth in 1987 when it appeared as a musical on the stage,
with gorgeous music, with Michael Crawford as a terrific
Phantom, and with an absolutely unbelievable set of special effects.

I saw it, and loved it, and I find it almost inevitable
that Martin Greenberg (this time with the aid of his lovely
wife) should conceive of the idea of collecting a group
of original stories, written by masters of macabre mystery, that were intended to capture some of the flavor of
The Phantom of the Opera.

No one story includes all the factors of the original;
they weren't expected to. They would only be retelling
Leroux if they did.

To be sure, they would, inevitably, include a lurker in
the depths, a mysterious figure of doubtful humanity; but
one story is almost a straight murder mystery; one is a
fantasy-edged bit of science fiction; one is a fantasy-
edged tale of revenge; one is a satire, uncomfortably
sharp, of modern television; and so on.

Each tale is different; each presents another facet of
the Phantom idea; so that each, in its way, is a commen-
tary on the original.

It's a great collection. You'll enjoy it.

THE OPERA OF THE PHANTOM

by *Edward Wellen*

Part One. 1871. *The Pied Piper of the Cellars*

Victor slipped softly as his shadow past the sentries and into the shell of the Opera House. By moonlight through the stark windows, he found the little staircase near what would one day be the footlights. The builders had stopped work on the new Opera House while the siege went on. Listening at the head of the stairs for voices or footsteps below, Victor heard the muffled drumbeats of Prussian artillery shells slowmarching ever closer to Paris.

He heard nothing else, and started down the staircase into darkness thick as mud. The steps led down to the cellars, where scenery and props would one day fill space and where workshops would ring with the music of hammer and saw, but where now the crypts held provisions for the siege. Victor hoped at the very best for a crack at these provisions, but at the very least there had to be fat rats. He tightened his grip on the club in his right hand and made sure of the empty sack hanging from his rope belt.

And rats there were. His coming stirred them up. The musty air came alive with scamperings and squeakings. He clamped the club under his arm, drew from his pocket a candle and matches, and struck a match. The phosphorescent streak blinded him long enough so that he saw nothing at first. Then, with the candle smoking off the charred tip of the wick, he caught only a few shiny red gleams and the whisking blur of sleek forms. And now with the candle burning clear he saw simply the cold sweat of the walls and the rubbled floor. The rats were not.

But a presence supplanted theirs. He felt the haunting *thereness* of something else: something he neither saw nor heard. It seemed near, and moving nearer.

Why did he stand frozen as in a spell, holding the light that singled him out from the darkness and that exposed his meagerness?

Make yourself even scarcer, his mind screamed at him.

He blew the flame out and freed himself to swing his club in a protective arc.

The menacing stillness outlasted his held breath, then the darkness split.

Someone had him full in the glare of a dark lantern suddenly unhooded.

He blinked up at a tall thin figure shrouded in black. He could make out only the yellow eyes, but they were more than enough to scare him into holding his ground.

The man looked as if he had expected bigger game. The yellow eyes regarded Victor as Victor might regard a scrawny rat not worth putting himself out for. Victor pulled his blouse together where the tear showed his ribs.

"A kid. How old are you?"

Victor weighed saying seven to gain sympathy and saying twelve to gain stature, then stared into those yellow eyes and found himself saying the truth. "Ten. Why? What's it to you?"

"A fresh kid. Ten, eh? I ran away from home when I was ten."

Victor felt like saying he bet that made the creep's parents happy.

The man moved the lantern nearer Victor and Victor was glad he had held his tongue.

"What are you doing here?"

"Who wants to know?"

"Erik."

"That's a hell of a monicker. Well, if it's any of your business, Erik, I come down here to catch me some rats."

"Rats?"

"Damn right. They make good eating—with the right sauce. Folks will pay three francs for a rat, same as for an egg." Victor bit his lip. He already had all the competition he needed; that was what had driven him to venture into the cellars of the Opera House. "I know a flic when I see one, and you ain't no flic; and if you owned this joint you wouldn't be sneaking around down here; so what's the diff if I help myself?"

Erik made a grand gesture. "This is my turf. As Moslems warn thieves: 'Hands off!' "

"I bet you ain't no Moslem, neither."

Erik gave voice to a strange sound; Victor realized it was a rusty laugh.

"So I don't scare you?"

"You're the scared one."

The air around Erik seemed to crackle with the aura of suppressed violence. "Why do you say that?"

Victor tried to hide his trembling. "Because you're afraid to show your face."

Erik remained still a long moment, then with a frightening controlled slowness unwound a black silk scarf from around his face. He let the light of his lantern shine full upon his face.

Victor would have run but for his feet.

"Well? What do you see?"

"You look like Death."

Victor made ready to fend off a blow, but Erik did not move.

Erik made his voice deep and hollow. "I am Death . . . to those who cross me."

A faint squeak from deep in the darkness reminded Victor that he could say the same. His shudder turned into a shrug. "Well, there's more than enough rats down here for the two of us, so I wouldn't be taking nothing away from you. What say you back off and let me get on with the hunt?'' He sensed the air crackle, and he moved swiftly from reason and challenge to temptation. ''I'll split my take with you, how's that?''

Again the rusty laugh. ''I'm not in the ratmeat business, but it's a deal—if you show me how good you are at nabbing them.''

''Ah. Sure thing, Erik, just stand back.''

Blackness. Erik had hooded the lantern before Victor finished speaking.

Victor, a bit shaky now that he found himself on trial, got his candle alight and stuck it upright in the wall, in a space between two blocks of stone. He put a crumb of cheese in the half-circle of light on the floor. He pulled back into shadow—away from the deeper shadow that was Erik—and held his club ready.

Erik's spinechilling laugh broke an eternity of inaction. ''How long must I wait for my share of nothing?''

Victor had grown stiff holding himself ready. He worked his muscles loose. He had never had this trouble catching rats before. It had to be Erik's fault. ''No fair. Not with you standing around. You scare them off.''

''Me? I can summon them at will.''

''Says you.''

''Says me.''

''So far it's just talk.''

''Wait here. I'll be back.''

The *thereness* of Erik vanished.

Victor eyed the candle. When it got down to an inch of stub, enough still to find his way out of this stinkhole, he would scram.

It got down to an inch, and less. He didn't know why, but he didn't want this species of Erik to think him afraid.

Victor began to hallucinate the darkness as a monstrous sleek rat. Its eyes, big as manhole covers, glinted red. It bared teeth big as guillotine blades.

He tried to keep up his courage by whistling a tune of the music halls.

He jumped. The *thereness* was there.

"*Merde!* About time."

Erik sounded defensive. "Sorry. I had to dodge a detail of soldiers." Then he sounded impressed. "I expected you to be gone."

He opened his lantern and set it down on the floor. Victor snuffed the candle and pocketed it. Erik drew something from under his cloak. Victor saw the shine on the object before he made the object out. It was a smooth black stick. Victor backed away and raised his own club.

The laugh, a lot less rusty by now though it had a lot to go before it sounded normal, human. "This, my ignorant little ragamuffin friend, is not a stick to beat you with. It's an oboe."

"What does it do?"

"What I tell it to."

Erik put an end to his mouth and made a run of funny sounds—an eerie mix of drone, blast, whine, and shrill—and all at once Victor heard a counterpoint of squeaks.

The rats came out of hiding. They ringed Erik in a mass. They sat up with their forepaws jerking as if they didn't know whether to cover their ears, to keep time, or to applaud.

Victor seemed to himself as much under the spell as the rats. They were dazed, charmed, confused, easy prey—and he had yet to move.

Erik took breath out to say, "What are you waiting for?"

Then it was massacre. Red slaughter.

Victor clubbed them to death, one right after the other.

Erik left off playing. He looked around with a twisted smile, then pointed to a huge rat still sitting prayerfully in a charmed daze. "There's one you missed."

Victor nodded. "I know about that one. That's a mama rat. Can't you see she's knocked up?"

Erik's smile took a greater twist. "Ah, a soft spot."

Victor bristled. "What do you mean soft? Let her have the babies and let the babies grow to be worth catching."

"An eye to the future."

"Sure. it makes sense."

The mama rat came to herself and whisked away.

It remained only to lift the dead by the limp tails and drop them into the sack. Victor counted them. One in five for Erik seemed fair. Victor set aside three of the fattest. "Three's your share."

Erik shook his head.

Victor made a face. "Not enough?" He added a fourth.

Erik toed all four toward Victor. "I don't want any."

Victor eyed him in amazement. "Not want any?" Amazement turned to worry. What would induce Erik to stay in partnership? "Then can you show me how to use that oboe thing?"

Erik laughed the hateful laugh. "Even with musical talent, which I doubt you have, for you whistle offkey, that would take years of practice. And by then the war will be over and the market for ratmeat gone."

"So you're not throwing in with me?"

"I didn't say that. We can fix times for raticide—if you keep your mouth shut about your source. I don't want the place overrun with rat-killers."

"I can keep my mouth shut. Cross my heart and hope to die."

But his mouth busted them up just when business got really good. His mouth passed along what his ears took in.

Erik was a strange one, no question. He had his moods. Victor found him oftener down than up—and when Erik was down Erik was way down, and when he was way down he talked real crazy. Like this day he snapped at Victor, "Don't call me Erik today. Call me Pluto."

"Huh?"

"Easy is the descent to Avernus—and long is the way and hard that out of hell leads up to light."

"If you say so." Victor should've let it go at that, seeing Erik was at his crepehanging worst. But Victor thought to snap Erik—or Pluto—out of himself. "I hear Bismarck is at Versailles."

The yellow eyes regarded Victor incuriously. "Who is Bismarck?"

"The top Prussian in the war against us. Don't you know? Don't you care?"

"I don't give a damn."

Like the man from Auriol. Everyone at Aubagne prayed hard for rain—all but one man. The priest said, "Why aren't you down on your knees? We won't get rain if we don't pray for it." "I'm from Auriol," said the man. "I don't give a damn about your rain."

Just so, it seemed, the war meant nothing to Erik. To him, the world out there was the phantom—and whether it stood at war or at peace mattered little.

Victor still couldn't let it go at that. "It's your war, too."

Erik spoke coldly. "Our war? The war isn't between me and this Bismarck. It isn't between a waif like you and this Bismarck. It's between the Prussian big shot and some French big shot."

"Will you say the same when Bismarck goosesteps into the Opera House?"

Erik laughed. "He won't know I'm here below."

"Don't kid yourself. People know about you." Too late Victor knew he had gone too far. He put up a hand. "Hold it, Erik—I mean, Pluto. Don't blame me; I ain't said word one to nobody. But folks are talking about a shadowy figure that haunts the Opera House. They call you the Phantom."

The yellow eyes blazed. Then they hooded. "That does it. Sooner or later, whether you want to or not, you're bound to lead the outside world to me." He put up a skeletal hand. "For my good and yours, you have to go away before that happens."

Victor's heart sank. But at least "go away," if it really meant "go away," rated above "drop dead." Before asking, he set himself to run for the stairs if he didn't like the answer. "Go away where?"

"For some time I've been thinking about that very thing. City life is bad for your health. Just look at you."

"Merde. What's wrong with the way I look?"

"You're too thin, too pale."

"Merde. Look who's talking."

"It's too late for me to change. Though in my earlier days I did roam with the Gypsies." He mused a moment. "I suppose they were my happiest days."

Who did the guy think he was kidding? He never had a happy day in his life. Now he wanted to ruin Victor's life.

Victor almost yelled in outrage. "Merde. You want me to wander with Gypsies, out in the open? I don't know no Gypsies. I don't want to know no Gypsies."

"Easy, Victor. Calm yourself. I had in mind placing you with a farm couple."

The outrage failed to subside. "Merde. I know farm couples. I don't want to stay with no hicks."

The yellow eyes blazed at Victor. "What farm couples do you know?"

Victor answered in spite of himself, sullenly. "There's some fat old bitch and her man that cart carrots and turnips all the way from Nanterre. I sometimes do deals with them. She's the sharp one, but I'm sharper, so it works out for me."

"When's the next market day?"

Unwillingly, Victor told him. "Thursday." And then had to tell him how many days till Thursday, for Erik had lost track.

"Very well. Thursday you'll take me to meet this woman."

"Merde."

"Among the carrots and turnips you'll be safe from the Cabbages."

Had Erik actually made a joke? Victor shot Erik a look, but Eric's natural rictus made it impossible to tell if Erik smiled.

"Merde. I ain't scared of no Cabbages."

"And I'll fix it with her for you to get schooling."

Now *that* scared Victor.

* * *

It did not prove hard to find the woman. There she stood, loudest of the loud, stoutest of the stout. The cart was her stall, and her man had unharnessed the spavined, swaybacked nag and led it off to a watering trough.

The Morilles had come to market. For a moment, though, Victor considered telling Erik that, this one Thursday, the woman had failed to show.

But the yellow eyes, though shadowed under the visor of a kepi, held Victor in true. With a grimace, Victor jerked his chin toward the woman.

Erik nodded, and Victor went to bring the woman to him.

The woman saw Victor—she saw everything—but kept him waiting while she finished putting down a sister marketer.

That one had just asked the world at large, "Anyone know where I can get *doigts prussiques*?"

These were the things folks had been speaking of—pins dipped in prussic acid for pricking Prussians—to allow a Parisienne to defend her honor.

Mme Jacqueline Morille shook with laughter. "Why? What honor would you be defending?"

This led to a hairpulling match Victor hated to see end. But Erik seemed restive and signaled with the yellow eyes and Victor tugged at Mme Morille's shawl.

She backhanded him away, quickly polished off her opponent, then whirled on Victor.

"Hey, you brat, what the hell do you think you're doing?"

He whispered in her ear.

She turned to look where he pointed, and he almost blushed at the figure Erik presented. He had felt self-conscious leading Erik here, had kept a pace ahead so it would not seem they were together. Erik was for sure one strange creature. Even kepi'd and caped, muffled to the eyes, he could not hide his oddness.

But Mme Morille appeared unfazed. "Three gold louis just to talk to him?"

Victor nodded. "Just to hear him out."

She shrugged, apparently sure she needed no *doigt prussique* to deal with that one, and sauntered over to the column Erik lurked behind.

Victor slunk in her wake. He watched her stick her hand out to get the three gold louis up front. She bit each of them before slipping them into a pouch that went down between her tits. Then she settled herself to listen.

They were deciding his fate, but he distanced himself from them disdainfully. Let them decide whatever the fuck they wanted. If the farm proved a soft snap, fine. If not, he would make his way back to the streets and alleys of Paris.

He caught the upshot of it, Jacqueline's firm promise. "He'll be like my own son."

And, without a word to him, but with a burning look of those yellow eyes, Erik slipped away.

Victor waited gloomily by the cart as it emptied long before noon. Then Armand Morille, wiping beer froth from his mustache, came back with the nag and harnessed it to the cart.

Armand stared at Victor when his wife informed him of this addition to the family. She jiggled the pouch and he broke into a smile and clapped Victor on the shoulder with a meaty hand. And so they set out for home.

Every quarter, at a given date, at a given hour, under a given milestone on a given road, the Morilles would find three gold louis and in return they would leave a scrawl from Victor wrapped in oilcloth.

Part Two. 1880. *The Clown of the Orchestra*

The Opera House stood whole, full of red silk, gilded carving, plush. It glowed. It had come alive.

In the darkest of the times leading up to this bright now, Erik had pleasured himself often thinking of the gamin he had saved from the grimness of the siege and from the bloody turmoil of the Commune. He could see Victor playing in the sunlight among the hens and rabbits in Nanterre, the pallor under the grime gone. Ruddy, maybe even tanned. And sleek as a sewer rat. Above all, that sharp mind burgeoning under the light of knowledge.

It had been hard to come up with the gold for his keep, but Erik had managed. And the Morilles had kept their end of the bargain, matching every three gold louis with a scrawl from Victor. Erik had saved every one, though one might have served for all.

Dear Monsieur Erik. I hope this finds you will. It's real nice here. The Morilles treat me swell. I get lots to eat. You would never know me, I filled out so much. I am getting big, so if you can spare a few extra francs for new clothes that will be great. Thanks. Your Victor.

Victor should have more reason to give thanks. He would have a university education. That called for more money than Erik commanded.

How to raise the needful?

Deep under the Opera House, Erik came up with the answer. He would compose an opera.

What theme? He had to pick a dramatic subject, a colorful background. Something noteworthy. Joan of Arc? Domremy. The Wild West? Laredo.

Wait. That Albanian legend he had heard on his Balkan wanderings with the Gypsies.

The bare bones: There lived in Scutari under the Turks a man who married a woman from the hill country of the Mirdita region. The wife's brother had become a bold outlaw with a price on his head for wreaking havoc on the Turks with sword and torch. The brother laughed at danger, and came often by night to see his sister and her two young sons. The husband, out of greed for the reward, informed the Turks. And one night, after the brother entered the house and—as was the custom—left his sword and dagger by the door, Turkish soldiers burst in and cut him down. The sister grieved, yet found comfort in her husband's supportive love. Then one night she came upon him while he counted once again his Judas pieces of gold. Light burst upon her, and she taxed him with betraying her brother. He confessed, but sought to temper her wrath by reasoning with her. Her brother's recklessness would have led inevitably to the same end. Why should a stranger get the reward and they remain poor? The gold would enrich their lives and the lives of their sons. To this she said nothing, and he believed he had won her around, and so he slept soundly. But the woman lay awake, and she heard the voice of her brother's blood, and she rose at midnight and took up her brother's sword and beheaded her husband. After this, she went to the bed of her young sons and looked down upon them as they slept. And she would have turned away, but the voice of her brother's blood spoke again. And she lifted the sword and cried out, "Offspring of a viper, you shall not grow up to sell out my kin!" And she brought the sword down twice more. And with the bloody sword in hand she fled Scutari and made for the mountains of Mirdita, where her kinsfolk honored her for her deed.

Now to flesh out the bones. The people of the story needed names. Liri would be the woman's name—and the opera's. Her brother the outlaw: Mehmet Tashko. The husband: Rustem Marku. The two young sons: Djordji and Leka Marku. The Turkish officer to pay the reward and to slay the betrayed man: Aziz-Bey.

Already Erik could see them, embodied in singers on the stage of the Opera House.

Before the curtain rose, he had to get them on the page.

Blank pages were here in plenty, his for the taking: the voluminous library of the Opera House held a store of sheets for the drones who copied music. Here, too, from the bright shelves and dusty archives he moonlight-requisitioned reference books on the art of composing, librettos and scores of the masters, and—for no good reason but that a skimming through intrigued him—a volume entitled *On a Theory of Semantic Phase.*

His tongue hung out one corner of his mouth as he wrote. Only when he knocked off for a bit—to chafe his

hands or to take a bite or a sip or to refill his inkhorn—
did he become aware again of the squeak and scamper of
his old companions the rats. At such a time, when he was
working on a scene in which the family listened to footsteps outside and awaited the knock at the door—the
Turks? Mehmet?—he put the eerie notes of their patter,
vocal and pedal, on the page. And into Liri's admonish-
ment:

> That knock!
> At our gate
> The hero stands.
> Your dear
> Uncle's fate
> Is in your hands.
> Of his
> Coming here
> Speak not one word.
> What is
> Never said
> Is never heard.

And often when Erik stole into the orchestra pit to pick
out notes and try chords softly on the piano, he saw in
the dark house the glittering eyes of his first audience,
his first critics.

He learned about his characters as he wrote them into
being.
More than mere greed for gold motivated the husband
to betray his brother-in-law, his fellow under Turkish op-
pression, his guest.

> Tongat jeta,
> Long life.
> Step right in.
> Our house your house.
> Welcome.
> We are kin.

For one thing, Rustem Marku, as a Christian, an infidel, felt pressure to prove his obedience to his Turkish overlords. For another, he viewed with jealousy his sons' hero-worship of their outlaw uncle. Rustem's *sotto voce* grumbling would play nicely against the boys' enjoyment of Mehmet's tales of harassing and outwitting the Turks—striking at outposts, waylaying tax collectors—in the unending struggle for Albanian freedom. An eagle swooping down.

> *The Turkish wolf's in my talons;*
> *His lifeblood I spill in gallons.*
>
> *(Good thing he's not in your beak;*
> *You'd lose him, so much you speak.)*

Liri, too, had complexity, depth. Sure, she mourned her brother's death at the hands of the Turks. The irony was that, deep down, she did not really care that much about him while he lived, for he had given her in marriage to Rustem Marku against her will and then had put her family at risk with his recklessness. Yet honor drove her to avenge his death.

> *Honor is all.*
> *Dearer than love,*
> *Dearer than life;*
> *Dearer than man,*
> *Dearer than wife;*
> *Dearer than self,*
> *Dearer than child.*
> *Must wash in blood*
> *Honor defiled.*
> *Honor's earthy, honor's gritty;*
> *Without mercy, without pity.*
> *Nothing means anything*
> *When honor's betrayed.*
> *Lek dukagini*

> *Must be obeyed.*
> *Honor is all.*

Erik seemed to remember that *lek dukagini* meant something like "the law of vengeance" or maybe "the code of the mountains." He didn't know the meaning for certain, but he felt sure that the phrase lent authenticity and that it would sound fine when sung.

At first, Liri would think her son might have let slip Mehmet Tashko's whereabouts—out of childish boasting. (Erik had suddenly decided to drop Leka and make Djordji an only child.) She would take Djordji to task for this, perhaps beat him. (Erik saw Djordji as Victor, with Victor's spunk. That would lend itself to comic recitative. *"Uncle Mehmet, take off your hat." "Small Nephew Djordji, why is that?" "I want to see the price on your head. The Turks put it there, so father said."* Djordji grew so real to Erik that Erik had to blink away tears when Liri slew Djordji. It was almost as if someone had killed Victor.) Only afterward would Liri find Rustem counting the gold coins—and realize that her husband was the traitor.

And when it came to killing Djordji, she should be terribly torn, have a beautiful aria as she contemplated the sleeping boy.

> *How beautiful he is!*
> *Yet beauty must die*
> *When, beneath it,*
> *Lies a lie.*
> *How beautiful he is!*
> *Yet duty calls me,*
> *Crying in blood*
> *What must be.*
>
> *How beautiful he is!*
> *Yet beauty must die*
> *When, beneath it,*
> *Lies a lie.*

It took no stressful thinking to decide what Liri did with the gold after she killed Rustem and Djordji. She would not take it along on her flight to the mountains. To keep the deed a pure deed of honor and to make of the gold an oblation, she would pour the coins into the well . . . the splashing a liquid run of notes of celestial purity in a moment otherwise silent.

During the writing, Erik changed his mind many times, and often at great cost. He saw that a short outburst at the end of the second act, when Liri confronted Rustem over the gold, would be more moving than an extended finale. He scrapped the long movement he had sweated over.

He ended with a revamp of the beginning. The overture would end with three wood-block beats, coinciding with the customary three knocks that signal the curtain's rise—and foreshadowing the three knocks Mehmet gives the door of his sister's house.

Now to translate the rough draft and the tortuous and torturous revisions into a perfect copy. Like the Opera House with its cellars hidden and forgotten.

The manuscript of *Liri*, tied in a blue ribbon, lay on the Managing Director's desk.

Erik had made many alterations that were not in the plans of Architect Garnier. In dead of night while the Opera House finished construction, Erik had fashioned hidden chambers, secret passages, sliding panels, peepholes in the walls. No trick at all, then, to force the manuscript of a new opera on the Managing Director's attention.

Through an eye in a painting of the Circe episode of the Odyssey, Erik watched Henri Valembert enter the office, stand goldknobbed cane and hang gray tophat, take off gray gloves, then preen his imperial while he stood staring down at the topmost manuscript in the pile on his desk.

M. Valembert checked a list, shook his head, riffled

through the manuscript of *Liri*, then lifted it gingerly by a corner and with the other hand tinkled his bell for the secretary.

She hurried in with pad at her breast and pencil in her hair.

He shook *Liri* at her. "Where did this one in the childish hand come from? I fail to find it on the list from the screening committee."

Erik's ears burned. Childish hand! He was self-taught, true, but *Liri* was a mature work.

The secretary looked, then flatly disclaimed knowledge and responsibility. Valembert gave her a sharp glance, then tightened his mouth and put *Liri* at the bottom of the pile.

"All in due time. Like the dancers of Joncquières."

At Joncquières, the Mayor's daughter wailed that she was a wallflower, so the Mayor ruled that all the girls sit on a long bench and that each gallant take the nearest when his turn came.

Valembert waved the secretary away, then sat down to read.

Erik watched him read and reject two new operas before he put on the gray gloves, picked up the cane and the gray tophat, and knocked off for the day. Erik fumed. At this rate. . . .

M. Valembert found *Liri* staring him in the face again the next day. He tinkled the bell. Again the secretary denied culpability.

Valembert screwed his mouth tighter, stuck *Liri* at the bottom, and read one manuscript before, claiming headache, he left for the day.

The following day, an edgy Valembert slammed cane and tophat on the desk, tore off his gloves and hurled them to the floor, then tinkled.

Erik saw two faces redden as Valembert pointed a trembling forefinger at *Liri* resurfaced and as the secretary stood with folded arms and shook her head.

The impasse ended with the secretary rushing out in tears.

Valembert snatched up *Liri*, swung it over the wastebasket, and made ready to tear it in two.

Erik's eyes blazed. Maybe a hiss of rage escaped him without his taking notice.

Valembert held himself in check at the last instant. Feeling used his face as an instrument. Fear, curiosity, uneasiness, speculation—these plucked his skin and fingered his features. With a shiver, he shook himself into action. He shoved his cane and hat aside to make room on his desk for reading, and with a scowl at the door to the anteroom, settled himself to go through the forward manuscript.

Erik watched. And smiled.

M. Valembert did not leave early this day. He tinkled the bell.

The redeyed secretary saw him at the cursed manuscript and got set to gush anew, but M. Valembert's face when it lifted wore a thoughtful smile and M. Valembert's eyes were not seeing her.

"If you will be so kind, mademoiselle, find M. Lefevre if he is in the building, and ask him to come to my office."

The secretary nodded happily, then noticed the gloves on the floor and approached to pick them up. Valembert good-naturedly stopped her.

"No, mademoiselle, leave that to me. Go, go."

Erik felt his heart beat an up-tempo tune. Claude Lefevre was a young and ambitious orchestra conductor Erik had heard Valembert tout as a comer. Erik had heard others speak of Lefevre and Valembert as very, very good friends.

Lefevre proved to have been in the Opera House, for he turned up in Valembert's office promptly.

He arched a smooth eyebrow. "You sent for me, Henri?"

Valembert indicated the manuscript of *Liri* and spoke lightly, laughingly. "Claude, here's something from an unknown, an obvious amateur."

Erik burned with humiliation, swelled with anger. If these two dared laugh at his masterpiece . . .

But Valembert's tone had turned serious. "Look it over to see if it has any worth. If so, maybe you can do something with it."

Lefevre eyed it doubtfully. "I'll certainly be glad to see, Henri."

Valembert gave him the chair and hovered over him as he read.

Lefevre started to read rapidly, at a skimming rate, then read more slowly, and even went back to begin over. At times he stopped to hum one of the musical phrases.

"Aha, aha," Valembert would say, and used every opportunity to pat him or poke him in their shared enthusiasm.

Lefevre looked up at last. "It has possibilities. Possibilities. But of course," archly, "it needs a lot of work."

"I leave it in your hands, Claude."

And in Lefevre's hands *Liri* left Valembert's office, and Erik's eyes followed him warmly.

Soon, soon, the notes and words of *Liri* would fill the great Opera House.

Alone, deep in the cellars, Erik lost some of his sense of elation, and he felt a bit uneasy about the superior attitude of Lefevre and Valembert.

Not alone; he heard the rats.

"Sing, my friends. The Opera House belongs to you and me."

In the eyes of the world, however, and in the exercise of power over performances, the Opera House belonged to Valembert and Lefevre.

Erik paced his hidden chamber as a prisoner might pace a cell. He needed to make sure that *Liri*, from con-

cept to execution, remained true to his vision. He came
to a dead stop of decision.

He gathered up his jottings and rough drafts. These
would prove authorship if it should come to that. With
these, Victor could come forward as the heir of the Erik
who had written *Liri*, and so entitled to receive the fees
and royalties.

Eric grimaced. Some pages showed signs of gnawing.
He shook his finger at the rats in the walls.

"My friends, you do not learn to sing by ingesting
notes."

He put the papers in the tin box he used to store food.
Liri went well with burnt almonds and patisserie foraged
from the refreshment rooms adjacent to the Promenade
Salon of the Opera House.

The rats sang their frustration.

He left their company when his inner clock struck the
first hour of twilight. Taking along the opera glass he had
found forgotten late one night or early one morning in
Box 5 on the grand tier, he made his way to the roof.

A mare's tail streaked the sky.

The right bank spread out around him like a palette,
with the Opera House itself holding the place of the
thumbhole. Pere Lachaise a blob of grayish green, the red-
tiled roofs of Montmartre a smear of dusky pink, the
Tuileries a dab of bright green . . .

His nostrils were working. A wind had sprung up and
carried with it the smell of spring. A sudden silence fell
on the rattling and creaking traffic below and the night
carried to him the distant refrain of a waltz.

He lifted the opera glass and looked down at the Seine.
Near at hand a flatnosed *pousseur* pushed a tight four-
some of barges. He outsped it, pulled the Seine along as
the light-bubbly river corkscrewed to the western hori-
zon, and past the marshy Grenouillere in the loop north
of St. Cloud he made out the outline of the mountain
looming over Nanterre: Mt. Valérien with its feckless
fort. A mere eight or ten miles from where he stood.

Nanterre had been within the lines of investment, but there had been no doubt the Prussians would break through in a gray-green flood. Still, he remembered thinking: Leave it to farmers to live through war. War manured fields, not city streets. Time had proved him right. Victor and the Morilles had come through.

What did he know of Nanterre? Hadn't a young woman named Madeleine created at Nanterre the shell-shaped tea-cake to sell in the Tuileries Garden? The *madeleine*. He could smell and taste the crumbs of the last *madeleine* he had eaten, just three nights ago, scavenged from a refreshment room after the echoes of a performance of *Fidelio* died down and the Opera House darkened.

With a sudden movement of his shoulders he shook off the past. He lived in the present. He had to move in the present. He had to do in the present. The time to set out for Nanterre was now.

He made his way down and let himself into Wardrobe. He loved to feast his eyes on the theatrical dazzle his lantern brought to light in Property Room and Wardrobe. Clothing of every style. Accessories to match. Feathers, buckles, buttons, straps, brooches, sequins. Those castanets, that flounced dress, that guitar: Carmen. He shook himself again and outfitted himself, costumed himself, for the journey.

A closefitting woolen skullcap covered his head. He found his size in boots—there would be mud puddles in the suburbs. He picked a sackcloth cowl—the hood and its shadow hid his face.

He eyed himself in a pier-glass. His figure seemed ascetic enough. Here was a monk—or the ghost of one. He brought the lantern to his face. As Victor would say honestly, Death.

Packet of proof tied snugly under the gown, he weighed taking sword cane and dagger. Beggars, thieves, pickpockets filled the ways. He passed weapons up. Death went in peace. That seemed more than Life could say. Death grinned.

* * *

When he set out, clocks were disputing twelve midnight. The flow of carriages and carts had abated, the few foot travelers he passed gave him the wall. By dawn he had reached the bridge at Neuilly-sur-Seine without encountering an unoccupied carriage-for-hire willing to take a monk smelling of death all or part of the way to Nanterre.

That suited Erik. Stretching his legs did him good. Spring air did him good. Death loved life.

Not life as embodied in most humans. Life as in himself, and as in an all-too-rare Victor.

He crossed the bridge at Neuilly. After a bit he found himself in true country. The fields were green and the trees in full leaf. He deliberately strode through the weeds and high grass for the chill freshness of dew and to stir up the shrill accompaniment of cicadas.

Then he came to the fork in the road and no signs.

Mt. Valérien, because a rise blocked the view, did not serve as a beacon.

As Erik stood wondering which way to take, a coach roared up behind him. Erik turned with a smile. The coachman would know the way to Nanterre.

The coachman had his whip in hand for it was a stiff pull up the hill.

Whether he thought Erik a highwayman or merely an obstruction, he gave Erik no chance to ask the way. He waved Erik aside, and when Erik failed to leap into the ditch, the coachman cracked the whip at him.

Maybe the coachman had mistaken Erik's stance. Maybe the boots went oddly with the cowl. Maybe Erik had looked as if he meant to start something. But no. Any obstruction, however innocent, would have drawn the same lashing out.

Erik watched the coachman coil to strike. Too proud or too disbelieving to dance out of the whip's way, Erik stood his ground.

The lash bit, drew blood from his cheek.

Still Erik did not leap aside. He flashed his eyes and

winged out his gown like some great bat, and the horses did not run him down but reared within inches of him and brought the carriage to a grating halt.

The coachman fell back against his seat with the slack, then shoved himself upright and with a curse slashed again at Erik.

This time Erik swayed aside and, his hand where his face had been, snatched the stinging end. Grinning at the pain, he took a twist and yanked.

The coachman, locked by his own grip to the whip handle, sailed from his seat into the ditch.

An imperious voice called from the coach. "Urbain! What's holding us up?" Like the crack of the coachman's whip, the crack of the voice enforced social distinctions.

Urbain croaked from the ditch. "Monsieur le duc, that bastard frightened the horses."

The passenger swung the door open.

Erik stared at the device on the door: a golden Y dividing a winedark circle into three parts. The design held Erik frozen while his mind raced back to the gilded Y on the great iron gate at the poplar-lined driveway leading to the chateau. Erik saw in his head the barbican wall enclosing the whole park, saw the two corner towers of the chateau, saw the corduroy of tilled fields all about the walls, saw the forerunner of this very same coach carrying the very same passenger, who now kicked out the step and stood on it craning to see what went forward.

Monsieur le duc Evariste d'Origny de Younceville, whitehaired now but jutting of nose and chin as ever if not more so, stared at Erik and struck some chord in him.

Erik remembered standing with his father, Andre Blanc, master mason of Barentin, a small town near Rouen, and with his mother, Madeleine, as the coach raised dust passing by. He remembered the passenger flicking only a glance at them. He remembered his mother turning pale. He remembered his father waiting for the coach to round the turn before he shook his fist at it. He remembered his father saying, "So he has come back. Let this remind you to stay in the house till he goes away again." And he remembered his father imprinting a hand on his mother's cheek.

He grew aware that the duc was speaking to him, cracking the voice-whip at him. ". . . out of the way, scum."

Erik's temples pounded like iron hooves. Out of the corner of his eye he saw Urbain creep around to come at him from behind. Erik whirled to blaze a look at him. Urbain scuttled to put the coach between them.

Monsieur le duc drew a pistol and pointed it at Erik. "Move aside, or I shoot."

Erik glared back without stirring.

Younceville smiled tightly and fired.

The bullet tore through the cowl, creasing Erik's shoulder. Erik weighed jumping Younceville before the man could get off another shot, but the pistol had a longer reach and a speedier throw. Erik spun, leaped the ditch, and took cover behind a tree.

When he looked, he saw Younceville draw himself into the coach. Urbain raised the step and closed the door, then mounted to his seat and with a triumphant shout cracked his whip. Hooves and wheels raised dust laboring up the hill.

Blood had not got past the packet of proof's cover sheet. The bullet wound called for no more than a strip torn from the hem of the gown. The encounter called for revenge.

But when Erik caught up with the coach at a busy wayside inn, and saw his chance—with master and man indoors at their several repasts—to loosen a wheel nut or hamstring the horses, he passed on. His quarrel was not with coach or horses but with master and man, and that settlement would come at a better time and place.

Erik paused only long enough to ask the way. A stablehand with a careless air and an insolent mien did—after a blazing look from Erik—deign hurriedly to stop and give a straight answer. This, friend, was indeed the road to Nanterre.

Along the way Erik found a fallen limb that made a fine walking stick, though he chose it for its heft. He listened and looked for the coach to overtake him. He held himself ready to leap out from behind a tree or hedge, to rest the reins, and then to deal with stunned master and man as Victor had dealt with the rats.

But he got good though grudging directions from farmers in the fields and reached the turnoff to the Morille farm before that could happen. Rather than lie in ambush on the main road, a wait that might last hours, he took the turning.

The cottage brought Erik a frisson of déjà vu. It stopped him in his tracks physically and threw him back mentally to the recurring dream of his wandering years. In that dream he saw himself returning to the loving warmth he had never known.

He got a grip on himself. Andre and Madeleine Blanc did not await him here, with or without welcoming smiles and outstretched arms. They were dead and gone, and in waking life they had been dead to him long before they were dead and gone.

He got going again. Before he reached the door a voice halted him.

"Hey!" The shout came from a pigsty just beyond the house. A man stood inside the pen among other heavy forms modeled out of mud. He looked Erik's way with a hard stare that carried. "What do you want?" The discouraging tone also carried.

"I'm Erik."

"Who?"

"I've come to see Victor."

Before the man could quiz further, the door opened and Jacqueline Morille thrust herself out. She directed a blast toward the sty. "Armand, you fool, this is Victor's

Erik." She faced Erik with a welcoming smile that faltered only briefly.

"You walked all the way?"

"Yes. Where's Victor?"

Armand had climbed out of the pen and came muddy and shitty to where they stood.

Erik looked at the pair while the pair eyed one another.

Jacqueline had grown even louder and stouter. Her healthy fat had given way to puffy flesh. Armand had grown redder and veinier of face. The froth on his mustache was that of age, not beer. But Erik was most mindful of his own chalk-white skin, the colorlessness of his hand on his pilgrim's staff as against the color of their flesh.

Jacqueline cupped her hands around her mouth and directed her volume at a figure far across the fields. "Victor!"

The figure, still as a scarecrow, stirred and set to hacking with its hoe.

Jacqueline called again. "Come here, my dear. There's someone to see you." She beckoned.

The figure straightened, downed the hoe, and came slowly toward them. Erik swelled to see how big Victor had grown, how well he had filled out.

With a grunt he might have meant for manners, Armand shouldered past Erik and shoved Jacqueline indoors. Armand and Jacqueline exchanged fierce whispers, then Armand stuck his face out the door. He smoothed his mustache, then gestured and made room.

"Come right in. Our house your house."

He looked at the stick. Erik leaned it against the side of the house before entering.

Jacqueline seemed a slovenly housekeeper but a hospitable one. She moved a stool from the wall. "You must be weary." As Erik sat down gratefully, she turned to Armand. "Give Erik a glass of wine. I'll get fresh water from the well." She picked up a jug from the table and went outside.

Erik heard a splash, then a young man's voice.

"What's up?"

Jacqueline spoke slowly and with heavy emphasis. "Victor, my dear boy, your patron has come to see you after all these years."

"My what? And why do you—"

She cut him off. "Come, Victor, over to the well. Haul the bucket up for me and fill this jug."

They spoke further, but faintly, and the ratlike squeak of the pulley covered even this.

Armand handed Erik a glass of wine and poured himself a fuller glass. Armand tossed his off first, and poured himself another before Jacqueline returned with Victor.

Her voice preceded her. "A pleasant surprise, isn't it, Victor? Now, Victor, brush yourself off; prepare yourself, Victor, to meet again your benefactor Erik."

And she led him in by the hand, the jug in her other hand dripping.

Erik did not know—nor care—which stared harder, he or the young man.

Victor? This dull-eyed lout? Erik found it hard to accept that the shrewd quick gamin Victor had grown into this lummox. What a letdown. Erik tried to hide his dismay, control his disappointment. What good had he done the kid by shunting him off to the sticks, by consigning him to a dulling routine?

Erik could not summon the energy to rise and shake hands, much less the emotional force to leap up and embrace. But he found his voice. "Good to see you again, Victor."

Victor shuffled his feet and looked down as if surprised to find them in motion. "Uh, it's real nice to see you too, Erik."

The poor lost soul. Nothing remained in him of the old Victor, the young Victor. Erik, whether out of guilt or pity, shoved to his feet and embraced Victor. He stepped back. He felt as embarrassed as Victor looked. But Jacqueline stood smiling approval with her head canted and her hands on her hips. Then she lifted the corner of her apron and wiped an eye.

"What a happy reunion. I'm getting misty-eyed."

The first false note—the first, at least, that Erik had caught. Jacqueline damned well knew this was no happy reunion.

Erik turned again to the young man. Could it be that nothing about him spoke of Victor because this was not Victor?

Victor had seen Erik at his lowest, his moodiest, and had borne with him. Victor would remember that.

Erik tried for a casual tone. "Do you remember Pluto?"

The supposed Victor looked puzzled and cast Jacqueline and Armand glances that drew no help except stiff smiles. He shrugged. "Sure. It means 'more than anything else, ahead of anything else.' "

Erik grinned tightly. The young man thought Erik had said *plutôt*. "So it does. And do you remember the mama rat you killed ahead of all the rest?"

More sidelong glances but no help forthcoming, the young man laughed uncertainly. "Yeah. That was something, wasn't it?"

"Ten rats at one blow." Erik laughed. "A masterful stroke, my boy."

Erik was not the only one who could tell a false note. Jacqueline grabbed a kitchen knife and moved to block the doorway.

"Armand, Leon, grab him! He knows!"

Erik bent to grab the stool by one leg. Before he could swing the stool, the two men were on him and clamping his arms. Erik thrashed wildly, but by weight, rather than skill, they brought him down. Then Leon pinned him and Jacqueline held the knifepoint to his Adam's apple while Armand took an iron skillet and clanged it on Erik's skull.

When Erik came to, he found himself sitting on the floor in a corner, naked and bound hand and foot with rough rope.

The three Morilles sat around the table with his clothing heaped up in the middle and with Jacqueline clinking the six louis d'or Erik had carried in his pocket. Leon was tugging Erik's boots onto his feet. Armand was leaning to the hearth to light a spill for his pipe. The spill was a page of the draft of *Liri*.

Jacqueline was first to notice that Erik had come around. "Back with us, are you?"

Erik asked hoarsely, "What happened to the boy?"

She disregarded the question. She pointed to the crusted crease in his shoulder. They had removed the sackcloth bandage, perhaps hoping to find something of worth under it.

"How did you get that?"

"Somebody shot at me."

"While you were stealing the gold, no doubt."

He let that pass. "What happened to the boy?"

She obviously relished breaking it to him. "Your precious Victor didn't last long. The little sewer rat caught a chill and died the first winter. We, of course, hated to see the flow of gold stop on that account. So we paid the village apothecary to scribble those notes. Speaking of writing. . . ." She turned to gesture at the opened packet and caught Armand lighting his pipe with the cover page. She scowled at Armand. "Stop that, you fool. Let's find out first what it is."

Armand took a petulant draw and blew a defiant puff. "You're the fool. You should've told him 'It's a pity you came all this way for nothing. Victor's away just now.' "

Jacqueline glowered. "I thought we could pass Leon off as Victor. It seemed a chance worth taking. Is it my fault Leon takes after you and botched the job?"

Leon looked up. "Hey! Don't go blaming me."

"Shut up."

Leon shut up.

Jacqueline tapped her fingers on the papers. "Back to this." She faced Erik. "Just what species of writing is this?"

Erik burned his gaze at her. "Music."

"Music?" She riffled through the pages. "Yes, I've

seen music. It's music, but it's not all music. What's the rest of it?''

"The whole thing is an opera—the music and the words."

"You wrote this? You made this up?''

"I wrote it. I made it up.''

"Well. Quite a cultured bag of bones, eh?''

Erik did not bother to answer.

Jacqueline smiled. "Music. One can't eat music or spend music." She gathered the papers together and tossed them into the fireplace. "One can feed fire with music."

Erik watched his proof of authorship go up in smoke, sink in ashes. He narrowed his eyes, and not against the smoke. "You should not have done that.''

Jacqueline seemed not to have heard. Her eyes passed indifferently over his naked bound form and fixed on the six louis d'or. With a sigh, she picked them up. "Well, these are the last we'll have from him.''

When she added the six louis to the hoard cached under a stone of the floor, without bothering to conceal from Erik the hiding place, Erik knew he was in her eyes as good as dead.

He strained at his bonds but could not loosen them or burst them. He saw Armand watching, fascinated. He blazed his eyes at Armand.

Armand tried to stare back, but his gaze could not hold and fell away. Armand appeared set on covering that by mocking. "Look at him. Walked right in without suspecting a thing. So green the cows could eat him.''

Leon laughed. "Better the pigs.''

Armand almost choked on the pipe stem, laughing around it. He pulled it from his mouth. "They won't find much nourishment in Old Corpseface, Old Skin-and-bones.'' Coughing, he put the pipe down.

Without a glance at Erik, Jacqueline said, "Don't waste time putting on a harlequinade. Finish him off.''

Armand finished off the bottle of wine first.

* * *

He lay deep in the sludge of the sewers, or buried in the mudflats of the Seine. No—the mud was not the same. This felt a much-churned mud, alive with forms vastly huger than rats. Forms that grunted and snuffled as they nosed him and trod him underfoot.

Erik surfaced to the sense of heavy bodies rooting around him. He squeezed his eyes tight for tears to wash his eyes clear of the mud, and a blur of light and shadow fixed the place. He lay, still naked and bound, in the pigpen, at the mercy of boar tusks.

First he writhed and kicked out to convince the hogs that something desperate and dangerous would strike back if they tried to make a meal of it, and to see if he could loosen the ropes. Then, through a throbbing on top of the throbbing from the skillet blow, and without letting up in the squirming and straining, he tried to think why he still lived—if indeed he had not come back from the dead.

Either Armand had been too sodden to make certain Erik was truly dead or Armand had counted on the blow and the bonds to render Erik helpless.

His vision cleared, and he felt repulsed by the evil ugly faces of the hogs. Then, without ceasing to ward the hogs off, he grinned at them. They were as nature had made them, just as nature had made him the thing that for a time had made its living by putting itself on show as a living corpse. Humans had penned them in, just as humans had in effect penned him into the cellars of the Opera House.

That did not make the hogs his friends. To them, this was not Man the Master. This was something Man the Master had thrown them to eat.

Erik felt about in the mud for something to grasp and wield—a sharp stone, a splinter of bone—anything to discourage the hogs and attack the ropes. And a bone buried deep in the mud came to hand.

Not a splinter, but a whole bone, a human thighbone. A small one.

Victor's?

Erik grinned sadly but nonetheless savagely. *Have you been waiting here for me all these years?*

He took a good grip of a knob end. He held it in one hand and both arms had to work as one. They worked as one now when the boar moved in on him, head swinging the tusks in a slashing arc. The bone smacked the snout a sharp blow. The boar backed off with a surprised grunt, but eyed him meanly.

Erik sensed a slight easing of his bonds. Moisture in the mud must have soaked into the rope. He could stretch the rope a trifle, give himself some slack.

His crossed wrists were tied in front and by bending he could reach the rope binding his crossed ankles. The same mud made the knots slippery to already benumbed fingers. But he kept at the knot holding his feet and at last dug a fingernail in under the uppermost loop of the knot. From there it was simple, though still not easy, and at last the knot loosened entirely and the rope fell away from around his ankles. He shoved himself to his feet.

Once he stood upright, and was—even though swaying—again Man the Master, he had no more trouble from the hogs. Boar and sows made way for him as he waded and slithered to the fence. He no longer needed to beat them off with the bone, but he held on to it.

Wrists still tied, and bone still in hand, he climbed stiffly and painfully out of the pen.

He leaned against the fence, gulping great lungfuls of cool air into him. He straightened. His gaze swept the rich farmland bleakly. Far off he saw a figure lending the landscape scale. He watched the figure lean on its hoe and lift one foot as if admiring the boot, and then the other the same way. Leon.

Erik grinned. He dismissed Leon for the moment and tested the knot fastening his wrists. The knot would not yield to his teeth. He drew another deep cool breath and faced the pen.

He caught the boar's eye and held it. He spoke low in his most vibrant, most urgent tone. "Sui. Come here."

The boar obeyed, maybe because Man the Master was

also Man the Server. It thrust its head between the rails, looking for what Man had brought it.

Erik slowly brought his bound hands to the boar's head, carefully worked the uppermost loop of the knot onto a tusk, then spiked it hard.

The boar drew back, pulling Erik flat against the fence.

Erik blazed his eyes at the boar. "Sui. Hold still."

The boar's eyes remained mean, but Man the Master's command prevailed. True, the mud did not give the boar's feet much purchase.

Erik worked the knot around on the tusk, then unspiked it. Now the knot had give, had play. Erik's teeth finished the job. The rope fell off.

He locked eyes with the boar again. He spat mud. "I'll feed you yet," he said.

And the boar moved his head in what might have been a nod.

Erik shot a look toward Leon to make sure Leon had seen nothing from afar. Mud made good camouflage. Erik rose from his crouch and strode to the cottage door.

His stick leaned still against the wall, but he stayed with the bone. He listened at the door a moment, then flung it open and himself in.

Armand stood in the center of the room, filling his pipe, and Jacqueline stood bent over the table, picking at a piece of ham on a plate. Both froze openmouthed as Erik rushed in upon them swinging the thighbone.

After killing Jacqueline and Armand, battering them past recognition to make sure, he held the jug high and poured the water over him to remove the worst of the caking mud, shit, and blood. Then he tore a blanket off a bed and rubbed himself dry. Still naked, he finished the ham and waited with the kitchen knife for Leon to come in from the fields.

After cutting Leon's throat, he pulled his boots off Leon's feet, then stripped all three bodies and dragged them one at a time to the pen and lifted them over the fence and dropped them inside.

Now he went to the well and the pulley sang its song as he hauled up bucketful after bucketful of water to wash himself clean on the spot. He returned to the cottage, dried himself off again, and put on his clothes and boots.

He pried up the stone in the floor and unearthed the hoard of gold. The bone he buried in its place.

It took no stressful thinking to decide what to do with the gold.

Liri, after killing her husband and her son, contemplates the bag of gold. She raises the bag high, much as a headsman might hold a severed head, and sings her song.

> *Behold!*
> *For this, the wicked word was told.*
> *For this, immortal soul was sold.*
> *Behold!*
> *A bag of gold.*
> *Behold!*
> *For this, there died an outlaw bold.*
> *For this, did bloody tale unfold.*
> *Behold!*
> *A bag of gold.*
> *Behold!*
> *For this, a mother's heart turned cold.*
> *For this, a youth would not grow old.*
> *Behold!*
> *A bag of gold.*

She dips the bag in the blood of Rustem and Djordji, then drops it into the well before fleeing to her tribal home in the mountains.

Erik raised the bag of gold, weighing it, then found a length of rope and slung the bag from his good shoulder, under his cowl.

There would be a horse and cart around, but he took up his stick and on foot set out for home.

* * *

Through the eye in the canvas of Circe and her swine, Erik watched MM. Valembert and Lefevre hard at work.

Swirling wine and flicking cigar ash, the managing director and the conductor sat at Valembert's desk and discussed staging the new opera *Illyria*, a work by Lefevre himself.

It took Erik a moment to realize that they had retitled *Liri*, that they had stolen his opera.

On his return, he had spent a full week mostly in sleep, healing mind and body—and now, just when he felt whole, himself again, came this new shock.

He grew stiff with wrath and a tear of rage glittered in his eye. He listened with divided attention, thinking ahead to what he could do to get back at them. He would send the rats up among the audience. Then, as the full enormity of their usurpation of the opera and betrayal of its spirit sank in, he made up his mind to plague them with better than rats.

He heard them conspire to put in a cloying and vitiating long movement—Lefevre hummed the theme for Valembert's benefit—just where Erik had scrapped the long movement he had sweated over, at the end of the second act. ("Brilliant, my dear Claude," said Valembert. "Thoroughly professional. It will certainly knock down any claim our crude unknown may put forward.")

He heard them add an anticlimactic ballet scene at the end—the mountain tribe celebrating Zoe's deed and return.

Zoe! They had even renamed Liri.

Now, heady with inspiration from the fumes of wine and tobacco, they turned to casting the opera.

They spoke of Céleste Mascarin, a coloratura soprano Erik much admired, for Liri-Zoe. Though offstage the Mascarin talked in a colorless tone, saving all her emotion for the stage, onstage she became liquid fire. He silently applauded the choice.

Maybe the opera would not be a total disaster.

But Marcel Rambol, tenor, to play Rustem (renamed

Baptiste; *Baptiste!*)? Totally wrong. Erik considered
Rambol a *cabot* in both senses of the word: "mutt" and
"ham actor." Plummy voice, indistinct consonants and
vowels, given to fluffing his lines and flatting his notes.
Walking through his roles when he found no occasion to
chew the scenery. In short, an absurdity.

And Georgette Amadou, a tiny lyric soprano in her late
twenties, to play Djordji? Merde. Erik had nothing
against a woman playing a boy. But thought of the Amadou as Djordji made Erik's heart sink apace. The re-
troussé nose would be bearable, but a mincing Djordji
would hardly evoke Victor.

Jules Janvier as Mehmet (now *Ali*)? Out of the question. The basso profundo had the voice but not the figure.
The audience would howl to think of the portly Janvier
swooping down like an eagle. Not on Turks, not even on
turkey cocks.

No, no, no, no, no.

Rehearsals confirmed his worst fears.

Erik made his way back down to the cellars after
watching one such rehearsal from the shadows of a box.
He shook so with rage that he did not care that along the
way a woman cleaning the stalls caught sight of him and
fainted.

Out of his rage came a thought. All sounding bodies
are in a state of vibration. All structures have a funda-
mental frequency at which they will vibrate if excited.

Yes, yes, yes, yes, yes.

Erik vibrated with excitement.

Music could shatter a glass or topple the walls of Jer-
icho. With the right vibrations he could bring down the
Opera House, shake it to pieces and collapse it into the
underground lake.

He brought himself up short. That might satisfy his
immediate urge to strike back, but it would also destroy
his permanent home.

For his own sake, for more practical and artistic revenge, he had to be more selective.

He reached his chamber and found his glance lighting on the volume he had borrowed from the Opera House library. He reached for it.

On a Theory of Semantic Phase, by one Professor Alf. W. Bahzan of the University of Leyden.

Till now, Erik had skimmed through only the first few chapters. The work demanded much of the reader. What he had been able to make of the words had seemed fascinating, but the mathematical formulae had proved too daunting to others before him and fully three-fifths of the pages remained uncut.

Now he went to work with letter opener to liberate the professor and settled himself to study.

The professor had some odd notions. He posited something in the human makeup, perhaps on the cellular level, that tells the body what shape to take.

But his basic message seemed to be this: When any two particularities of animate matter—however far apart in time and/or space—are in *semantic phase*, they cohere in, and stereotaxically actualize, an idea that otherwise hovers in the limbo between possibility and reality.

Erik puzzled over this. *Semantic phase* seemed something other than, and something more than, sympathetic vibrations. It seemed to deal with the effect of words on mind and body.

The professor took it as self-evident that the mind can bring about physiological change. If the mind feels "This is more than I can bear," the body gets a backache. If the mind feels "I can stomach this no longer," the body gets a bellyache.

The professor went beyond this to hold that sound—not mere noise but sound with sense—could remold human clay.

When in semantic phase, the professor said, molecules would shift shape. The mind's vision would become the body's reality.

Erik remembered stories around Gypsy campfires of

werewolves and vampires. By woodsmoke and nightchill, it had been easy to believe in such transformations. Why not believe now? He knew what wonders music could work. He had seen Gypsy violinists pluck heartstrings and loosen pursestrings.

With the right instrument, the right sound, he could—

The double bassoon. That would be his instrument. They called the double bassoon the clown of the orchestra because of the comic sounds it made as a solo instrument. Erik grinned. He had seen some vicious clowns. He himself . . .

The glissando. That would be his sound. It all rested in the demonic nature of the glissando. The screaming glissando of the eagle that froze its prey.

He ventured out one evening, and in a music store near the Opera House bought the best double bassoon in stock. If the little old man wondered how his strange customer would draw the wind for it, he did not voice the thought.

He grinned. Gold that a Liri would have dropped into the well at the Morille farm had paid for the instrument that would play the accompaniment to Liri dropping gold into a well. It seemed mystically right.

The sound had to be precise. Erik scraped his double reed and adjusted his lip pressure to get the sound recipe he wanted.

He had time, but not all that much. He overheard Valembert and Lefevre, in their anxiety to establish authorship, decide to schedule the premiere of *Illyria* for six weeks hence. Lefevre reluctantly agreed to let other conductors take over performances already on the schedule while he single-mindedly polished *Illyria*.

Erik just as single-mindedly applied Professor Bahzan's formulae, as Erik understood them, to the glissando. This involved adding mordents and pralltrillers. These melodic graces on the awkward and blatant double bassoon would have been tricky for a virtuoso. Erik often had to laugh in earnest and in frustation at his own clownish efforts and effects. More than once he was on the point of giving it all up. But at last he got it just so.

It worked almost too well, for it worked on him. The sound involved his whole being, the harmonics possessed him in every cell.

He felt rather than heard the vibrant glissando swoop ominously—and with it, there swooped a shadow of satanic mischief.

When he finished playing, he broke into nervous laughter, as at having escaped a spell, a doom the sound laid on him.

He had the sense that the sound was in tune with something in the universe, in phase with the selfsame notes playing elsewhere and/or elsewhen.

Sweat filmed him. If he had not concentrated on getting the sound, and had allowed some stray thought to invade his mind, who could fathom what change he might have suffered?

Damned if he would play the damned glissando himself again. He cased the instrument and put it away forever and from memory scored the double bassoon's part. And even then he could not look at the notes on paper without a shiver, though with a grim smile.

Erik watched the musicians show up for rehearsal and waited for the bassoonist to find the changes on his music stand.

The bassoonist stared long at his new score before hesitantly approaching Lefevre.

"Pardon, maestro, but you did not tell me about this."

"About what?" Lefevre took the sheet loftily. He scanned it and frowned. He jerked his head in the direction of Valembert's office with something between puzzlement and pique, then testily handed the part back to the bassoonist. "I did not have time. Let me hear you play it."

"Of course, maestro. This is the first I've seen it, you must understand."

"I understand, I understand. Play."

The bassoonist experienced a delay in reaching certainty of pitch; it took the double bassoon a while to attain a balance of losing interior heat to the colder rehearsal room. The other musicians exchanged smiles. Lefevre looked on sourly; his fingers moved not in sympathy with the bassoonist's fingering but as though they itched to tear the sheet of music—or the musician, or both—to bits.

But then after repeated tries the glissando came nearer Erik's conception, and the other musicians left off smiling and whispering and Lefevre began nodding.

"Again, again. That is more like what I had in mind. I can see the audience gasp with awe as the gold pours into the well."

Erik started. By the slant of sunlight pouring in through the window he knew it to be Valembert's usual time to arrive at his office. Erik hurried through his secret passages to the place behind Circe and her swine.

Valembert had indeed arrived, and Erik caught him just after Valembert had relieved himself of cane and hat and was in the act of stripping off his gloves. Valembert paused with one glove still on and reopened the inner door the better to hear the compelling sound from the rehearsal room.

The bassoonist had mastered the glissando, and Valembert stood with head canted listening.

Erik threw his voice so that it seemed to come out of nowhere, out of everywhere. "Valembert, you are hand in glove—forever."

Valembert stood rooted long after the glissando had died away. Then he pulled himself free, shut the door, and stared around his office in a daze. With the blankness of habit he resumed taking off his glove.

He came alive with a gasp of pain, and frowned down at his gloved hand. He tugged, gently at first, then madly.

He let out scream after scream as the tugging grew more painful and more bloody.

M. Valembert was not on hand for that night's performance of *Die Zauberflöte*. Nor would he return to the Opera House ever again.

To the end of his days he would travel the Continent from consultant to consultant for the thing that had happened to his hand.

It seemed that the glove had fused to the hand; that the suede had all the sensitivity of the flesh bonded to it; that there was no telling where glove ended and hand began, that surgery would be necessary to remove the glove, yet surgery was impossible.

Erik, however, enjoyed that performance of *Die Zauberflöte*. In fact, Erik applauded Mozart from the shadows of M. Valembert's otherwise unoccupied box. Erik enjoyed not only his fellow composer's work but the audience and the Opera House itself.

In the distant ceiling, through the dusky glow of gas and gilding, he could make out dimly the grand frescoes by M. Baudry. The auditorium's plaster nymphs and cherubs found counterpoint in the perfumed, powdered and pomaded ticketholders.

Between acts, Erik peeked out at the humming crowd strolling and gossiping in the corridor. Out of the sounding sea of voices he picked the name Younceville.

Erik's eyes flashed and his ears pricked up.

"Yes," someone said, "Evariste's back from his plantations on Martinique, and I hear he's brought some goods with him."

"What? Rum? Bananas?"

"Brown sugar."

Erik looked and saw the nose of a tall man cut through the crowd as the fin of a shark cuts through the sea. And as the crowd parted, Erik saw a beautiful black woman on the arm of the Duc d'Origny de Younceville.

The next act was to begin and they were returning to their box.

Erik made note of the box and though he could not see into Younceville's box from Valembert's he took in the rest of *Die Zauberflöte* with savage joy.

No one among those attached to the Opera House linked M. Valembert's strange misfortune to *Illyria*. No one raised the specter of a jinx, even though the demonic glissando evoked eerie sensations in all who heard it.

The double bassoonist seemed to grow paler and edgier as opening night approached, bringing nearer his glissando solo, but those who knew him put that down to stage fright.

Otherwise, everything moved smoothly.

For Erik, too. By opening night he had built a closet, a space just large enough for him to hide in if he stood, in a back corner of Younceville's box. This he fashioned as a hollow pillar, and he built another in the other corner to balance it and so help it pass unnoticed. He gilded these, and aged the gilt to match the Opera House's omnipresent gilding.

And by then, too, he had installed a speaking tube that ran from the cellar to the orchestra pit, up through the conductor's wooden music stand fixed on the little podium. He masked the opening in the front of the stand with cloth painted the color of the stand.

On the day of opening night itself, Erik could spare little time to check that everything went well. Several singers had words about how they would line up hand-in-hand for the applause, but everything material backstage, down to the dressing room trays of *papillotes*, the little pieces of paper used for curling hair, was in place. He found the mammoth Janvier well muffled up against drafts. He caught a glimpse of Céleste Mascarin's perfect rondeur of hip, of her lovely face in the cheval glass as the Mascarin powdered her shoulders, of her *oreilles de chien*, the long curls that seemed all right for the Mascarin but all wrong for Liri; but that had to suffice. He must station himself in the pillar before the doors opened and the seats filled.

By the flicker of the flaring gas jets, Erik watched through the peephole in his pillar as Younceville took a pinch of snuff from his *tabatière*. Eager though Erik was to observe the performance of his opera, however mutilated by the miscreants, he found himself fixing on the back of Younceville's head.

The overture. The three knocks. The curtain.

He tried to hear the singing of his words through the stupid and incessant chatter of Younceville and party, and at times barely held himself from shouting at them to shut up.

Younceville and his party had taken the pillars for granted, not once remarking on them, though one woman complained that she had never realized how cramped these boxes were.

Erik grew as stiff with inaction as with rage. It took all his self-control to keep from giving his presence away. Even between the acts he did not dare stir. The curtain had risen at nine-thirty on the dot. Erik had been inside the pillar at least an hour before that. The opera had a good hour-and-a-half to go before the glissando. He stayed still and waited, straining for his cue.

It came at last. Liri raised high the bag of gold and sang her aria.

For once those in the box fell silent, caught by the moment or sensing something in the air. The *aigrette en diamants* of the mistress scarcely waved.

Now Liri opened the bag and poured out the gold and as she did so the double bassoon sounded its demonic glissando.

Erik threw his voice at Younceville.

"Younceville, stand up. Younceville, you are a living Y."

The hand of Younceville's mistress fell away from Younceville's thigh as Younceville stood up. As in a trance, Younceville lifted his arms in what might have seemed to onlookers imitation or mockery of the heroine's elevation of the bag of gold. His hands were empty, however, and the arms thrust up and out and the legs were tightly together. He formed a recognizable Y.

Before the last notes of the glissando sounded, Younceville came out of his trance, found himself paralyzed so, struggled to move arms and legs, and toppled, still a rigid Y, into the stalls.

Orchestra and singers fell raggedly silent.

Down in the orchestra pit Lefevre stood frozen in almost the same Y pose. Then he broke free and signaled the stage manager. The curtain came down.

Attendants rushed to rescue Younceville and the people he had fallen upon. Only one other person seemed seriously hurt, and this man, eye bleeding thanks to Younceville's signet ring, they helped to an exit in the wake of Younceville, who proved awkward to maneuver through the aisle other than sideways.

Erik had slipped from the pillar and leaned over the mistress unnoticed to look down and see how Younceville fared. The man seemed alive, but alive as one with a stroke. And so it would prove; Younceville lived on another dozen years, a Y to the end. But Erik, satisfied, patted the mistress consolingly on the back and was gone before she turned around.

Meanwhile Lefevre had leapt to the stage; from there he frantically sought to stem panic. "Ladies and gentlemen! Quiet yourselves! Shortly the opera will continue from where it left off!"

By now Erik had reached the cellar and the speaking tube and stood ready.

As Erik had hoped, Lefevre began again with the glissando, Younceville having spoiled the end.

And as the double bassoonist sounded the demonic glissando, Erik intoned for Lefevre's ears only:

> "Your mouth is a rose,
> Your teeth are pearls,

A button your nose,
And raven your curls."

They had scheduled *Illyria* for two weeks, for the usual four performances a week, but the curtain came down on it during the first performance, before the spectacular ballet at the end, and never rose on it again.

THE PHANTOM OF THE SOAP OPERA

by Henry Slesar

It was inevitable that I would be compared with Gaston Leroux when I decided to write the chronicles of the Phantom of Studio 43. (Actually, the story had already surfaced in the public press, in a trash barrel of a gossip column, with three factual errors per column inch). But when my name was finally linked with the Phantom, everyone missed one small mystical detail, that I had been born on the very day of Leroux's death, a coincidence which could have led to lurid speculations about reincarnation. Let all speculation end with these pages. This is the whole story of the Phantom of Television Studio 43, defantasized and demysticized, and all the more fantastic for being the unembellished truth.

My first disclaimer is this. I was never a victim of the Phantom, and might not have encountered him at all if I hadn't deliberately chosen to invade his dark kingdom. Most of the Phantom's mischief was confined to the television studio in downtown New York where *Before the Dawn* was taped each weekday, and writers of daytime serials are rarely on the set when their lines are spoken. Even if their laborious chores allowed them time for such visits, producers and directors discourage them. Writers tend to stumble over cables. They gawk a lot. Worst of all, they get collared by actors with persuasive suggestions about ways to fatten their roles. Television studios are not their natural habitat, and Studio 43 wasn't mine.

That was one important reason why the Phantom's deadly, ghostly hand never reached out for me.

I like to think there is another reason: that the Phantom simply didn't include me in his plan of Revenge, that he recognized my innocence in the great Sin that he believed had been committed against him. Of course, your acceptance of this theory depends on whether or not you accept my explanation of the Phantom, his identity, and his demonic purpose. There are some people (mostly in the Police Department) who were and remain skeptical.

In an introduction of this sort, it's customary to thank those who provided supportive facts of one's narrative, just as Gaston Leroux did in his *Phantom of the Opera*. I'm sorry to say that I can name only two people who were of the slightest assistance: Mike Zurman, the associate producer of *Before The Dawn*, and a police officer I'll call Harry, who prefers, like the Phantom himself, to remain anonymous.

They said it began at the thirtieth anniversary party. As usual, "they" were wrong. There had already been half a dozen "accidents" at Studio 43 that could have been laid at the feet of the Phantom, but it was just as easy to blame a falling baby spot on a rusty connection, a sudden fire on a crewman's careless smoking habits, an outbreak of stomach virus on a shared pizza with everything on it including salmonella. But when *Before the Dawn* turned thirty (an achievement, considering the short life span of most television shows), the Phantom struck in a way that was unmistakable. He threw a pie in the face of the whole ensemble.

Well, not really a pie. It was the anniversary cake, a square yard of angel food and chocolate icing and fluffy billows of whipped cream. It had been ordered from Latanzi's in downtown Manhattan, with special attention to its photogenic quality, the show's producers hoping for party coverage in the fan press and perhaps even *People* Magazine (Mike Zurman dated a girl whose mother knew a man whose sister worked there). *People* never showed up, and missed a great photo opportunity: half a dozen members of the cast, including the celebrated Nina Kemper, covered with angel food, chocolate, and whipped cream.

No one could explain how the cake was intercepted. Solly, the dullwitted security guard, claimed he never received it, but also admitted that he had strayed from his post on more than one occasion that afternoon (the champagne was flowing freely). The delivery man from Latanzi's swore that a "man in uniform" accepted the boxed cake and signed a receipt with a scrawl that was indecipherable. Nobody noticed that the cake hadn't arrived until Gordon Knapp, the producer, decided it was time for a group shot and realized that there was only a square yard of bare white linen on the refreshment table. Where was the cake? The question was answered a moment later, when twenty-one pounds of baked goods descended from above and smashed moistly into the group, splashing its icing in a wide perimeter, setting off a chorus of shrieks and imprecations. Only one person, Mike Zurman, had the presence of mind to look up at the catwalk and saw what appeared to be a blurred pair of silver-gray legs, vanishing among the tangled cables overhead. It was Harry the Cop who later remarked that the security uniform was also silver-gray.

Solly wasn't accused, however; he was on the studio floor with the rest of us, a comic glob of pink icing in the form of the letter B smack in the middle of his astonished face. But it was the last day Solly was to wear his uniform. The studio management blamed him for both the theft of the cake and for allowing the practical joker into the studio. As to the identity of the culprit, the most favored theory was that it was some disgruntled fan, perhaps unhappy about the breakup of one of the six or seven romances currently spinning in the story line. Viewers hated breakups, which is why they were so frequent on *Before the Dawn*. It's axiomatic in this business. If you're after ratings, never give the audience what it wants.

There was only one serious injury among the victims,

but it was purely emotional. At first, we thought Nina Kemper was joining in the outburst of nervous laughter that followed the bombing; then we realized it was hysteria. For some reason, perhaps because of my owlish appearance—I wear large round glasses, and people are always mistaking me for a physician, although I'm squeamish even about applying Band-Aids—Nina chose to seize my arm and plead with me to take her "somewhere." I was new to *Before the Dawn* at the time, having signed on as associate headwriter only three months ago, but Nina, like half a dozen other actors, had already gone out of her way to be ingratiating, acts of kindness somewhat soured by a warning label which read: Caution: Actor Friendships May be Dangerous to your Story Line. At any rate, there was no gallant way to refuse, and a few minutes later I found myself in a narrow booth at the Three Turtles, an establishment popular with the cast and crew simply because it was the bar nearest the studio.

I sat through two drinks all by myself while Nina repaired the damage in the powder room. By the time she emerged, the only hint of her experience was in her eyes. They were oddly unfocused, the pupils dilated, and I suspected that the actress had done more than comb cake out of her hair. As a result, I assumed that her first statement was inspired by something out of a pharmacopoeia.

"I think it's my husband," she said. "I think it's Jules. Please don't laugh! I've been so afraid to tell anyone my theory, but I thought a writer . . . Well, writers have imagination, don't they?" She looked at me imploringly.

I tried desperately to use my writer's imagination, but all I could come up with was a lame scenario in which an estranged, prankish spouse drops a cake on his wife and her associates as an act of spiteful malice. Then I remembered something that blew that theory to bits. Nina Kemper had been widowed almost two years ago.

"Isn't Jules—well, dead?" I asked.

"That's why I haven't said anything. People are so *funny* about things like this. Although maybe now, because of Shirley—"

"Who?"

"Shirley MacLaine. Thank God for that woman, she's made it so much less *embarrassing* to say what you feel, what you *know* is true, about Death and all that. Do you know what I believe? I believe the *Beyond* is coming closer, that it's no longer as distant as it used to be. I think it has something to do with the planets, with anti-matter and black holes and all those other funny things they're finding out there . . .''

She stopped and ordered a drink, and I was grateful for a momentary respite. A devout Skeptic, I'm always unnerved by conversations on occult subjects, and usually found myself nodding in apparent agreement rather than waste energy in useless rebuttal. But I couldn't resist at least one question.

"Are you saying that it was a *ghost* who dropped that cake?"

"Please don't use the word 'ghost.' I *hate* the word 'ghost.' We've made it sound so trivial, a joke word. Casper and the Ghostbusters and all that. Say 'spirit.' Say '*revenant*.' What a terrifying word! It gives me chills just to say it."

"The cake," I reminded.

"I know—you don't think spirits can manipulate solid matter. Haven't you heard of poltergeists? If it *was* Jules, it wouldn't be the first time he's done something like this. Do you remember that light *crashing* on the set last year? I know, you weren't there, darling, but you must have heard about it."

"I heard something, yes."

"Did you hear *where* it fell? On Felicia's bedroom set!" Nina's show character was named was Felicia. "I was doing a run-through not three feet from where that light dropped. If I'd been walking downstage instead of across, it would have killed me!"

It wasn't quite the story I'd heard; Nina was on her lunch break when the accident occurred, but I didn't interrupt.

"And the fires! Do you realize the abnormal number

of *fires* at the studio? Ask Gordon Knapp! He's always complaining that our insurance premiums are exorbitant because of all those little fires that keep breaking out!''

''I *did* hear that there have been . . . accidents.''

''There *are* no accidents,'' Nina said gravely. ''That's what Shirley MacLaine says.''

''I think Freud said it first.''

''Things fall, things crash, things disappear, people trip, people get sick . . .'' She stared into the red depths of her Bloody Mary. ''But that isn't the only reason I think Jules is responsible.''

I said nothing, recognizing her need for the dramatic pause.

''It's because I've *seen* him, darling.''

She lifted her eyes, challenging me to protest. I bit into a pretzel instead.

''It's true. I've seen Jules—in that same fur-trimmed coat he used to wear when he played Randolph. Oh, it was all so terribly quick! Just a flash of his image, after the studio was dark . . .''

''Maybe you saw Tom Derringer,'' I suggested carefully. Tom was the actor currently playing the part of Randolph Moore.

''No. Tom wasn't at the studio that day, he was in Virgin Gorda or someplace. It was Jules I saw, looking just like Randolph, or Randolph's ghost, if you can imagine such a thing.''

The ghost of a fictional character? Even my writer's imagination didn't stretch that far.

''It was my husband, darling, I swear it on his grave! Not that he's in it. He's right here, on 23rd Street! He's still in the studio, where he was killed!''

''He wasn't *killed*,'' I reminded her. ''I was told Jules died of a heart attack, during rehearsal.''

''He died when he tried to lift that chair—that tiny little uphosltered chair that someone had *nailed* to the floor! It was an act of murder, pure and simple!''

''I heard it was nailed down because the damned thing was always falling over during taping. No one on the crew wanted to admit the nailing, because of what happened.''

"If there wasn't a *murder,* Jules wouldn't be haunting the studio now. Everyone knows that a murdered spirit can't rest until he's avenged!''

"Well,'' I said uneasily, "it's a theory. I just think it's a funny kind of revenge, making all that mischief in the studio. Couldn't it simply be that this show is . . . well, accident prone?''

"It's *death* prone, darling.''

She gave the line her most dramatic reading, almost turning "death'' into a three-syllable word. But then she was silent, and a new expression crossed her handsome if slightly overpowdered features, a look I can only describe as fearful.

"I'm sorry,'' she said. "I've never told anyone this before, and maybe I shouldn't, in case . . .'' She stopped again, and like most writers, I felt compelled to finish her sentence in my own mind. "In case,'' she might have said, *"Jules is listening . . .''*

The next day, I had lunch with Ted Hauser, the headwriter who had made me his "associate,'' but I didn't tell him Nina's theory on the assumption that she intended it to be confidential. But I did ask him about the phrase "death prone.''

"It's true,'' Ted said, surprising me. "There have been a peculiar number of deaths. I mean, in the studio itself.''

"Like who? Besides Nina's husband?''

"Simon Wales, for one. The actor who played Raymond Moore before Jules replaced him.''

"I never heard of Wales,'' I said. "But then, I only started watching the show six months ago. How many Raymonds have you had?''

"Tom Derringer is number four.''

"How far back does the character go?''

"At least twenty years,'' Ted said. "Mason Trumbull created the role, of course, until he got too long in the tooth. You know the way the Suits are.'' He meant the management executives who ran the show. "They hate to see their core characters age. So one day, I was told to write Raymond out for a couple of months. I sent him to South America to build a banana factory or something, and his plane crashed in the Peruvian jungles. It must have done him some good. When he came back, he looked twenty years younger. He also looked a hell of a lot like Simon Wales."

"And what killed Wales?"

"He choked himself to death. Strangled on a piece of meat."

"Doesn't anybody here know the Heimlich maneuver?"

"There was nobody around. He was alone in the studio when it happened, after hours, having a beer and a sandwich and studying next day's script. Simon had trouble with lines."

"Wait a minute," I said. "I think I remember reading about that. Only I thought it was his heart."

"That was what they printed, cardiac arrest. It sounded better than Death by Roast Beef, and it was literally true, of course. Whose heart *doesn't* arrest when they die?"

"Name another case."

"Lois Sturtevant," Ted said promptly. That surprised me, even though I knew that Gordon Knapps' secretary had committed suicide after her boyfriend, one of the crew members, walked out on her—on the show, too, for that matter.

"I thought Lois died in her apartment."

"She did," Ted said. "Keep this quiet, okay? Lois took that overdose right here in the studio, in Gordon's office. Then she calmly left, hailed a cab, and went home."

That was worth a "my God," so I said it.

"They found the pill bottle on her desk, that's how they know. Lois was more than a little weird; her love life must have pushed her over the edge. For a week before her suicide, she was going around telling people that the studio was haunted."

That got my attention.

"Haunted," I repeated carefully. "By what?"

Ted shrugged. "A ghost, what else? Maybe Simon Wales."

"Not Jules?"

"Jules was still alive then."

"Did Lois describe the ghost?"

"Hey, what is this?" Ted asked, looking at me curiously. "You planning to write a book or something? You've got enough on your plate right now."

"I'm just interested, that's all."

"All I remember her saying is that she saw this *person* walk right through a wall. She was looneytunes. People walk through walls in Spielberg movies, not in real life."

"What about the cake man?"

"Who?"

"The man who threw the cake! Mike Zurman saw him on the catwalk, and he vanished into thin air. Maybe it was Lois' ghost."

"There are doors up there, not just walls."

"Doors?" That was news to me.

"Of course. The whole studio's a maze of doors and crawl spaces and underground passages, didn't you know that? That's the way they built theaters back then."

"I forgot this was a theater once," I said.

"It was a movie house called the RKO Grand Palace about thirty years ago, and it was a legitimate theater *before* it was converted into a movie house. Their big hit was *Ben Hur.* They had a chariot race right on stage."

"Wow," I said.

"That's what Mike Zurman told me—he's the local historian. His great-grandfather used to manage the place."

I knew the building was enormous. I remember Gordon Knapp telling me that at one time the network produced *two* daytime serials out of this same facility, with room left over for the storage of random props. If there *was* a ghost at work in Studio 43, he had plenty of living space—if that's the word.

"Stop worrying about ghosts," Ted said, "and start

worrying about that new story line for Felicia. The audience is getting fed up with her usual bitchy tricks. We need something new, something really *rotten* for her to do.''

As it turned out, Felicia—or rather the actress who portrayed her—did something really rotten the next day. She disappeared.

A soap opera set is always a scene of controlled panic. Some of the best acting takes place before the broadcast. The performers appear calm, untroubled, undaunted by the fact that they memorized their lines only the day before, that the dress rehearsal had been a preview of disaster, that there were a hundred things that might go wrong during a taping. But the one event calculated to shake their professional equanimity is the nonappearance of a cast member. Nina Kemper had attended the dress; she had coolly dispatched her lines without hesitation; as always, she had her moves down so perfectly that they appeared choreographed. Nina was reliable. But fifteen minutes before taping, Nina wasn't there.

Joe Manley, the director of the day's episode, sent half a dozen production assistants in search of her. They covered every possible site, from dressing room to powder room to wardrobe, from her Village apartment to the Three Turtles, although Nina had never been known to drink in the daytime. They made frantic calls to her agent, her lawyer, her mother in L.A., her two ex-husbands, her current boyfriend. None of them knew anything. Nina had simply vanished, just as if she had—what? Walked through a wall? I was the only one who asked the question, and only of myself.

Gordon Knapp made a quick decision. They would tape "around" Felicia that day, and then extend the next day's taping schedule. He was assuming, of course, that Felicia would reappear. She didn't. The only solution became a temporary recasting of the role. An actress named Amanda Parr was hired, and with a professionalism that never failed to impress me, stepped into the role within a matter of days.

It was only a stopgap solution, while the search for Nina Kemper went on, hampered by the fact that the Suits managed to keep the fact of her disappearance a secret from the public. The official explanation was a sudden breakdown of her health, that she was in need of a rest, that she would soon be back, bitchier than ever. I couldn't blame their circumspection. More than any other daytime serial, the rating strength of *Before The Dawn* depended upon one central character, and Felicia, as played by Nina Kemper, was definitely IT. Her permanent loss was unthinkable.

By the end of the week, the police were quietly involved, which is how I met Harry.

I was surprised to find myself among the interrogees, considering my short tenure on the show, but my post-party drink with the actress qualified me as one of the "Last Seen Withs."

Harry was surprisingly small for a cop; he must have just come in under the qualifying wire. He was also older than the "detective" image I carried around in my Writer's Imagination. He made up for both deficiencies by a bright-faced enthusiasm for his job. When I told him the substance of my conversation with Nina Kemper (I was no longer reticent under the circumstances) he listened eagerly, and never even smiled at the improbabilities of her "ghost" story. As it turned out, it wasn't the first time he'd heard it.

"She said something to this guy Tom Derringer about it, you know him?"

"Yes," I said. "The actor who plays Randolph Moore."

"Same part her husband played, right? Jules, the one she says is haunting the studio?" I nodded. "Day before she disappeared, she asked this guy Derringer if he ever walked around the place at night, wearing some kind of fur-trimmed robe. Derringer thought she was nuts."

"It's a robe the character usually wears. Randolph Moore is supposed to be an eccentric multi-millionaire . . ."

"She told Derringer that she'd seen a ghost wearing the robe. When he laughed at her, she got sore and slapped him. Then she went kind of hysterical. Said something about . . . proving it."

"Proving what? How?"

"Don't ask me," Harry shrugged." "Maybe she was going to hire a medium, a ghostbuster, who knows? But since this happened the day before she took off, it might be important. If you think of anything, let me know, okay?"

I said okay.

I was lying in bed that night, waiting for my ex-wife to call me just before I was ready to fall asleep. Knowing my habits after fourteen years, she was an expert in this form of harassment. For some reason, the phone didn't ring (it turned out she was in Florida with her boss), but the insistent silence only made me more awake. I stared at the ceiling and started thinking about Nina Kemper's disappearance, wondering how I would solve the problem if it had been projected in a story meeting.

The first scenario that came into my mind was Nina behaving like one of those airheaded movie heroines determined to find out who's rattling the chains in the family cellar (or more currently, what slimy outerspace monster was coiled around the refrigerator). Could she have been so anxious to prove her "ghost" story that she wandered into the bowels of the old Palace Grand Theater with a lighted candle, wearing a loose-fitting nightgown? It seemed improbable. Even if Nina's theory was ridiculous, her fear seemed genuine enough. Besides, there was no easy access to the underground storage rooms; according to Gordon Knapp, they had been sealed up decades ago to lower heating and cooling costs. And Nina claimed to have seen the robe-wearing spirit in the studio itself.

I tried simple logic. (1) Assuming Nina *had* seen this

apparition, the chances were good that (2) it was a living man who had (3) stolen or borrowed the fur-trimmed robe worn by the character of Randolph Moore, and if so (4) the theft of the robe might have been detected by (5) the wardrobe lady, Sophia Lenz. As you might gather, for all its absurdity, I was already forming the notion of a resident "phantom" at Studio 43.

I was in for a surprise the next day, when I cornered Sophia, a dwarfish grayhaired lady, and asked her about the robe. She tittered and opened a closet. The robe was there, all right, and so were five counterparts. It seems there were always half a dozen of Randolph's trade-marked attire on hand at all times. They were of differing lengths, reflecting the four different actors who had played the role over the past twenty-two years. If the studio ghost did exist, he had a choice. He also had a key. According to Sophia, the wardrobe room was carefully locked every night.

I examined the six robes, not knowing exactly what I was looking for, but already too involved in the mystery not to be intrigued by the idea of "clues." The pockets were empty, and all of the robes seemed to be in the same slightly threadbare condition (the TV camera is unusually kind: the Moore living room, somewhat shabby on the set, looked like a grand salon on the tube.)

I had almost given up hope of learning anything of value when I detected a metallic glint in the closet. Something had definitely caught the light, and it took me a few moments to realize that there were metal particles on one of the robes, barely visible traces of some silvery substance. I brushed my hand over it, and some of the flakes came off on my palm.

I didn't wash my hands when I left the studio, and on my way home stopped in to see the one man I thought might provide the answer. He wasn't a laboratory technician. He had no technical training whatsoever. His name was Linus; he owned the neighborhood hardware store, and he never failed me. He said it was nothing more than silver paint. Old, old silver paint.

* * *

That night, the silver paint still glistened on my hand when I picked up my beer at the Three Turtles and brought it to the booth where Mike Zurman waited for me. Mike, Ted Hauser, and I had struck up a friendship after discovering we all had a certain mutuality of interests, or perhaps I should say agonies. Mike was also divorced, his wife constantly tormenting him about his alimony payments. Ted had been separated from his wife for only a few months, but there was rampant bitterness between them. Usually, all we talked about was our marital and ex-marital woes, but tonight I was more interested in Mike's ancestral memories.

"It's true about my great-grandfather," Mike said, with his customary gloom. "I never knew him, of course, but my grandfather used to tell me stories about him, about what an impressario he used to be. I grew up thinking he was famous, and then I realized that nobody even remembered Max Zurman. . . . All that's left of his memory is one chapter in an old book of theater history."

"Do you have the book?"

"Yeah, someplace. It was written about 1935. There's a chapter on his production of *Ben Hur*."

I put the next question lightly.

"Anything in it about the theater being haunted?"

He looked at me sharply. "Yeah, I heard that you've been asking about Lois' ghost."

"It's not just *her* ghost," I said. "Nina told me about one, too, just before she did her vanishing act."

"I hope she didn't 'vanish' the way Lois did. If we lose our Felicia, the next thing Studio 43 will be is a parking lot."

"You don't think Nina was suicidal, do you?"

"Not that I know of. But then, I didn't figure Lois would kill herself either, just because Charlie disappeared."

"Charlie. Is that the stagehand?"

"He was an electrician. Big good-looking guy, always

wore a rough-looking plaid shirt. But then, they all do, don't they?''

"Why did he leave the show?"

Mike shrugged. "Maybe because Lois was putting too much pressure on him, maybe she was pregnant—who knows? Charlie was good, too. He was working on a whole new wiring system for the studio when he walked out without handing in his notice. Never even collected his last paycheck.''

"Mike," I said, "where would I get a copy of that book?"

The next morning, I was plowing through a third revison of the new story projection when a studio messenger dropped off a package. It was a battered book with a frayed cover, so faded that I could barely make out the title, "Landmarks in the American Theater." A three-by-five index card marked the chapter on Max Zurman's 1924 production of *Ben Hur*. There was a hand-tinted photograph of the chariot race scene, staged on a gigantic moving belt before a rotating diorama. The colors had faded, too, with the exception of the silver paint on the chariots. I found myself staring at the illustration, and then at the palm of my hand.

Now comes the difficult part of this chronicle. We all consider ourselves the hero, or heroine, of our own life, and heroes have standards of behavior that are universally acknowledged, like loyalty, self-sacrifice, and courage. It's not easy to admit failure in all three of those sterling qualities. I can expect no more from the reader than a grudging respect for my candor. The only excuse I offer is that my first encounter with the Phantom might have unnerved an even stronger personality than my own.

I will take credit for one act of "bravery." I ventured into the Phantom's domain alone, just like one of those dumb movie heroines (candle and nightgown, remember? Only I was equipped with flashlight, jeans, and running shoes.). I had thought of asking Mike to accompany me, but I was more afraid of ridicule than of a ghost whose existence I denied.

I'll also take credit for locating the entrance to his underground kingdom, but that proved to be simpler than I thought. There was a door, and it hadn't been "sealed off" at all; it was simply rusted shut through disuse—until someone made it viable again. It was accessible through the studio basement, a vast area of damp brick and squat machinery that provided both heat and air conditioning to the studio above.

There was a building engineer in charge of the power plant who was so grateful that someone showed an interest in his job that he answered my most important question readily. Yes, there was a way into the "old" cellar of the theater. He had shown it to someone only a few months ago, he said, and now he showed it to me. It turned out to be the original electrical room of the old theater, long since abandoned, an awesome display of antiquated switches that looked as if they belonged in Dr. Frankenstein's laboratory. On the opposite end was still another door, that opened into the dark labyrinth that I still see in my dreams.

Until I ventured into that man-made canyon, I had never realized that darkness wasn't an absolute. This was more than the absence of light; it was an inky pall cast over all things like a damp, heavy cloth; it had weight and odor and sentience. The beam of my flashlight was no more than a thin white thread in the black folds, but I didn't have far to venture before it picked out one of the objects I had expected to find. Once it did, I left hurriedly and gratefully. When I returned to the studio, gasping, I felt like a diver coming back from the Stygian depths of the ocean floor.

I caught up with Mike Zurman at the Three Turtles just before he became too drunk to understand the meaning of my discovery.

"It's the chariots," I said. "Ben Hur's chariot, or maybe Messala's. It's still there, down in the basement of the theater, with the silver paint coming off in little flakes."

"So?" Mike said.

"What if the flakes on Randolph Moore's robe came from those painted props? What if someone is wearing it down there? Maybe sleeping in one of the chariots?"

"The ghost?" He looked at me with swimming eyes, but his state of near-intoxication made him reckless. He grinned and said: "Maybe it's my great-grandpa. Let's go have a look!"

Company was exactly what I wanted.

The engineer was gone for the day, but that didn't interfere with my return to the black labyrinth, this time with two flashlights and a companion. It made all the difference; I almost felt lighthearted as we explored that dank subterranean world.

Mike chortled with pleasure when he saw the prop chariots. He was more excited by these artifacts from his family history than he was by my theory about the silver flakes and fur-trimmed robe. He didn't care about the Phantom; he was like a child who had wandered into an attic full of antique toys. As for myself, I discovered something which also drove the purpose of our mission from my mind, an incredible device with monstrous gears, obviously the machinery which drove the moving belt upon which chariots and horses had once thundered across the great stage. Then I heard Mike's strangled cry of horror, and his light was extinguished.

I think it was the diminished light which frightened me more than his outcry. I flicked my own beam in its direction, but Mike wasn't there. I called out his name, but there was no answer. I know I was shaking because the beam wobbled uncertainly over the props, and trembled even more wildly when it suddenly illuminated the single most terrifying image I have ever seen: the ghastly, bony face of a *Thing* seated at the reins of the farthest chariot. I had only one thought. That I had found my Phantom, and it wasn't human; that I was being punished for all my skepticism by an encounter with something from Beyond. *The Beyond is getting closer* . . . Who had said that to me?

Now the shameful part: I turned and ran. I didn't make

any attempt to assist Mike Zurman, assuming that he needed assistance. I swung the beam of my flashlight toward the place of exit like a lifeline, and followed it to safety. I thought about nothing but escape, and it was only when I was back among the comforting hum and clank of the subbasement machinery that I felt any remorse.

I breathed easier when Mike himself reappeared, apparently unaware of my cowardly retreat. In fact, he apologized for dropping the flashlight.

"I couldn't help it," he said. "When I saw that corpse in the chariot—"

"Corpse? You mean it was a dead body?"

"What's left of one, anyway. It must have been there for months—it's all sort of eaten away. I guess there are rats down there." He shuddered. "They ate everything but his plaid shirt."

"Plaid," I repeated stupidly.

It was three weeks before the inquest was held, and I could only find one mention of the result in the press. I'm including it exactly as it appeared.

"ACCIDENTAL" VERDICT IN SOAP OPERA STUDIO DEATH

March 9. The death of Charles M. LaPorte, head electrician on the daytime serial "Before the Dawn" was declared "accidental" by a coroner's jury today. According to testimony, Mr. LaPorte had been working on a new electrical system for Studio 43 on E.23rd Street which houses the program's production facilities. He had decided to explore the original power plant located in the subbasement of the building, a plant abandoned almost fifty years ago when the building had been a movie palace. In the opinion of the medical examiner, the technician tripped in the darkness and struck his head, causing a fatal concussion. He is survived by a wife and four children in Marina del Ray, California.

Obviously, there were omissions. There was no mention of the fact that Charles LaPorte had "tripped" right into a stage chariot. There was no description of the state of his "decay," which was probably too gruesome for a family newspaper. There was no background story on all the other catastrophes which had plagued Studio 43. And the item left me wondering if Lois Sturtevant had known about those "survivors" in Marina del Ray.

I told only one person what I really thought about Charlie LaPorte's death.

"I think he was murdered, Harry."

I was gratified when Harry the Cop didn't respond with a skeptical smile, but he was a polite guy.

"You think your Phantom killed him?" he said.

"Just listen for two minutes. I don't have any facts, just a theory. Call it a story projection. Okay?"

Harry nodded.

"LaPorte decides to find the old electrical room in the subbasement. He finds a door nobody's opened in years, and wanders into the Phantom's home territory. The Phantom is annoyed. He doesn't want visitors. He tries to hide, but LaPorte gets a glimpse of him just the same. He's superstitious, and thinks he's seen a ghost, but he's afraid of being laughed at. He tells the only person who won't laugh. He tells his girlfriend."

"And Lois Sturtevant goes around telling other people."

"Right. Then Charlie goes back to the subbasement, maybe to work, maybe to look for the 'ghost' again. Only this time, the 'ghost' sees him first."

"Clubs him in the head, drags him into one of the stage chariots, and leaves him there to rot."

"So Charlie disappears. And when those child support payments stop coming to the wife in Marina del Ray, she comes looking for him . . . That's when Lois finds out about the hidden family, and decides that life isn't worth living . . ." I stopped, suddenly dissatisfied with that beat in the story. "Or maybe there's another answer," I said.

"Such as?"

"Maybe Lois decided to look for Charlie herself. Maybe she went to the subbasement, just like Charlie did . . ."

"She didn't die down there," Harry cautioned. "She killed herself, remember?"

"It wasn't a typical suicide, was it? How many people would take a lethal overdose in an office, and then go home to die? Have you ever heard of a case like that?"

"So you're blaming *two* murders on your Phantom."

"Or more," I said.

I don't think Harry had much faith in my theory, but he indulged me in one way. He agreed to make a personal inspection of the subterranean world beneath the main studio. It would be strictly unofficial, since he doubted he could get Department approval for an action unconnected with a crime.

A few days before the search, Mike Zurman discovered the architectural plan of the old theater among his great-grandfather's private papers. What made the blueprints useful was a comparison of the old structural plan with the new. The primary change was in the number of outside entrances and exits, especially after the building's conversion from movie house to television studio. In order to keep security costs at a minimum, accessibility to the outside had been reduced to three: a front door, a back door, a fire door. But there had been less effort (and money) expended on reducing the numerous doors, stairwells, crawlspaces, closets, and other storage areas in the interior. If there was a secret resident, he would have plenty of places to hide, even from a diligent cop armed with a powerful portable lantern. At least, that was the explanation I gave when Harry's search of the subbasement yielded no sign of the Phantom.

"What I think," Harry said bluntly, "is that famous Imagination of yours is working overtime. Why would anybody want to live in a place like that? *How* would he live?"

"Maybe he's got no place else. Maybe he's one of the

Homeless. Maybe he's stealing small change from the studio people, or maybe he's selling off the old stage props . . .

"And what does he eat?"

"He could sneak out to MacDonald's every night, or steal the leftovers from the coffee wagon . . . You've got to admit it would explain a lot of the things that have happened around here."

"And what explains the fact that I can't find any evidence of him? Unless you count this."

He took something out of a plastic bag. It was a red rose, on a long stem. It wasn't fresh, but it wasn't desiccated, either. I picked it up and went speechless, but Harry perceived the question in my mind.

"Yeah, I found it in the basement. Just lying on the floor. Don't ask me how it got there. Do they have roses on the table at MacDonald's?"

Despite this strange discovery, it was obvious that I had lost Harry's attention. And twenty-four hours later, I no longer had time to worry about the Phantom, the death of Charlie LaPorte, or anything else but the writing of *Before the Dawn*. Because Ted Hauser, the headwriter, was suddenly put out of commission. It happened in a flash, and I mean literally. Ted was electrocuted.

The first rumor was that it had happened at the studio, but Ted visited the set even less often than I did. The second rumor proved true, that it had occurred at home, one of those frequent household accidents we're always being warned about. With all those warnings, it was hard to understand why Ted had been foolish enough to let a portable electric fan fall into a bathtub, with Ted immersed in it. The third rumor, that Ted had been killed, proved untrue. By some miracle, and because his next-door neighbor was an ex-fireman who knew his CPR, Ted survived.

I was among the earliest visitors to his room at Mt. Sinai, but it was more than a sympathy call. Gordon Knapp, concerned about a slowdown, wanted me to check in with Ted before assuming his duties. But I was in for a shock myself. With his first hoarse whisper, I knew Ted wasn't interested in *Before the Dawn*. He was concerned about a different kind of plot—against his life.

"It wasn't an accident," he said. "*She* did this to me! We had another one of our fights, on the phone . . . I told her I was going to take a bath . . ."

"Who, Ted?" I asked, although certain he meant his wife.

"I never keep a fan in the bathroom, it's March, for Chrissake! She picked it up from the kitchen and sneaked into the bathroom. She still has a key to the apartment, and I don't lock the bathroom door when I'm alone—"

"My God," I said, genuinely horrified. "You actually saw your wife do this?"

"It couldn't have been anybody else! She opened the bathroom door, and turned off the lights . . . I thought the electricity had gone off, a fuse or something. Then she plugged in the fan, and just before she tossed it in the tub I heard her whisper . . ."

"Whisper what?"

" '*Now I'm writing YOU out, Hauser!*' "

I was already tingling with anxiety, but those words increased the voltage. Everything was wrong about that statement. Why would Ted's wife call him "Hauser?" Why would she talk about "writing him out," a soap-opera catchphrase if there ever was one? Besides, she had already "written him out" with the separation agreement that allowed her to live rather more comfortably than Ted himself. Why cut off her income by trying to cut off his air supply?

Ted never brought charges against his wife—no pun intended. They would have been unsupportable. The night of his electrifying experience, Mrs. Hauser was playing poker with her girlfriends, and winning big. If it *was* attempted murder, someone else was responsible. I had no doubt that it was the Phantom. More important, I no longer had any doubt about his identity.

His name was Mason Trumbull.

The logic had struck me before, when I learned that

two possible victims of the Phantom had both replaced Trumbull in his long-term role of Randolph Moore. Both deaths had appeared "accidental," but so had the death of Charlie LaPorte and the near-death of Ted Hauser. The whispered words of his would-be assassin were the final proof. Ted had "written out" the character of Randolph. If Trumbull, deprived of his twenty-year role, was seeking revenge, Ted would have to be on his Little List.

There was one more necessary step. I had to make sure that Mason Trumbull was still alive, and a viable Phantom.

It wasn't an easy task. I needed help, and the only person who knew Trumbull well enough was Gordon Knapp, the producer.

I was hesitant about approaching Gordon. He was a tall, rangy man with a quick smile, who cultivated his reputation for equanimity in the face of a frenetic business; his own favorite catchphrase was "My door is always open." But while Gordon's door may have been open, his mind wasn't. He listened to your suggestions and complaints with eyes concealed behind tinted glasses, thanked you politely, and ignored everything you said. In fact, I was so persistent that Gordon, uncharacteristically, showed his annoyance.

"You might as well ask me where elephants go to die," he said. "Trumbull was finished, played out, *ausgespielt*. I don't think he ever got another job after he left the show."

"After he was fired, you mean."

"The guy had a twenty-year sinecure. How many actors work almost every day for twenty years?"

"But you think he's still alive?"

Gordon shrugged, and I could see that it didn't matter to him one way or another. "If Mason Trumbull died, his obituary would be too small to notice. Come on, we're not talking Olivier here . . ." He sighed. "But no, I have no reason to think he's dead. I think he's either right here in town or on the West Coast. Those are the only two worlds he knew."

I was tempted to mention the possibility that Mason was living in a third world, a subterranean one.

"Do you remember the name of his agent?"

Gordon frowned. "Why aren't you home writing breakdowns? Do you realize we're only a week ahead on scripts?"

I decided to take a chance. I told him my theory. From the minute I used the word "phantom" I knew it was a mistake. Gordon started to fidget, and kept glancing at the doorway of his office as if considering a call for help.

"I realize it's farfetched," I said. "But maybe the shock of losing the role derailed the guy's trolley. He could be looking for revenge against everybody responsible. Like Simon Wales . . ."

"Who died of an ordinary heart attack."

"Trumbull could have nailed that chair to the floor. He could have known there was a scene which called for Wales to lift it. He could have seen a rehearsal, or appropriated a script. . . . Even if he couldn't count on Wales having a coronary, he must have known it would be a shock. The guy's something of a practical joker—the cake business proved that."

"So you think *that* was Trumbull, too?"

"He had a grudge against the show. He would have been there for the thirtieth anniversary if he hadn't been dumped. So he let the world know how he felt . . ." I took a deep breath. "And then there was Jules, the next Randolph Moore."

Dryly: "You think the Phantom choked him to death with a roast beef sandwich."

"Trumbull could have just . . . choked him. Left the remains of his sandwich in his throat. How do you tell the difference?"

"And now," Gordon said, "You think he's after Ted?"

"He blames Ted for writing him out." I paused. "Although, when it comes right down to it, it wasn't really Ted's idea, was it? I mean, re-casting a major character is a policy decision."

Gordon's spine stiffened against his leather chair.

"Meaning what, exactly?"

"I wonder if Trumbull realizes that the headwriter couldn't have been solely responsible. I mean, that there were other people involved in the decision, that Ted was only following orders."

"You mean me, right?" Now Gordon removed the glasses entirely so he could glare at me more intensely. He looked ten years older without them, and a lot less affable.

"I'm not trying to alarm anybody," I said. "I just think we ought to find out where Mason Trumbull is."

"I thought you already knew," Gordon said, now with a full-throttle sneer. "He's downstairs, in the basement. Next time you see him, tell us he owes us some back rent."

I think it was then that I realized what I had to do. I had to spend some time in the Phantom's domain. I had to set up a vigil in order to prove, to myself if no one else, that the Phantom really existed, that he was lurking below the studio waiting to strike the next vengeful blow.

I don't want to give a false impression. I wasn't trying for Hero status. I had no intention of attempting to overcome or capture the Phantom, whether it was a disgruntled actor or some homeless derelict or even Something from Beyond. All I hoped to find was some evidence of my theory, some shred of proof to inspire others to put an end to his menace. I would have preferred a companion, someone like Mike Zurman, but I knew that my only hope for success lay in stealth, and an incursion by two people doubled the chances for failure. This was something I had to do alone.

I spent the next twenty-four hours working harder than I've worked in my life. With the help of two other members of the writing staff, we ground out eight days of synopses to keep the show going. Then I went home, slept six hours, left a message on my answering machine that I was in the Hamptons, and got dressed for the occasion. Black jeans, a black turtleneck, and running shoes so dirty that might as well have been black. I looked like an over-the-hill commando. But I felt as heroic as Elmer J. Fudd.

The most frightening moment of my ordeal came at the very outset. I didn't dare open the door to the underground cavern until I had turned out all the lights in the furnace room. That proved to be a test of willpower that I almost failed. Finally, my trembling fingers managed to push the switch down. I let my eyes become adapted to the dark, and pushed hard on the door. It opened on an even greater darkness, and I was tempted to reach for the small flashlight I carried in my hip pocket. Somehow, I resisted the temptation, and to my indescribable relief, within ten minutes my eyes adapted even to this inky nothingness. It meant that there was some trace of light, perhaps only phosphorescence, somewhere in the black void. But was it enough to risk moving farther into the interior? If I were to stumble over something, trip over an object (the word stirred a chilling memory of Charlie LaPorte) wouldn't I risk being seen by the Phantom, whose eyes were probably far better "adapted" to this perpetual night? I was frozen with indecision. I reached out like a blind man and took a few cautious steps forward.

Then I became aware of the music.

I don't think I've ever heard a more incongruous sound than the distant voice which suddenly emerged from that subterranean dark. It was a woman; was it Diana Ross? She was singing about love and disappointment. I was almost disappointed myself when I realized that it was a radio or phonograph. The banality of it! I had expected more from my Phantom.

When I heard the murmur of an announcer's voice, it gave me courage to move on. I used the sound as a homing device, praying that I wouldn't be fooled by the underground echoes.

I must have taken half a dozen wrong turns, until something warned me that I was about to run into a wall, maybe that sixth sense the sightless are believed to develop, a tingling of the nerve endings on my skin. I stopped and put out my hand. There was a wall, all right, cold and damp. Then I touched something else: small bits of jagged metal. I recoiled, and touched it again. Then I realized what it was: a ring of keys.

If there were keys, there had to be a door.

Carefully, I lifted the ring away from the hook on the wall, and then went in search of a keyhole.

The music helped me find it. Not because it grew louder as I approached, but because it stopped, suddenly, with a stillness as total as the darkness. I held my breath and listened, hoping my sightlessness would also be compensated by an improvement in my hearing. (As you can see, I was becoming less of a Skeptic throughout my adventure.) Whether my ears were keener or not, I did hear a slight sound. The sound of human respiration . . .

I was sure that only inches separated me from the Phantom, that he was behind the door waiting to spring out at me with an already bloodstained knife. I considered flight.

But then somebody *whimpered*.

Don't ask me how, but I was sure that whimper came from a woman's throat.

That decided me. I stopped calculating risks, and began trying every key on the ring until I found the one that made the huge metal door handle turn. I pushed open the door, and found myself in the living room of Randolph Moore.

To be more precise, it was the *old* Randolph Moore living room, the set that had been retired after twenty years of service on *Before the Dawn*. It still bore a superficial resemblance to the newly-designed set. The fireplace was in the same location, but the mantle portrait was different; the chairs and sofas were upholstered in brocade, now more threadbare than ever; the tasseled lamp shades were there, and the mock-Aubusson carpet, and, of course, there was the presence of Randolph's two-timing sweetie, the Registered Bitch of *Before the Dawn*: Felicia, also known as Nina Kemper, wearing her famous slinky black evening dress that was badly in need of mending and dry-cleaning.

Nina didn't emit glad cries when she saw me. She retreated into the room, covering her mouth as if to stifle a scream. I realized she didn't recognize me in my commando attire (I was usually a Suit) and later I learned that she simply assumed I was her jailer returning in yet another guise. When I finally identified myself, she threw her arms around me and played the best hysterical scene I've ever witnessed, on or off the screen.

I finally calmed her down and brought her to the sofa; its wobbly legs almost didn't support our weight. There was a sideboard with half a dozen filled decanters, and I went to get her a drink, but she stopped me with a shrill laugh.

"They're all fake," she said. "Just like on the show. He fills them up with colored water. Nothing is real here, everything's a prop! Please get me out of here, please!"

I assured her that I would, that she had nothing more to worry about, but I had the uneasy feeling that I was reading lines from a script. I wanted desperately to ask her questions, but there was another question that had to be answered first. How did we get out of there without the Phantom's interception?

"I don't know where he is!" she told me. "He goes away for hours at a time. He comes back with food, and flowers—"

I looked at the oriental vase that usually contained artificial blooms. It was filled with roses.

"Maybe we'd better get help," I said, and picked up the telephone. I felt ridiculous when I remembered it was only a prop. I hung up and said: "Never mind. We'll get out of here the way I got in." I started to guide her to the door, but she seized my arm.

"No!" Nina said. "He might be on his way back, he might see us! The man is crazy, he's dangerous! He talks about getting rid of people all the time. 'Writing them out!' He said he's going after Tom next, and then Gordon Knapp. He hates Gordon most of all . . ."

"Then it *is* Trumbull," I said, without any sense of triumph.

"Only he thinks he's Randolph Moore! He does! He calls me 'Felicia' all the time; he keeps bringing me her clothes to wear . . ."

"Did he hurt you any?"

"No," Nina Kemper said. "You know Randolph, he's a gentleman." She laughed with controlled hysteria. "Except when he's killing people, of course. He can't afford to be polite then, that's what he told me . . . Did he kill Ted Hauser? He said he'd stolen his apartment key . . . He's always stealing . . ."

"Ted's okay," I said. "And we'll be okay, too, as soon as we get out of this place."

I tried not to show how scared I was. I had thought about bringing a weapon, but doubted I could bring myself to use one. Now I regretted it. I looked around the room, trying to improvise. There were no fireplace tools. The lamps were the heaviest objects, but too unwieldy. I spotted a tall wardrobe, and opened its doors. It was filled with clothing, obviously purloined from Wardrobe, out-of-date dresses, formal suits, an assortment of uniforms, including the silver-gray costume of a studio guard. But no weapon.

"It doesn't matter," Nina whimpered. "You can't hurt him. Sometimes I think he's not human any more. Maybe Mason died, and this is his revenant . . ."

"Don't be silly," I said as sternly as I could manage. "He's a lunatic, not a ghost."

"He makes himself look so different! If you could see him—"

"He's got a whole studio at his disposal. Wardrobe, makeup, everything. That doesn't make him superhuman." I was fumbling in all the drawers, in futile search; but suddenly, there it was. A gun, a souvenir of one of the many murderous story lines of the show.

"You don't think *that* will you do any good?" Nina said. "It's just another prop!"

"How will Trumbull know for sure?" I stuck it in the

waist of my pants. For the first time, I *felt* like a commando. "Now let's get out of this place," I said, trying to sound like one.

There was no longer any reason not to use my flashlight. With Nina clinging to my arm, I manipulated the beam until I located the route back to the furnace room. It was closer than it appeared to be in the dark, but it seemed to take longer to reach.

Nina was still trembling when we were safely inside the furnace room, and just as apprehensive as we made our way upstairs. I was steady as a rock, but I was roleplaying. I soon found out how shallow a performance it was when I saw the man in the fur-trimmed robe in the long corridor that led to the studio. It was too far for me to see his face, but there was no doubt that I had finally met my Phantom. I almost wanted to cry out a greeting, but my appearance was obviously unfriendly. He turned his back on me.

I hardly knew what I was doing when I yanked the prop gun out of my belt and yelled at him to stop. The Phantom of Studio 43 never lost his dignity; he continued down the hall, without any visible hate, and then veered sharply into a doorway. I heard the click of a latch, and started to follow, but Nina dragged me back.

"No!" she said. "Let's get out of here!"

"That was *him*," I said pointlessly. "We've got to do something before he gets away—"

She let me drag her to the door. It was marked "VIEWING ROOM—AUTHORIZED PERSONNEL ONLY."

"He's watching tapes," Nina said. "He does that all the time. He watches tapes of the old shows, when he was Randolph."

"But don't you realize that we've got him trapped? There isn't any other exit from the viewing room."

"You don't know him," she said. "He'll find some way out—he always does! I really believe he *can* walk through walls! Look, I don't want to sound ungrateful—

but I need a bath! If you want to hang out around here, fine. I want to go home!''

I didn't see how I could refuse, although I wasn't very happy to be left alone with the Phantom.

The moment Nina was gone, I decided that I needed company. There was a pay phone at the end of the corridor. While I kept an uneasy eye on the Viewing Room door, I dialed the police and asked for Harry the Cop. Luckily, he was there.

"Don't tell me," Harry said. "It's the Phantom, right?"

I did tell him. I stumbled over my words in my desperation to convince him, and managed to give him a faintly coherent account of Nina Kemper's rescue. The fact that the Phantom was "trapped" didn't impress him; he told me he would cover every exit of the studio and dispatch as many men as possible to make sure the Phantom didn't get away. I was impressed with my persuasiveness. Then Harry told me why he was suddenly so much more cooperative.

"This guy Derringer, the actor? He fell or was pushed off his penthouse terrace tonight. He's dead."

I looked toward the Viewing Room door and wondered if I should leave even before the police arrived. I think I'd used up all my Hero potential.

It was the sirens that caused the next problem. The sound of them wailing outside the building must have broken Mason Trumbull's happy reverie. The Viewing Room door opened, and out he came. For a moment, he posed himself in the dimly-lit corridor, his body erect, glaring at me with what I felt sure would have been an expression of haughty disdain, if I could have seen his face. Then, for the first time, I heard him speak.

"I will never be caught," he said. *"It isn't in the script."*

Perfectly cued, the front door of the studio burst open and the heavy tread of the arriving police shook the floorboards. Still, the Phantom didn't appear agitated. He simply turned, his fur-trimmed robe flaring out behind him, and headed toward the stairway, returning to his subterranean lair to conceal himself once more in the cloak of protective darkness.

Harry was such a reassuring sight I wanted to hug him. He was less pleased with the sight of me, especially when I told him that the Phantom was no longer in the trap.

"It doesn't matter," he grunted. "I've got every exit bottled up and a dozen cops to search every inch of this building. He won't get away. Now give me that thing before you hurt yourself."

I handed over the prop gun, and watched while Harry's blue dozen fanned out in every direction, armed with enough flashlights and firepower to dislodge a small army from Studio 43, to say nothing of one actor, no matter how elusive. I took my first full breath of the night, finally confident that the Phantom's days were numbered. I walked into the set of the new Moore living room and collapsed on a sofa, enjoying the anticipation of my fifteen minutes of fame that lay ahead, certain that I would be credited with the Phantom's discovery and capture. For someone who has lived his adventures only on paper, it was an exhilarating prospect.

There were two things I hadn't counted on. One was the fact that Nina Kemper, for reasons of her own, decided to completely *deny* both her captivity, her rescue, and the very existence of the Phantom of Studio 43. The second was the fact that Harry the Cop, along with more than a dozen of New York's Finest, failed to apprehend the Phantom, who eluded what must have been the tightest net ever drawn around a building.

It was some time before I solved the puzzle of Nina Kemper's strange behavior. It was Gordon Knapp who was responsible. The producer, undoubtedly speaking for the Suits, suggested that Nina had nothing to gain, and a great deal to lose, by admitting to having been the prisoner of a still-mythical "phantom" in the bowels of the studio where *Before the Dawn* was produced. The story was too incredible, he said, and would only support another rumor: about Nina's pharmaceutical habits. It would be better to forget the whole thing, he said, especially since the police had certainly driven Mason Trumbull permanently from his low-rent housing.

There was, of course, the problem of Yours Truly.

That was solved easily enough. A week after the great Phantom hunt, Ted Hauser, home from the hospital with a clean bill of health, handed me a clean bill of divorcement from *Before the Dawn*. He was clearly shamefaced when he gave me the required six-week notice on my thirteen-week contract, and he didn't offer any other explanation except, "You know, those guys upstairs . . ." And, of course, it was all the explanation I needed.

As for Harry, his explanation was even less satisfying.

"He couldn't have been there," he said stubbornly, over the last cup of coffee he and I shared together. "Don't tell me he was hiding in any secret passages or junk like that, because I've got every blueprint ever made of Studio 43, before and after."

"But I saw him, Harry," I said, feeling the tears of frustration in my eyes. "I saw the Phantom just when the police were arriving. I heard him *speak,* for God's sake! And why nobody believes me about finding Nina Kemper in that room downstairs . . . I mean, isn't that room evidence enough?"

"Okay," Harry said. "So somebody fixed up a room for themselves in the basement, using old props. Some homeless guy . . ."

"It was Mason Trumbull, and he's a killer, and you let him get away, Harry."

"He'd have to be a ghost to get past us," Harry said, his mouth grim. "The building was sealed up tight as a drum, and we covered every room, every closet, every crawlspace, every *everything* for almost eight hours. The guy would have to be invisible, he'd have to walk through walls. Do you honestly think this Phantom of yours can really walk through walls?"

I didn't have any answer. Except: maybe yes. Maybe Nina had been right, that it was Trumbull's ghost haunting the studio.

Harry paid for the coffee. He must have heard about my job.

Mike Zurman was also feeling sympathetic, too. One morning, he called and told me that he heard ABC was looking for a new associate writer, but he wasn't sure for which show. I was about to hang up and call Jozie Emmerich to check out the rumor when Mike said, hesitantly:

"I suppose you heard about Gordon?"

"No, what about him?"

"Somebody tried to kill him."

My hands went clammy on the receiver.

"My God, when? Do they know who it was?"

"It happened night before last. He got home fairly stoned from a party and found somebody in his apartment. A burglar, I guess. The guy must have panicked, because he grabbed Gordon and pushed him right through the window."

I remembered how Tom Derringer died, in a fall that was yet to be judged accidental or deliberate. But according to Mike, there was one major difference between the two events.

"Gordon lives on the third floor," Mike said. "He was cut up more than he was bruised. He's at Doctor's Hospital right now if you want to send a get-well card. Although I don't suppose you do."

I decided to do something better than that. Don't ask me why, considering the way I had been treated. Maybe it was because I took a certain grim satisfaction in the moment.

When I arrived at the hospital, I saw a uniformed policeman stationed at Gordon's door, and realized that Gordon had already decided to take the Phantom seriously. But true to his nature, he denied having asked for police protection.

"Then it was Harry," I said. "Harry knows what happened to you, doesn't he?"

"Yes," Gordon admitted. "He was here yesterday. We talked about the burglar."

"It wasn't a burglar, Gordon," I said. "You know damned well that it was Mason Trumbull. You were next on his list, didn't Nina tell you? Or have you got Nina completely convinced that there was no such person as the Phantom?"

"If that's all you came to tell me—"

"I just want you to be careful," I said, maybe too smugly.

The ABC job didn't materialize, but a week later my agent called to ask if I would be interested in writing some episodes of a proposed new cop show. I was glad to get away from New York for a while, so I booked myself on the next available westbound flight.

There's no place where I feel so *alone* as on a plane, thirty thousand miles away from everything that keeps me attached to the planet. Maybe it was because I was ruminating about the cop show, and cops made me think of the great Phantom hunt—maybe it was the altitude, or the alienation, or the two Bloody Marys that were also so much more potent in the air—but suddenly I realized exactly what happened that night, and how the Phantom walked through the walls of Studio 43.

The answer was in the tall closet in "Felicia's" home-like prison in the subbasement. I had stared at it without connecting it to later events. It was a police uniform.

Mason Trumbull had simply gone back to Randolph Moore's living room, slipped into his police clothes, and joined the hunt for himself. And when the police left, defeated by the wily Phantom, the Phantom left with them.

I had to wait four more hours, until the plane landed at Los Angeles Airport, before I could call Harry and tell him.

He listened in silence, and I expected some sardonic reply, but instead he asked one question.

"You say you *saw* the cop uniform in that closet?"

"No question about it."

Harry grunted. "Interesting. Because there *wasn't* any cop uniform when we took inventory."

"Doesn't that prove it?" I said, feeling the glow of exoneration, wishing now that I wasn't so far away from the scene of my success. "I just thought I'd let you know as soon as possible. Especially because of Gordon Knapp. If I were you, I'd keep that police guard on him twenty-four hours a day."

"What police guard?" Harry said.

THE OTHER PHANTOM

by Edward D. Hoch

At this time the Opera ghost had not been seen for nearly a year, and there were those who believed him to have been a flesh-and-blood creature who had died, deep underground near the lake where he was rumored to have lived. Others, however, offered a much simpler explanation. The great Paris Opera had simply been closed for three months, between engagements, while some needed painting and maintenance work were completed. Those who held to this theory were convinced the ghost or phantom would return quickly enough once the new season got under way.

In that summer of 1887 the attention of many was focused instead upon construction of the Eiffel Tower in preparation for the 1889 International Exposition. Gustave Eiffel's structure, the tallest on earth, was the center of controversy, denounced by Dumas, de Maupassant, and even Charles Garnier, architect of the Paris Opera. They viewed it as an intrusion onto the city's skyline, "arrogant ironmongery" that should not be tolerated. The city promised to demolish the Tower in twenty years. but there were those who doubted the promise would ever be kept.

One such doubter was Franz Vinding, who'd made something of a career of being the city's chief cynic. His column in the daily press had taken the lead in opposing construction of the Eiffel Tower, and now that the first girders were going up he'd taken to lunching in a small cafe across the way, where he expressed his views to anyone within earshot.

"Are you still at it, Franz?" Bernard Mosaven asked, stopping by the table where Vinding was dining alone. "Why do you come here if the sight of the Tower upsets you so much?"

"I glory in bad taste," the journalist responded. "Come, Bernard, sit and drink a glass of wine with me."

"Only for a few moments." Mosaven pulled out a chair. "At least the building of the Tower has given you something to write about other than the Opera ghost."

Franz Vinding chuckled, revealing a row of irregular teeth in need of dental work. He was a stout man whose love of food seemed reflected in the gradual deterioration of his body. "The Opera ghost! Must the public forever suffer these foolish illusions? There never was a ghost of any sort, and there most certainly was never an Opera ghost! My colleagues in the press have much to answer for."

"Perhaps you'd change your mind if you ever came face to face with the Phantom yourself." Bernard Mosaven delighted in tormenting the older man. Their long-standing rivalry dated from the time a few years back when they'd reviewed the Opera productions for competing Paris newspapers. Mosaven was out of journalism now, employed by the company building the Eiffel Tower.

"I would love to meet the charlatan!" Vinding replied.

"You would run! You would die of heart failure!"

The journalist's eyes glistened angrily. "Are you issuing me a challenge, Bernard?"

"Take it as you wish."

"Call up your Phantom of the Opera from his depths and I will happily face him! It should provide me with an amusing column for my paper."

"The Opera ghost has not been seen of late," Mosaven admitted. "But I have no doubt he is still in his lair deep underground."

"I will go to the Opera. I will spend the night there and dare him to show himself. Will that satisfy you?"

"Alone?"

"Alone! If I survive you will pay me twenty-five gold louis. I will use the money to campaign against your Tower. Agreed?"

Bernard Mosaven hesitated only an instant. "Agreed!" He reached across the table and the two men shook hands.

When Nadine Bucher heard of the bet she was furious. She stormed into the newspaper office where Vinding was working on the following day's column, a comely blond tempest not to be turned aside.

"Franz, what is this foolishness about a wager with Bernard? Have you lost your mind?"

"Not at all, my dear," he told her with a smile. "It seemed an easy way to earn twenty-five louis."

"By spending the night alone in the Paris Opera? You must be crazy. People have died there. Remember all the trouble back in '81?"

"The Phantom has not been seen in nearly a year. The madman has died of old age, or merely tired of his game."

"And if it is a real ghost?"

"Then I will have an exclusive story for Friday's edition."

Nadine Bucher had been a friend of both men for several years, and Vinding suspected she was more than a friend to Bernard. He was touched by her concern for him, but of course it did nothing to change his mind. He would rather have been championing some more immediate cause like the demolition of the Eiffel Tower, but the Opera ghost would have to do. If he could humiliate Bernard in Nadine's eyes, it would be well worth a night without sleep.

She eyed him now across the desk. "You are a stubborn old man!" she told him and turned on her heel. She did not see the look of genuine anguish her words caused. Franz Vinding was still in his fifties, and until that moment had never thought of himself as being old. To be branded as such by this woman he admired was a terrible blow to his pride.

"I'll show them," he decided. "I'll show them both. If the Opera ghost does appear, I will be ready."

A distinguished journalist like Vinding had no trouble gaining permission to spend the night alone at the Paris Opera. The watchman, a gray-haired old actor named Ramos Chastel, met him at the the door shortly after eight. "Come in, sir. Your friend Bernard Mosaven has already arrived and is waiting for you."

Chastel led the way backstage, past the scaffolding that had been erected for the painters. Franz glanced up. "It seems a shame the Opera House must be repainted less than ten years after its opening."

"It is a good time to touch things up, to keep it as new and sparkling as it has always been," Chastel told him. "It will be ready for the September opening of *Don Carlos*."

"I hope so. I'm planning to be here on opening night."

The scenery for the opera had already begun to arrive backstage, in the building's huge storage area. They passed large flat crates marked *Don Carlos Act III* and *Don Carlos Act V*. Finally they reached the great dark stage itself. "Do you want a lantern?" the watchman asked.

"I've brought my own," Vinding said.

Suddenly from the front of the orchestra came the sound of hands clapping. "Bravo, Franz!" Bernard Mosaven shouted. "Bravo! You have lit up the stage!"

"I'm here as we agreed," the journalist answered sourly. "If you are to join me for the night's stay, I will no longer be alone."

"Never fear, I will leave you to the Phantom. You will see me again at dawn, if you are still alive!"

"Bring the twenty-five gold louis with you," Vinding reminded him as the younger man made his way up the aisle to the exit.

The watchman left him, too, and Franz settled down at a little table and chair on the stage, his lantern casting a circle of light that seemed a slight barricade against the surrounding darkness.

Vinding had been sitting there for some time, half dozing as the hour approached midnight. Suddenly he awakened with a start. There may have been a noise, or perhaps it was only his subconscious mind that signaled a message. He reached into his coat pocket and brought out the army revolver with which he'd equipped himself. Then he stood up and stared for a moment into the darkness.

"Who's there?" he asked. "Is anyone there?"

No answer came.

In waking, a subconscious thought had worked its way forward in his mind. He remembered it now and moved forward, heading toward the backstage storage area.

Something, something here—

There was the squeak of a floorboard off to his right and he was immediately on guard. He raised the lantern high over his head, and saw in the shadows the dim figure of a man.

"Who are you?" Vinding asked.

The figure took a step forward and the journalist saw the long black cloak, the mask that covered the entire face—

"The Phantom!" he breathed, almost to himself. He raised the revolver in his other hand.

The figure leaped forward, and Vinding saw the lantern light reflected on the blade of a dagger.

The body of Franz Vinding was found in the morning, when the painters arrived to continue their work on the Opera House. Before eight o'clock, Inspector Clovus of the Paris Police was on the scene. He glanced over the assembled workmen and let his narrow eyes settle on a gentleman dressed for the street. "Who are you, sir?"

Bernard Mosaven introduced himself. "I fear this terrible tragedy is the fault of a stupid wager. I dared Franz to spend the night alone in the Opera House, and was to pay him twenty-five gold louis if he remained until morning. When I arrived a half-hour ago, the painters had already discovered his body on the stage.''

Inspector Clovus, a short man with a large mustache, stepped forward to view the body. "Knife wounds?"

"Three, Inspector," one of his men answered. "He couldn't have lived more than a few minutes."

"What are these words?" He indicated three scrawled French words that seemed to be written in the victim's blood: *Fantome non acte—*

"Phantom no act," Mosaven said. "He was telling us that the Phantom of the Opera is real. He had the greatest story of his career and he never had an opportunity to write it."

"Is there any doubt the dead man wrote that?" Clovus asked.

"None," the officer said. "His index finger still has blood on it."

"Where is the night watchman?"

The man named Chastel was brought in. He stared dumbfounded at the body on the stage, unable to explain it. "I would swear that no one entered the building after Mr. Vinding. The killer must have been hiding here all the time."

"The Opera ghost? The one some call the Phantom?"

The watchman stared down at the bloody message. "I have never believed in him till now."

"You're certain all the doors were locked?"

Ramos Chastel nodded. "Every one. Nobody could have entered, except through the stage door where I sit."

"You heard nothing? You never checked to see that Franz Vinding was all right?"

"Mr. Mosaven told me they had a bet. He said Vinding was supposed to remain there alone for the entire night. I stayed away."

The inspector nodded, then turned toward Mosaven. "When did you leave the building?"

"Shortly after Franz arrived."

"Were you seen by anyone?"

"No. I believe the watchman was away making his rounds."

"I'd have been checking that the doors were locked," Chastel explained. "If Mr. Mosaven had gone out in my absence, the door would have locked after him. No one could have entered."

"But Mr. Mosaven could have remained in the building, correct?"

"Remained?"

"Remained hidden," the inspector said.

Bernard Mosaven turned to face him. "Why would I have remained?"

"In order to kill Franz Vinding. Your animosity toward one another is well known, especially over the new Eiffel Tower."

"My God! He was my friend! I didn't kill him!"

"Then am I to believe a ghost did it?"

One of his men came up to Inspector Clovus. "Sir, there's something you should see. We found some bloodstains in the wings, some distance from the body."

Inspector Clovus followed the man to the spot indicated. There were indeed a few small bloodstains on the floorboards. "At least thirty feet from the body," the inspector mused. He knelt down and produced a magnifying glass from his pocket. Crawling along the floor between the bloodstains and the body he found more traces of blood. "The body was dragged across here and the bloody trail was wiped up."

"Then the man's dying message is a hoax."

"Not necessarily. The wounds may not have been immediately fatal. Left alone by the killer, Vinding may still have lived long enough to scrawl those words." he got to his feet. "Mr. Mosaven, I'll have to ask you to accompany me to my office for further questioning."

"This is outrageous!" Bernard stormed. "You can't believe I killed him!"

"We shall see."

* * *

The Surete offices were alive with activity when Inspector Clovus returned. He saw at once the blonde young woman who waited on the visitors' bench and leaped up when she noticed Mosaven entering behind him.

"Bernard, I just heard the news about Franz! I came here to find out what happened."

"The inspector thinks I might be implicated in his death because of our foolish wager."

"I knew this would come to no good!" She turned to Clovus. "I did not approve of Bernard's goading Franz to stay in the Opera overnight, but I assure you he did not kill the man. Bernard would be incapable of harming a fly."

Clovus merely responded, "We are investigating all the possibilities, mademoiselle."

He questioned them both at length, about the wager and about their relations with the dead man, but in the end he was no closer to a solution. Would a man like Mosaven commit murder to save himself twenty-five gold louis? It seemed unlikely. Still, there was the dispute over the new tower, in which the younger man had an interest as an employee of the company. And, Inspector Clovus admitted to himself, there was this lovely young lady. A man like Mosaven might kill for her.

"It was the Phantom that killed him!" Nadine said at last. "Why won't you accept Franz's dying word for it?"

They had discussed the words written in blood by Vinding, but the inspector was oddly dissatisfied with them. "Why would he write *Phantom no act*, a somewhat odd phrase, when the words *Phantom is real* could have been written just as easily and made his point more directly?"

"You are the detective," Bernard pointed out. "While you puzzle over it, I have other duties to perform. Am I free to go?"

Clovus sighed. "You may go, but I will want to question you again. I am not yet ready to conclude that Vinding was killed by your so-called Opera ghost."

He watched them leave together, and even walked to the front window to observe them outside the building.

Nadine had taken Bernard's hand, and they were walking side by side across the street to the park. To share their mutual loss, he wondered, or—?

Clovus was still pondering the case after dinner that night. Instead of going home he ate in a cafe near the Surete and decided to visit the Opera after dark. He wanted to view the scene of the crime at night, by lanternlight, as Franz Vinding would have seen it in his dying moments.

The watchman admitted him and he made his way through the storage area to the great stage itself. Clovus had never been a fan of the Paris Opera, and he marveled at the vast space that seemed necessary for the elaborate productions. He stood at center stage, hands on hips, and stared up into the darkness. Are you there, Phantom? Are you watching me?

He took his bull's-eye lantern and retraced the route Vinding must have followed from the table and chair to the point where he was stabbed. When he reached the fatal area, he began to examine the crates and boxes piled there.

Suddenly there was a sound above his head. Acting on reflex, he threw himself to one side as a heavy sandbag counterweight came crashing down with a bone-breaking thud. It had missed him by inches.

Clovus rolled over on the dusty floor, out of range of the lantern's glow, and pulled out his revolver. "Surrender or I'll fire!" he shouted. "This is the police!"

There were running footsteps on the catwalk above his head, and then the sounds of a struggle. He heard a man's grunt, then a scream, as a black-caped body hurtled down from the darkness onto the stage.

Inspector Clovus rose unsteadily to his feet, gun poised, and crossed the stage to where the body lay. He adjsuted the bull's-eye lantern and saw the mask across the face. Those who had seen the Opera ghost described him as wearing just such a mask.

He felt the man's pulse, but he could see from the angle

of his head that the fall had broken his neck. The Phantom was dead.

Clovus removed the mask and stared into the face of the watchman, Ramos Chastel.

"If you will put down your gun," a voice behind him said, "I will tell you why he murdered Franz Vinding."

Clovus slowly turned and stared into the eyes of a second masked man, dressed almost identically in a black cape. "Who—who are you?"

"My name is unimportant. I have been called Erik, and the Angel of Music, and the Opera ghost. Some of the more sensational writers speak of me as the Phantom."

"Then you really exist."

"Oh, yes. I live beneath the Opera and I harm no one unless it becomes necessary. This man tried to kill you, as he killed Vinding last night. We tussled and he took an unfortunate fall from the catwalk. He wore the mask and cloak while pretending to be me."

"Chastel, the watchman? But why?"

"To safeguard his secret. I overheard your conversation this morning when the body was found. I saw Vinding's message in blood and I knew what it really meant." The voice was full and melodious, almost like that of a singer. "Vinding observed something as he entered the backstage area. He saw crates of scenery for the September production of Verdi's *Don Carlos*. One of them is clearly marked *Act V*. As a former opera reviewer Vinding must have remembered that Verdi rewrote *Don Carlos* three years ago, in '84, to eliminate the first act. It is always performed now in just four acts, not five."

"If there is no fifth act, what is in the crate?"

"Vinding must have wondered the same thing. When he tried to examine the crate he was stabbed. The killer then dragged him back across stage to his table and chair, rather than attract attention to the spot near the crate where he was really killed. Vinding was not quite dead and after naming the Phantom he attempted to write *no*

act V, but he died before he could finish it. I looked in
the crate earlier today. It is carefully packed with rifles
and ammunition, perhaps for a new French Revolution.
I leave it to the authorities to uncover the exact nature of
the plot. But certainly the Opera storage area was a perfect hiding place for the arms, at least until September.''

Clovus turned to gaze at the body on the floor. ''You
have done us a great service, sir, not only in saving my
life but in—''

He looked up and saw that the masked man was no
longer there. He had faded back into the shadows from
which he came.

DARK MUSE

by Daniel Ransom

Hanratty came in that rainy Thursday afternoon and found what he'd dreaded he'd find.

Another song waiting for him on the battered Steinway that provided half the entertainment in Kenny's Lounge, the other half being Hanratty's cigarette-raspy forty-two-year-old voice. Hard to believe anything that rough sounding had ever sung "Ave Maria" at St. Mallory's Catholic High back in Shaker Heights.

Another song.

He lit a cigarette and sat down at the Steinway and started playing the notes and singing the words that had been left there for him. This one was a ballad called "Without You" and it was so heartbreakingly good that even the janitor, turning the chairs back up and polishing the floors, stopped to listen. As did the bartender shining glasses.

When he finished, Hanratty's entire body was shaking and tears collected in silver drops in the corners of his blue eyes.

It wasn't just the song that had gotten to him—though God knew it was beautiful enough—it was the mystery behind the song.

For the past three months now Kenny's Lounge (if you were wealthy and inclined to cheat, then you knew all about Kenny's Lounge) had been enjoying standing-room-only business and it was exactly because of all the new songs that Richard Hanratty had been writing that the crowd wanted to hear.

There was only one trouble with all the adulation being bestowed on Hanratty. He didn't deserve it. Literally. Because he wasn't writing the songs.

Once a week he'd come into work, he was never sure which day it would be, and there on the Steinway up on the circular little stage with the baby blue spotlight that made him look a little less fleshy and a little more handsome than he in fact was . . . waiting for him there on the Steinway would be a brand new song all laid out in perfect form on sheet music in a very precise and knowing hand.

Hanratty had no idea who was leaving these songs for him.

Hanratty said, "You think over my offer?"

Kenny Bentley said, "You want a lot, Richard. Too much."

"You think they're coming here to see you—or hear me?"

Kenny Bentley sighed. He was forty-one, slender, and had apparently taken as his hero one of those gangster B-movie actors from the forties who seem never to be out of tuxedo or into daylight. He wore his dyed black hair slicked back and wore contacts so dark his eyes sparkled like black ice. He carried a gun in shoulder rig in an obvious way. It added to the sense of danger he liked to create right down to the small jagged scar under his left eye which Hanratty felt sure Bentley had put there himself for effect. Bentley—even that was phony, Hanratty learning from the bartender that Bentley's real last name was Sullivan.

They were in Hanratty's dressing room. It smelled now of mildew and martini, the one drink Hanratty allowed himself before going on. The walls were covered with big black and white blowups of movie goddesses from the thirties and forties. Hanratty's favorite was of Rita Hayworth in a silky, sensual slip. He didn't think he'd ever seen a more erotic woman. The rest of the room was taken up by a couch, a full length dressing table with bubble lights encircling the mirror and various kinds of makeup strewn across the chipped and faded mahogany surface. Hanratty was secure enough in his masculinity that wearing makeup had never bothered him.

He said, taking a slightly defensive tone that sickened him to hear, "I'm just asking for my fair share, Kenny. Business has nearly tripled, but you're paying me the same."

"That another new song I heard out there?"

"Is that an answer to my question?"

Bentley smiled with startling white teeth a vampire could envy. "I still can't figure out where you got so much talent all of a sudden."

"Maybe my muse decided to pay me a visit."

"Your muse." Bentley bit the words off bitterly. "You're a lounge piano player for twenty-some years who's had three bad marriages, ten cars that the finance company has all repossessed, and you've got a slight drinking problem. The few times you ever played your own compositions before, the whole crowd went to sleep and I had to force you to go back to playing standards. But then all of a sudden—" He took out an unfiltered cigarette from a silver case that cost as much as Hanratty's monthly rent. The smoke he exhaled was silver as the case itself. His hair shone dark as his eyes. He gazed suspiciously down at Hanratty. "Then all of a sudden, you start writing these beautiful, beautiful songs. I don't understand and something's damn funny about it. Damn funny."

"Maybe it just took time for my talent to bloom," Hanratty said. There was a note of irony in his voice. He was uncomfortable talking about the songs. They weren't, after all, his.

A knock sounded tentatively on the door just as Bentley was about to say something else.

Bentley went to the door, opened it.

She stood there, Sally Carson, looking as overwhelm-

ingly voluptuous as ever—almost unreal in certain ways—
spilling out of the tiny pirate's costume all the waitresses
wore at Kenny's Lounge. She was six feet or better, with
a breathtaking bust, and perfectly formed hips and legs.
She also owned one of those tiny overbites that add just
the right sexy bit of imperfection to a beautiful woman's
face. Only one thing was wrong with Sally and that was
all the makeup she wore around her right eye. It looked
as if she'd put it on with a spade and Hanratty knew why.

She was Kenny Bentley's current girl friend and Kenny
Bentley, a man who brought new meaning to the term
insanely jealous, had obviously worked her over again
last night. If you looked carefully at Sally—as Hanratty
did dreamily many times—you also noticed that her nose
had been fractured right up on the bridge. Another memento from Kenny.

"What the hell is it?" Bentley demanded. "We're
talking business."

Sally suddenly lost all her poise and confidence. She
shied back and said, "You said to tell you when the
Swansons arrived."

"Oh. Right. Thanks."

And with that, Bentley slammed the door in her face.

Hanratty said, "You shouldn't treat her like that,
Kenny. She's a hell of a nice woman. Smart." He wanted
to say *too smart for you* but he knew better.

Bentley stubbed out his cigarette. "I'll go half your
demand, Hanratty. Half but no more."

Hanratty shrugged. "I'll have to think it over, Kenny."

"You do that." The suspicion was back in his eyes.
"In the meantime, I'm going to find out what the hell's
going on here."

"What's that supposed to mean?"

"It means that no broken-down lounge singer suddenly
comes into talent. There's just no way, Hanratty, just no
way." He started toward the door and paused. "In college did you read a book called *What Makes Sammy
Run?*"

"As I matter of fact, I have."

"Well, you know how Sammy Glick steals that poor jerk's movie scripts and sells them as his own?"

Hanratty felt his face redden and his hands fold up naturally into fists.

"Well, something like that's going on here, Hanratty. Something very much like that."

With that, he was gone, the sound of the slamming door reverberating like a gunshot.

Hanratty had a cigarette, just one of the innumerable vices he'd never been able to give up, and tried to calm down. He thought of how ironic it was that he'd just become so self-righteous when Bentley had accused him of using somebody else's material. Wasn't that exactly what he was doing?

He thought again of the tentative call he'd made this morning to a New York song publisher. Inquiring about how you went about selling songs . . . But then he'd backed off and told the woman he'd call her back soon. Without knowing where the songs came from, it would be a dangerous thing to start peddling them . . . At the least it could lead to embarrassment, at the worst to prison.

He jabbed out his cigarette and went over to the walk-in closet to select one of four lamé dinner jackets. There was a green one, a red one, a blue one, a black one, festive and tacky at the same time, and just what you'd expect from somebody who had spent his life—despite big gaudy dreams of being a star in his own right—singing other people's material, tapping parasite-like into creativity not his own.

As usual, the smell of moth balls startled his senses as he pushed the sliding closet door back. It always reminded him of his parent's attic back in South Dakota. He reached in for the blue jacket and felt another familiar sensation—a slight draft, one whose source he'd never been sure of. It was inside the closet only occasionally and he'd never checked it out but tonight, with twenty minutes to go and no desire to sit at his dressing table and brood, he decided to get on his hands and knees and find out just where the draft came from somewhere in the darkness at the east end of the long closet.

He had just gotten down on his hands and knees and started to crawl into the closet, the draft becoming much stronger and colder the more deeply he went inside, when an abrupt knock came on his door. Instead of responding to the knock, he decided to go a few feet closer to the wall. He put his hand out and felt for the first time a piece of plywood about three feet by three feet that had been nailed against the wall itself. Given all the nailheads his fingers found there in the gloom, Hanratty could tell that the plywood should have been firmly affixed. But it wasn't. Not at all. It almost came off in his hands. He put fingers on either side of the plywood and felt an opening whose chill metal surface told him that it was a wide piece of duct work now closed off for some reason. He wondered where it led and why it had been closed off. Then, just as he sensed a sweet odor—perfume coming from duct work?—the knock on his door became adamant. He reaffixed the piece of plywood as well as he could, crawled backward out of the closet, and then went to answer the door.

There, in his standard white bartender's uniform, stood David Sullivan. David was twenty-four, a former second-string tackle for the Browns, and now a guy trying to get himself an MBA at the local state university while working nights here. Sullivan was big, as you might expect, and handsome in the way a somewhat forlorn St. Bernard is handsome. Hanratty knew why he was forlorn. Sullivan was in love with Sally Carson.

"I talk to you a minute, Richard?"

Sullivan was a good kid and Hanratty both liked him and felt sorry for him. "Sure. Come on in."

Sullivan did so, closing the doors. His brown eyes watched curiously as Hanratty wiped closet dust from his hands. Hanratty thought of explaining, then saw that Sullivan's business seemed to be a lot more urgent.

"What's going on?"

"You saw Sally?" Sullivan said. His voice was trembling.

"Yeah, kid, I did."

"That bastard. That's the third black eye in less than two months." He made a fist the size of a melon. "You know what I want to do—"

Hanratty lit a cigarette, exhaled smoke. "Look, kid, I don't mean to hurt your feelings, but remember the last time we had this conversation?"

"I remember, Richard. You told me that if she really wanted to get away from him she would."

"That's right."

"Not any more."

"Oh?"

"She snuck over to my place about dawn this morning and really broke down. Just laid on my couch and cried and cried. She was really scared."

"Of Bentley?"

"Right."

"Why doesn't she just leave him?"

Sullivan said, "She thinks he'll kill her."

Hanratty frowned. "Look, I take no back seat in my loathing of Kenny Bentley. I know he likes to cheat his employees every way he can, and I know he likes to harass and debase people every way he can, and I know that he gets some kind of sick kick from beating up his woman-of-the-moment. But I can't say that I see him as a killer. Not on purpose anyway."

"She thinks he may already have killed one of his women."

"What?"

"Two years ago. She ran into a waitress who used to work here and the waitress told her that there was this really gorgeous but very quiet waitress named Denise Ayles who worked here while she was going to the Harcourt Academy. She got involved with Kenny very briefly but started to back away once she saw what he was like. Only he wouldn't *let* her back away. He kept coming at her. Then she just vanished."

"Vanished?"

"Right. Vanished. The waitress said she called the police and had them look into it, but all they concluded was that Denise Ayles, for reasons of her own, just took off." He made the melon-sized fist again. "You know damn well what happened, Richard. He killed her and got rid of the body."

Hanratty's jaw muscles had begun to work. "I guess that wouldn't be out of the question, would it?"

"Not with Bentley."

"And the cops lost interest?"

"Bentley had an alibi. He was in Vegas."

"Then maybe he didn't kill her."

"You know Bentley's friends. He could buy an alibi with no problem."

"I guess that's true."

Big, shaggy Sullivan looked sorrowful again. "I don't know what to do about Sally."

"Just kind of ride with things, kid. See what happens."

"If he lays a hand on her again, I'll break his neck, Richard. That's a promise." The cold rage in his otherwise friendly gaze told Hanratty that this was no idle threat. Not at all.

Hanratty reached up and put his hand on Sullivan's shoulder and said, "Let's just see what happens, all right? I don't want to see you *or* Sally get into a jam, okay?"

Sullivan sighed, calmed down somewhat. He even offered a quick flash of smile. "I don't know why you stay here. Especially since you got hot as a songwriter the past few months. You ever thinking of selling your songs?"

Hanratty wanted to say: Kid, I'd love to. If they were really *my* songs."

He played the new song for them that night, "Without You," and you could sense how the audience liked it. Enough to set down their drinks; enough to quit copping cheap feels in the shadows; enough to quit shedding tears over lovers who were never going to leave their spouses. How intent they looked then, sleek pretty people in sleek pretty clothes, the sort of privileged people Hanratty had always wanted to be—and now, as always when he played one of the songs left so mysteriously for him—now they paid complete attention.

By the time he got to the payoff, his voice straining just a little to hit the final high notes, he could see their eyes shine with the sadness of the song itself. The lyrics got to Hanratty himself, always did. Whoever was writing them knew the same kind of tortured loneliness Hanratty had felt all his life but had never been able to articulate, not even to himself. But it was there in the majestic melancholy of the music itself, and only reinforced by the words.

They applauded till their hands grew numb.

A few of the drunker ones even staggered to their feet and gave him an ovation.

And there was one more phenomenon Hanratty took note of—the look certain of the women had been giving him. Not as if he were a too old, too chunky, too cliched piano bar man but instead a very desirable piece of work. The same kind of looks the bartender David Sullivan was always getting.

Finished with "Without You," and realizing that he had now run through the six songs that had been left to him over the past few months, he sat down and began playing the standards Kenny Bentley insisted on, everything from Billy Joel to Barry Manilow, with a few Broadway tunes thrown in to give the proceedings a more mteropolitan air.

And he lost them then, as he always lost them then.

They started talking again, and grabbing cheap feels, and giggling and arguing.

Without the six original songs composed for him by the phantom composer, Richard Hanratty's act had gone back to what it had always been—background music.

* * *

Three hours later, finished for the night and sitting in his dressing room with a scotch and water and a filter cigarette, Hanratty stared at the six pieces of sheet music that he felt could secure him the sort of future he'd always wanted. If only he could be sure that once the songs became hits nobody would show up to claim them . . .

He got the chills, as happened many times after the show, because even playing ballads you worked up a sweat. He needed to get out of his jacket and shirt, wash up in the basin in the corner, and put on a turtleneck and regular tweed sportcoat.

He splashed water on his face and under his arms and then slapped on Brut and deodorant. Feeling much cleaner, he stepped to the closet and picked out the turtleneck he'd worn to the show tonight.

Because the club was so quiet—the unregistered aliens Bentley liked to hire for less than minimum wage sweeping up the floor now, David Sullivan preparing the bar for tomorrow—he was able to hear the whimper.

His first impression was that it belonged to an animal. A cat, perhaps, caught somewhere in the walls.

Then he remembered the piece of plywood over the duct opening in the closet wall. A cat lover, he wondered if a feline of some kind might not be caught down there.

He went over to the drawer and took out a long silver tube of flashlight and then went back to the closet and got down on his hands and knees and put his hand on the plywood rectangle again.

Still loose, it was easily pulled away from the nails mooring it.

He pushed the beam inside the wide mouth of metal duct and then poked his own head inside.

He saw what was down there instantly and just as instantly, he recoiled. His stomach knotted, he felt real nausea, and he banged the crown of his head pulling it from the duct.

He'd seen what had made the whimpering sound all right.

My God had he seen it.

* * *

After he had composed himself, and still armed with the flashlight, he replaced the piece of plywood, moved backward out of the closet, stood up, finished dressing, and then went out into the club to speak with David Sullivan.

"Bentley around?" Hanratty asked.

Sullivan sighed. "No, he and Sally split already."

"Good."

"What?"

"Oh. Nothing." Instinctively, Hanratty knew enough to keep what he'd seen to himself. "I'm going down to the basement."

Sullivan grinned. "It's okay, Richard. We've got a bathroom up here." Then, more seriously, "What's down in the basement?"

"A subbasement, if I remember right."

"Yes. We're close enough to the river that the sewer system runs right next to the subbasement, which used to be kind of a retaining wall before this part of the city burned down in the early part of the century."

Now it was Hanratty's turn to grin. "How do you know all this stuff, kid?"

Sullivan snapped his white bar towel like a whip. Hanratty had no doubt who the kid was whipping. "Well, when the woman you love spends all her time with a jerk like Bentley, you've got a lot of time to read." Then he shrugged. "Actually, I heard it on the news the other night. This whole area of the sewer system has become a refuge for some of the homeless who are wandering around."

"Poor bastards," Hanratty said. He nodded to the fifth of Chivas sitting next to the register. "How about a shot?"

"Sure." Sullivan poured and handed the shot glass to Hanratty. "It's on Bentley."

The first level of the basement was what you would expect to find—essentially a storehouse of supplies to keep the lounge running, everything from large cardboard boxes of napkins and paper plates to crates of glassed olives and cocktail cherries. The majority of the storage room, naturally enough, was taken up by tall and seemingly endless rows of brand name booze. The basement walls had been finished in imitation knotty pine and the floor had been given a perfunctory coat of green paint. Everything was tidy and dry and smelled of dust and the vapors of natural gas from the large furnace unit in the east corner.

Duct work of various types ran everywhere. It took Hanratty ten minutes to figure out which of the pieces of silver metal fed into his closet. Once he concluded that he'd found the right piece, he found its track along the ceiling over to the door to the subbasement, which was just where he suspected it would lead.

He had not forgotten what he'd seen in the duct work earlier. He would never forget.

It waited for him on the other side of the subbasement door. He could sense it.

He clicked on the flashlight, felt his stomach grab in anticipation, and put his hand on the door leading to the subbasement.

It was locked.

He spent the next five minutes trying everything from the edge of a chisel to a screwdriver—he found a tool kit in the corner—but nothing worked. The lock remained inviolate.

He raised his head, finally, and shone the light along the duct work leading over the door and beyond. He needed to find a section he could pry open.

This time from the tool kit he took a hammer and an even larger screwdriver. He went to work.

In all, it took twenty minutes. He cut his hands many times—he'd done sheet metal work two summers in college and it had always been a bitch—and he was soaked and cold with sweat.

His work complete, he two took cases of Cutty Sark, piled one on the other, and used them as a ladder.

Then he crawled up inside the duct work and started

his inching passage down the angling metal cave till he reached its end.

His first reaction, once inside, was of claustrophobia. He thought of all those horror films he'd seen over the years about being buried alive. What if he never got out of here . . .

He moved forward, knowing that was his only hope.

Fortunately, the passage was straight, no sudden turns that would block or trap him.

After five minutes or so he began smelling more than dust and sheet metal and the rat droppings that he crushed beneath with his hands and knees. He began smelling—river water.

Then the duct ended abruptly and he let himself drop from it to a huge concrete tunnel that was obviously the sewer system David Sullivan had been talking about. Everything smelled fetid. As he played the flashlight around on the walls, he saw red, blue, yellow and green obscenities spray-painted on the filthy gray arching walls. Rats with burning, hungry eyes fed on the carcass of what had apparently been an opposum. Broken soda bottles, crushed cans, sticks with leaves that trailed like dead hair all floated in the foot of filthy water that ran down the curving floor of the sewer.

He spent the next few minutes getting oriented, moving the beam around, fascinated and sickened at what he saw. To think that people actually lived here . . .

Then he heard the whimpering again and when he wheeled around he saw, high up on this side of the wall, a ragged hole in the concrete.

The creature he had earlier glimpsed was, Hanratty was sure, inside that hole.

Steeling himself for his second glimpse of the thing, he walked through the dirty water until he was directly beneath the hole.

"Why don't you come down?"

Nothing.

"Why don't you come down?" Hanratty said, his voice

reverberating off the peaked ceiling and the vast stretch of concrete cave.

Still nothing.

"I won't hurt you. I want to help you." He paused. "You've been leaving those songs for me, haven't you?"

The whimpering sound—this time it was more like mewling—began again.

He stood on his tiptoes and played his light inside the dark hole a few feet above him. The opening made him think of a bird's nest. The reeking dampness choked him.

The opening was perhaps four feet deep and three feet high. Inside he saw a six pack of Coke, a loaf of Wonderbread, an open package of Oscar Meyer luncheon meat, several magazines including *Vogue* and *Harper*'s and then female clothes of all kinds, from undergarments to dresses and sweaters. Spread across the floor were several mismatched blankets. At this point he raised the beam and waved it in the rear of the opening, where it angled down sharply to meet the retaining wall behind.

This was where he found her.

This time her face wasn't deeply pitted with what appeared to be radiation burns of some kind. Nor was her head sleek and bald and likewise tufted with terrible burns. No, this time she wore a mask to cover her hideousness, a rubber Cinderella mask from the Disney version of the classic fairy tale.

She said something he could not understand. The mask made her words incomprehensible. She tried again and this time he heard, "Stay away."

"I want to help you. You're the one who writes the songs, aren't you?"

"Stay away."

If he hadn't seen her face without the mask, he would have taken the rest of her to be a quite beautiful woman with perfectly formed wrists, ankles and neck, and a pleasing swell of breast beneath her ragged man's work shirt and heavy blue cardigan and baggy jeans.

"You live down here, don't you?"

She cowered in the rear of the opening, covering the eye-holes in the mask as his beam bore in.

"Why would you live down here?"

But as soon as he'd spoken he knew exactly why she lived down here. Her face. That horribly scarred and boiled face.

"Would you come out of there so we can talk?"

She shook her head.

He went back to asking questions. "You work your way up the duct work and leave the songs on my piano in the middle of the night when nobody's there, don't you?"

Faintly, she nodded.

"But why? Why do you want me to have them?"

Once more she spoke and once more he had a difficult time understanding what she was trying to say. Finally, finally, he heard properly. "Turn out the light."

"Why?"

"I want to take this mask off so you can hear me more clearly."

"All right."

He clicked off the light, lowered the long silver tube of flashlight.

He heard the rumple of rubber being pulled off. The opening was now a black pit with no detail whatsoever.

From the gloom, she said, "At night I lie here and listen to you play the piano and sing. You have a very sad voice."

He laughed. " 'Sad' as in pathetic."

"No, 'sad' as in troubled. Hopeless. And that's why I write the songs for you. Because you and I share the same kind of pain."

"You could make a fortune with your songs."

Now it was her turn to laugh, but when she did so it sounded morose. "Yes, I suppose I could get my face on the cover of *People*."

"No, but—"

She sighed. "I write for my own pleasure—and yours, I hope."

"Believe me, I love your songs."

"You may have them."

"What?"

"I'm making a gift of them to you."

"But—"

"That's a very serious offer, Mr. Hanratty. Very serious. Now, I've talked enough and so have you."

"But I'd like to help you in some way."

She sighed once again, sounding old beyond imagining. "You can't help me, Mr. Hanratty. Only one man can. Only one man." She paused and said. "Now go, Mr. Hanratty. Please."

Her voice was resolute.

"I appreciate the songs."

"If they make you wealthy, Mr. Hanratty, promise me just one thing."

"What?"

"To never fall in love as foolishly as I did."

"But—"

"Leave now, Mr. Hanratty. Leave now."

He heard a rustling sound as the woman crawled to the back of her lair, lost utterly in the darkness.

He stared a moment longer at the wall of gloom keeping her hidden from him, and then he jumped down to the watery floor, and started his way back through the duct work and to Kenny's.

In the morning, he called New York and a music publisher who at first would not even take his call. But finally, adamant, he convinced the secretary to put him through to her boss, who turned out to be a woman with a somewhat mannered accent and a strongly cultivated hint of *ennui* in her voice.

He made the call from his small apartment cluttered as usual with scabrous cardboard circles from delivery pizza, beer cans and overflowing ashtrays. Grubby overcast light fell through the cracked window and fell on his lumpy unmade bed.

She was about to hang up when he said, "Listen, I'm

sure you get thirty calls like this a week. But I really do have songs that could make both of us really wealthy. I really do.''

"That will be all now," the woman said. "I'm quite busy and—"

"Two minutes."

"What?"

"I just want two minutes. I'm sitting at an upright piano and all I need to do is set the phone down and play you one of these songs for two minutes and—"

A frustrated sigh. "How old are you?"

"Huh?"

"I asked how old you are."

"Mid-forties. Why?"

Her laugh startled him. "Because you're like dealing with a little boy." She exhaled cigarette smoke. "All right, Mr. Hanratty, you've got two minutes."

So he played. With fingers that would never be envied by concert artists. With a voice that not even the raspiest rocker would want. But even given that, even given his hangover, even given the grubby winter light, even given the mess and muck of his apartment—even given all that there was beauty that morning in his apartment.

The beauty of the deformed woman's pain and yearnings and imprisonment in a face few could stand to gaze on.

He played much longer than two minutes and somehow he knew that the woman on the other end of the line wouldn't hang up. Because of the beauty of the melody and the poetry of the words.

By the time he finished the song, he'd forgotten where he was. He had given himself over completely to the music.

When he picked the receiver up again, he was sweating, trembling. "Well?" he said.

"How soon can you catch a flight to New York?"

"A couple of hours."

"I'll have a car waiting for you, Mr. Hanratty." As

hard as she tried, she could not keep the tears from her voice. The tears the music had inspired.

Hanratty went to New York with a checking account of $437.42. He returned with a checking account of $50,437.42—and a contract that promised much, much more once Sylvia Hamilton, the music publisher, interested top recording artists in these properties. She was talking Streisand, for openers, and she was talking quite seriously.

As he deplaned, he caught the white swirling bite of the blizzard that had virtually shut the city down. He had to wait an hour for a taxi to take him directly to Kenny's. Bentley had not wanted him to leave in the first place and told him that if he took more than two days off, he'd be fired. In an expansive mood now, Hanratty planned to finish out the week at the lounge, and then head immediately back to New York where Sylvia (a not bad-looking older lady whom Hanratty felt he was going to get to know a lot better) was already finding an apartment for him.

Coming in on the crosstown expressway was an excruciating crawl behind big yellow trucks spewing billions of sand particles beneath whirling yellow lights into the late afternoon gloom and watching the ditches where obviously overworked and weary city cops were checking to see that the people who'd slid off the road were all right. Fog only added to the air of claustrophobia Hanratty felt in the back seat of the cab that smelled of cigarette smoke and disinfectant.

He saw the red emergency lights a block before the Checker reached the lounge. They splashed through the blizzard like blood soaking through a very white sheet. His stomach tightened the way it always had when he'd been a little boy and feared that a siren meant that something had happened to one of his parents or to his brother or sister.

Something was wrong at Kenny's.

The police already had sawhorse barricades up, but in

this kind of weather they were almost pointless. It was too bitterly cold to stand outside on a night like this and gawk at somebody else's misfortune.

He paid off the cabbie and fled the vehicle immediately.

A tall, uniformed officer tried to stop him from going into the brick-faced lounge but after Hanratty explained who he was, the cop waved him in.

"What happened?" Hanratty said, his voice tight.

"You better ask one of the detectives."

What surprised him, two steps across the threshold, was how strange the familiar place appeared. Violence had a way of doing that—of altering forever a setting one once took pleasure in.

From behind, a voice said, "May I be of any help?"

He turned to see a gray-haired detective in an expensive gray suit and a regimental striped tie step forward. He wore his ID tag pinned to his left lapel.

Hanratty once again explained who he was.

"You're the piano player."

"Yes," Hanratty said. "Why?"

"Sullivan said you'd vouch for him."

"David? The bartender?"

"Right. We've got him in custody."

"Custody."

The detective, who looked as much like a banker as a cop, nodded. "For killing the owner of this place, Kenny Bentley."

Hanratty felt a shock travel from his chest all the way out to the ends of his extremities. He could easily enough imagine the scenario Detective Keller (that being the name on the ID) had just sketched out. Sally Carson had come to work beaten up once again and David, unable to control himself, had grabbed Kenny and—

"Stabbed," the detective said. "In his office."

Hanratty was jarred back into reality. "You said stabbed?"

"Yes."

"No way."

"What?"

"David might beat him to death. Or choke him. But stab him—no way."

"You may be a great piano player, Mr. Hanratty, but I can't say that I put much stock in your abilities as a detective."

As he finished speaking, a white-coated man from the crime lab came out of Kenny Bentley's private office and drew Keller aside.

Hanratty looked around again. The chairs had not been taken down from the tables. The lights behind the long, elegant bar had not been lit. The stage seemed ridiculously small and shabby. Even the Steinway lacked sheen.

"I need to go have one more look at the body, Mr. Hanratty," Keller said. "You'll excuse me."

Without quite knowing why, Hanratty said, "Mind if I go?"

Keller offered a bitter smile. "You hated him, too, and want to make sure he's dead?"

"Oh, I hated him. But that isn't why I want to go."

"No?"

"No. I just can't believe David is the killer."

Keller shrugged and exchanged an ironic glance with the crime lab man. "Well, if you enjoy looking at corpses, Mr. Hanratty, then I guess I can't see any harm in your coming along."

The office showed virtually no sign of struggle. The flocked red wallpaper and gaslight-style wall fixtures and huge leather-padded desk all suggested Kenny Bentley's fascination with the Barbary Coast of the 1900s.

Bentley sat in his tall leather desk chair, dumped face forward now on his desk. A common wooden-handled butcher knife protruded from the right side of his spine. It had not been pushed all the way in, a good three inches of metal blade still showing.

Hanratty said, "Even if David had stabbed him, you don't think he would have pushed the knife all the way in—with his strength and his anger?"

Keller's eyes narrowed. Obviously Hanratty had made

sense to him no matter how much he didn't want to admit it.

Hanratty moved around the desk. Kenny Bentley's body already smelled sourly of decay.

"Hey," Keller said, "don't touch anything."

"I won't."

Hanratty examined the proximity of a pencil to Bentley's right hand. Then he leaned over and stared at a single word scrawled in a dying man's clumsy script.

The word was Harcourt.

Keller must have caught Hanratty's surprised expression. "Something I might be interested in, Mr. Hanratty?"

Hanratty shook his head. "Guess not." He took his cigarettes from his trench coat and stuck one carefully between his lips. "Maybe I'll go have myself a drink."

Keller, no longer so unfriendly said, "Maybe seeing him dead proves you didn't hate him quite as much as you thought, huh?"

"Oh, no," Hanratty said. "It just proves that I hated him even *more* than I thought."

"What?" Keller said.

But Hanratty didn't answer. He just went out of the office and across the small dance floor to the bar where he had himself several good belts of Chivas while the police finished their work.

Two hours later, Keller came over and said, "Afraid we're going to have to throw you out, Mr. Hanratty. We're closing down for the night."

The ambulance people had come and gone, as had at least a dozen other people. Now Kenny Bentley was headed for the morgue.

Hanratty set down his drink and said, "Fine."

He went outside. The wind and snow whipped at him. Whatever kind of drunk he'd been building was quickly banished by the chill. He walked ten blocks, along a black wrought iron fence on the other side of which was the sprawling river, its pollutants frozen for the moment by ice.

When he figured he'd spent half an hour, he turned around and walked back the way he'd come, back to Kenny's place.

He had a key to the back door so getting in was no problem, even if the police signs warning of CRIME SCENE were ominous. Inside was shadowy and warm. He went to the dressing room. He took off his trench coat and went immediately to the closet where he lifted off the plywood rectangle that covered the duct.

This time, he made the trip in less than fifteen minutes.

When he'd constructed another jerry-rigged ladder and gotten up on it and clicked on the flashlight, he got a brief glimpse of her without the Cinderella mask. She must have been sleeping and he'd surprised her. The lair was the same as before, reminding him of an animal's cave.

This time he recognized the horrible raw burns for what they were. Not radiation but acid.

As she grappled on the mask, he said, "I know who you are."

"I knew you'd figure it out."

"You worked for Kenny Bentley two years ago and went to the Harcourt Academy, which is a music school for particularly gifted people. Kenny got jealous of you and threw acid on you and you were so ashamed of your looks that you took up living down here where nobody could see you."

"Please turn out the light."

"All right."

Once again, he spoke to her in darkness. The sewer system echoed with their voices. The amber eyes of rats flicked through the gloom.

"I went to doctors," she said. "But they couldn't help me."

"Why didn't you turn Kenny in?"

"Because I want my own kind of vengeance. Just seeing him go to prison wouldn't have satisfied me."

"They think somebody else killed him. A nice young kid named David Sullivan."

"I know. I crawled up the duct and heard the police talking and then arrest him." Pause. "Get ready to catch something, Mr. Hanratty."

From the blackness a small white oblong of paper drifted down to his hands.

"That's a complete confession, Mr. Hanratty. Your friend will be freed as soon as you hand it over to the police."

"I'm sorry," he said.

"You know something, Mr. Hanratty, I sincerely believe you are."

The gunshot came just after her words, defeaning as the noise of it bounced off the walls of her small lair, acrid as the odor of gunpowder filled his nostrils.

"My God," he said. "My God."

He stood there on his rickety makeshift ladder for a long time, thinking of her hideous face and her beautiful songs.

When he jumped free of the boxes and stuffed the envelope into his trousers, he realized he was crying, the way he sometimes cried when he played her songs.

He paused for a moment and shone the flaslight up the wall and across the dark opening again.

Finally, he did the only thing he could do. He walked away, the sound of his footsteps softly splashing the fetid water loud inside the huge cave of the sewer.

He hadn't quit crying yet and he wondered if he ever would.

TOO HIDEOUS
TO BE PLAYED

by J. N. Williamson

Four in number—possibly more than four hundred in combined years—the old people clad in bathrobes, jammies, and slippers sat round a sturdy table in the nursing home rec room. Although sturdy, the table had been donated years ago by a surviving grandson who hadn't known what to do with it.

Three of the four old people knew better than to lean on the end of the table closest to the temporary stage. As a consequence, the rock group that was present to entertain them had the distinct impression that a portion of their elderly audience was shrinking from them in disgust, or horror, even before they began to make their sounds.

The fourth oldster (who did not know the table leg was braced in place) was a recent transfer from another home, and the three ancients with knowledge used their arthritic fingers to draw him from the danger. Thereby they came into contact with him—touched him, elicited reaction from him—for the first time.

They did not know his name, or nationality, had no idea how many institutions he had lived in, and none of them was prepared for the way his fleshy arm felt when their well-meant fingertips sank into it. But the young rock performers saw their faces and wondered if they had not made a mistake in keeping this engagement.

They also wondered if, behind the mask he wore, the

strange-appearing man causing the three elderly people at the table to recoil was actually as old as they.

Two of the retired regulars at the table were men who resembled parentheses when standing, facing one another; the third was a woman who never stood and looked to have been the permanent objective for persistent snowfall. Her reaction to touching the newcomer was an expression of repellent disgust which she conveyed to the three young men and one young woman constituting the rock group when, politely, she glanced away. The quartet began to play, proximately and unconfidently, with their eight eyes fixed upon the genuine stranger in the drab rec room, making a total of fourteen, round eyes turned to the sagging, once-obese old man who stared expressionlessly back at them from behind his full-face gauze mask.

The woman who never stood, physiologically able to do so but spiritually incapable of attempting the venture, had exerted a minimal amount of pressure on the inner meat of the stranger's right forearm. The cloth of the institutional robe concealing it had not kept her from sensing a clamminess that carried ominous forewarnings beyond her capacity for analysis. Her smile, when she stared at the musicians, was lopsided, attentive, and nervous.

Both male old persons at the table whom she knew—one short of stature but so frail he seemed taller, one tall but with his head and neck protruding at a horizontal plane with the rec room floor, to the degree that he looked drastically shorter than the other man—had clutched the stranger firmly. Respectively, the short senior citizen had imagined his hand went almost to the wrist in the fatty portion of the shoulder, and the tall septuagenarian was ready to swear his own fingers met after pinching through the third man's flaccid bicep.

All of them were wrong. They were simply victims of unfamiliarity with the sort of superannuated human being who, during his salad days, had rarely confined his appetites (literally or figuratively) to salad . . . who had in fact refused to restrain or moderate any of his appetites and who, now at the stage of unprepared-for elderliness, found himself dismayingly unable to dine or otherwise comport himself with the same single-minded absorption in sensual pleasures or escapes. He had been extremely old for such a period of time that he was not so much dieting as helpless, for years, to do justice to the gigantic framework which had been the hallmark of his personal youth as well as his middle years. Consequently, the once-formidable folds of flesh that had made him seem monumentally distinctive, granted him an ambiance of the Gargantuan *distingué,* were not aesthetically unlike the uncut and uncombed mane of snowy hair hanging from the head of the former beauty seated beside him, pretending he had disappeared.

As that which must pass for music was expelled from the expensive stringed instruments of the slightly rattled visiting entertainers, only the tall senior with the bent rooster neck continued gazing at the home's newest resident. He was not to be put off by the fellow's accent or the layers of gauze bandage enmasking his whole head, save for the eyes. A man of property but no compassionate offspring, the tall man had lived beneath the roof infinitely longer than he had ever intended, or wished; for want of anything better to do with the time vouchsafed him, he had endeavored for months to improve the administration of his fellow residents' time. In reality, he had neither said a word to anyone or so much as formulated a plan of action. He had merely turned his habitual businesslike attention to the clear need for better utilization of the limited hours left to those who were dying there, with him, and definitely planned to make his position crystal clear. When he was good and ready. The arrival of this new chap, this upstart, complicated matters. It seemed to mean the need to pose the questions of what he had been and how he might contribute, whether he was cut from the right stuff to serve as a lieutenant—of whether he had money, was *anybody.* Of just who the hell he was.

And why did he wear that damned gauze, anyway? The

flat, deep eyes seen through the slits were like those of a
decent poker player—or a snake! Damned black holes.
They gave nothing away, they seemed to focus on the
scruffy brats as if he could scarcely wait for . . . something. If he was badly scarred, if the fat fool had AIDS,
someone had t'get him *out* of a place where clean, decent
folks lived! Irritably concerned, the tall oldster shifted
his gaze to the four youngsters who imagined they were
there as an act of charity.

The rudimentary musicians were where the pingpong
table generally stood, and went unused; this dreary, late-
winter afternoon it was pushed back against the wall.
Wires and cords leaped from silvery instrumentation as
if the group were trying to become a sort of collective
Frankenstein monster. They had the customary meaningless or vaguely pornographic name such groups awarded
themselves as if bestowing a prize nobody else wished
to claim, but neither the stooped, retired leader of
commerce nor the once-mammoth, silent man in the
masklike gauze knew what it was, or cared.

Each gentleman had, however, noticed the finger-
snapping, palm-clapping girl whose role in the hypothet-
ical entertainment—apart from decoration, or moral
support for the young males—did not become instantly
clear. Her quiescence was more than compensated for by
the shriek seemingly emitted by her appearance. Hair that
might once have been any hue was close-cropped but
encouraged to rise in a porcupine-stiffened hedge of orange, blue, yellow, red and green. Her boots were flesh-
colored; since they pulled on and were buttonless, she
seemed toeless and her calves were completely without
definition. What she wore to cover her young bosom could
have been the one blouse she had as a careless child, and
the same held true for a woolen skirt that stopped short
of her dimpled knees. God remembered, possibly, the
features He had made for her face.

When she took a cue from the arguably psychopathic
leader who had been barking into the microphone, ignoring the electronic feedback bounding from the walls

like the crackling of lightning in a James Whale film—
when she handled the microphone and pressed it to her
crimson gash of a mouth, began to croon into it—her
shredded grade school blouse was forced against two dis-
associated buttons, threatening a moment of acute embarrassment for the audience. Yet she had also donned a
voluminous cape into which she demurely curled herself
while she sang. With her bare thighs showing beneath
the cloak, she appeared to be draped by the banner of an
emerging nation—or clad in nothing but a red bath towel.

The astonishing thing about the singer, to the oldsters
seated at the unsteady table and those trembling others
ringing the room in wheelchairs or jammed together on
cracked sofas, was the fact that she sang wonderfully.
Plaintively, if shrilly, in need of vocal coaching; touch-
ingly, movingly, in the way that a single rose found
blooming near a charnel house can evoke tears.

"Why, she's good," the tall businessman whispered.

"Pretty voice," said the woman who did not rise, bob-
bing her snowy pinnacle.

The short, frail man whispered the singer's name,
hurled their way by the group leader when he had introduced her: "A good day . . . the day of my life . . .
Chris Day." Then he peered down at his finger-laced
hands.

"She is," said the man in the gauze mask, "a bit of
heaven." He spoke so softly only the white-haired woman
and the tall man heard him, and the former tightened her
lips without turning toward him. The latter observed no
movement in the area of the bandaged man's mouth. Yet
his oddly accented voice drifted, grew louder, nearly insistent. "She . . . is the angel. Of music . . ."

Hush, the aged businessman said with embarrassment,
but only to himself.

At the mike, the girl—she was no more than twenty-
one despite the cheapening, gaudy makeup and its exces-
sive use—microscopically swiveled her head. She sang,
"Pity me . . . pity me" directly to the listeners clustered
at the end of the essentially three-legged donated table.

Her plucked brows raised above eyes made black as pitch
by contact lenses. "Be qui-et, oh," she sang to the
stranger, the newcomer, "if you waaaant to know." She
dropped her voice to a whisper. "Pity, pret-ty me."

And the applause, when the group stopped, was polite.
Not held spellbound. Not awed. Not discourteous; not
bored as was generally the way when entertainers were
coaxed to perform there for nothing, for no tangible reasons. Polite.

But the gauze-faced man stood like the film of a toppled tree run backward, the great, sagging remnant of
his flesh drooping beneath his thin robe like rain-soaked
branches. His massive hands began to applaud slowly,
steadily, rhythmically. Insistently, for the short ancient at
his table tottered to his feet to join in, the perpetually
seated woman cooperatively resumed clapping, white hair
loosened and cascading around her face.

Then the tall, pragmatic senior glanced disapprovingly
up, ready to demand that the fat stranger take his seat.
This was not a vaudeville theatre, a music hall, an opera
house. This was a colorless institution of literal, last re-
sort and enthusiasm, zest, enchantment were out of order. Unseemly.

But he saw that the lower part of the gauze masking
which concealed the standing man's face looked sucked
in. It formed a smile like that of a toothless or skull-like
thing—almost as if hearing the young woman with the
ridiculous hair and apparel sing, or seeing her peer directly at him, had infused the stranger with new life . . .
regenerated the collapsed mounds of flesh that had somehow sustained him—or had been sustained—for this moment of rebirth.

Suddenly, too, the former businessman did not wish to
draw attention to himself or for the queer, obsidian eyes
behind the strips of white gauze to turn in his direction
and peer down.

"*Be* Desdemona," cried the newcomer, the man no
one knew. Around them, silence had collapsed when his
singular clapping persisted and, while he had not raised

his voice, its unfamiliarly accented inflections suffused the bleak room. "Be her, Christine. Again."

Each young man grouped where the pingpong table belonged glanced quickly, hastily, from one to the other. The audience was not supposed to speak; they had not known it could. The indescribable leader scratched himself in the region of his zipper.

The vocalist lowered the microphone she shared, took a single step toward the table, the oldsters, the standing man in his cranial cosmos of cotton. Her hair of many colors trapped dying afternoon light from a window of the room in which there was virtually no recreation; her cloak hung loosely, exhibiting her two-button child's blouse and skin possessing the definition her underpinnings lacked. She was a riot of colorful youth discarded, beauty as garbled statement. "I'm just me," she said, not quite reasonably. "I can't be somebuddy else."

"Don't you know you must be?" The once-corpulent man straightened to his entire height. Behind the white gauze, his lips stretched across their hidden universe; behind him, other men entered the room. "I have never," he said gently, softly, "become . . . used . . . to eternity."

Chris Day laughed. "Well, jees, I mean," she said nervously, "who *has?*"

"I went on crying," the old man said as if he had not heard her, not then. "For you, Christine. For me. Are your eyes still blue behind the artifice?" He took one, lurching step toward her. For a man who had been Gargantuan, it seemed a floating, a curious, motion; he'd become a balloon with most of the air gone from it, yet a word from her and he could sail to the ceiling, beat himself to pieces with ecstasy. "Are you still a little child? An innocent?"

"Christ on a cross, Pops," said the performer with the largest guitar. "Like cool it, okay? All right?" But he remained where he was.

"And if I kiss your feet once more," murmured the man in the white mask, "will you weep, again, for me

. . . allow me to replenish those tears I have lost, permit them to mingle with those I can no longer shed?''

Chris gaped at the old man rolling toward her. He fell to his knees and narrowly retained his balance with the aid of one flesh-encased arm desperately outflung to his table. Hastily, she pulled back a boot-clad foot. "You poor man," she said, amazed. "What are you on?"

"Don't oblige me to weep alone forever, Christine, my Desdemona," he pleaded with her. "Together, our music—real music—will ascend to the stars, will fill the universe!" Unseeable, his face was turned up to her, the dual darkness deep within the slits of gauze seeking her love, her sympathy at least, almost absorbing her. "Give me time, my angel—a week, five days!" But she did not respond and the taut smile implied by the curving of the gauze vanished, his face fell slack. "Or see behind my mask!"

The attendants who had been summoned by the old, tall man with the commitment to organization came into the kneeling ancient's field of vision, then. Turning his great, globular head slightly, he saw the legend *RAUL* emblazoned over the uniform pocket of a muscular aide with shining, swarthy skin and a grinning mustache. Neither attendant was overtly menacing; both men threatened all he had lived for. "Easy does eet," said Raul between perfect teeth, rippling bare biceps—his sleeves were rolled up past the elbow—when he reached down. "She don' wandto see your face. You don' show eet to no one, remember?"

Imperiously, "*One*-two-three-*four!*" the lead guitarist counted off, striking two clamorous chords on his gleaming Les Paul-model Gibson. At once, the other young males helped in his effort to conceal everything, to control the situation.

And Chris Day, lifting her mike, screamed the first notes of her next number, fanned the cape out from her sides, was down to one button. Two retirees sitting at the far wall instantly adjusted the instruments in their ears. The white-haired woman who never stood staggered to her feet, uncertainly, face pale as an avalanche. The shorter, thinner of the old men remaining at the table hurriedly assisted her; together, they started toward the door.

"Stop it! Cease!" The aged man wrapped in gauze from pate to shoulders was shouting but simply in the hope of being heard. He sought to rise from his knees, concealed face turned in supplication toward the shrieking young woman. "Some music is so hideous it must not be played!" The attendants grappled with his enormous arms and he managed to scrabble away from them momentarily. But he also dislodged the wobbly leg and the table, on which their soft drinks and snacks had been strewn, crashed deafeningly to the floor. "It's horrible," he yelled, knees crunching chips, scuttling not toward the girl singer but to the one old man who remained, gaping with terror, in his chair. And he shouted over his shoulder, "It is horrible like the *grave*, my poor, mad Christine!"

When Raul and the other aide wrested one arm behind his back, he still succeeded in peering with his unreadable eyes into the face of the tall and distinguished resident of the institution. "I know you have seen death's heads," he began from his knees. "Skulls of the dead, terrible because they once bore the features of the young and the normal." Abruptly, painlessly, he was hauled to his feet. "Is my face worse than what you have seen, *mon ami*—eh? What do you think?"

The tall man glanced from the blank, masked head to the two belonging to the aides, to the girl and the rock group, to his clasped hands.

"Why not tear off the mask I wear? Do it; go ahead! *See* it—discover my identity so I can come back for you, as well!"

Then the muscular attendants were thrusting the raving ancient past the seated gentleman whose horror had kept him from moving, or speaking. It was not until the stranger had been led to the door of the room that he glanced around, wished he had accepted the challenge. Gotten it over with.

It was then young Chris Day finished singing her sounds, held up a pale, open hand to indicate her need for a break, and departed the temporary bandstand. In time, the tall man looked up and saw that she had popped out one contact lens and that the shining eye beneath it was a perfect sky-blue. The other, the black eye, saw his startlement and winked at him.

Chris' crimson cape swept out behind her when she passed and he heard her gentler, plaintive voice singing to herself, softly, "If you waaaant to know" and, "Pity, pret-ty me."

He caught his breath, stared after her, hoped with all his customarily uncharitable heart that they had locked the stranger in his room and hidden the keys.

An instant later, he heard the duet begin.

THE FINAL THRESHOLD

by K. Marie Ramsland

Meg watched the satin, gilt-edged box as if to unlock it with her eyes. She reached for it, hesitated, thought she saw its white sides expanding. She held her breath as her fingers strayed to the lid . . .

But not here!

Feeling in her pocket for the stolen key, Meg pressed the box to her ripening breast, grabbed her porcelain ballerina doll, then scampered down a dim hallway. There was no time to waste now that Christine Daaé had disappeared and the managers and cast from the *Opéra Populaire* were forming plans of vengeance. She arrived at Christine's dressing room, listened at the door, heard nothing, let herself in.

There was magic in this room, enough to make the weak mind mad. Meg recalled the day she'd encountered Christine here, just returned from a mysterious absence. Shoulders slumped, the budding prima donna had been staring into her wall-sized mirror.

"Christine," Meg had asked, "are you all right?"

Christine's frown had deepened, her lips pressed against speech.

Meg had gently touched her shoulder. "We missed you. Where were you?"

Half to herself, still gazing into her own dulled eyes, Christine had whispered, "Within."

"With him? Your tutor?"

Jealous, Meg had known of the man only as one senses

138

a piece of music in the glimmering eye of a satisfied composer.

Christine had remained silent.

"Who is he?" Meg had pressed. "Tell me, please!" She'd thought Christine had begun to hum. She'd stepped closer, heard the words "no one" cross the pale lips, then, "No one you'd want to know."

Head in the clouds, Meg's mother had said about this difficult, golden-haired diva. Meg had tried again. "What is he like, your tutor? Is he handsome?"

Christine's lips had moved wordlessly. Then she'd whispered. "He'll always be with me singing his songs."

Shivering at the singer's spooky innuendo, Meg had chosen another tack. "Where can I find him? Where does he live?"

"Inside . . ."

Exasperated, Meg had pressed again, "Christine, this isn't like you! Share him! Overnight, he's given you a name, made you famous! I, too, want to be recognized! I hate being just one of the *ballet de corps*, where no one knows me! I'm afraid I'll only be ordinary, nameless . . . *faceless!* With his instruction, I could be so much more! Please help me!"

Christine had only laughed, a short, cruel laugh. "No one knows you . . ."

"Please!"

Christine had finally turned, locking Meg into her gaze as firmly as if each had pressed her thumb to the other's throat, strangling, strangled. Meg thought she'd slip to the wooden floor in a faint before Christine had finally broken the spell. "What you fear," she whispered, "is what you will become."

"What *I* fear!" Meg had been incredulous. "*I'm* not frightened of what I could be, with his help! It's *you* who fail to take advantage . . . !"

"Yes!"—still a whisper—"I'm afraid." Christine had reached to the mirror, uttering words incomprehensible to the young dancer. "You don't know the price," she'd said, her eyes wide, "the unending night, your darkest dreams! I am only a mask . . . for . . . oh, horror!"

More riddles! "Of course there are sacrifices, Christine, but I'm ready!"

Christine had shaken her head. "No one is ready for *that!*"

The conversation had soured in Meg's memory. She'd begun to despise the vacant *chanteuse*, once her friend, who sang with such an unearthly voice and who refused to divulge her secrets. Now Christine was gone, and with her the coveted name of her music master.

But Meg had a plan! Once she had seen Christine disappear through the dressing room mirror. Her tutor, no doubt, was "within!" Meg knew just where to go.

Alone now in the darkening room, she placed the precious box at her feet and stood erect before the reflecting glass. She felt "all-overish"—her mother's word—at once chilled and flushed. Black hair and eyes gave her swarthy, twilit face the look of death. But she smiled, stroking her cold reflection as if to infuse it with the warmth of her fingertips. She imagined her visage as it would soon be sketched onto posters, caught proudly in daguerreotype, recognized in exclusive clubs. Christine's tutor must now unleash in her—"little Meg Giry"—a powerful transforming glory!

The *petit danseuse* whirled extravagantly on practiced toes. Her mother had promised she'd be an empress—that's what the Opera Ghost had said! But to be an empress was to be locked away, shielded from the people. Meg wanted praise for her dancing, for her grace, for her poor, humble features. She'd find Christine's tutor, she'd . . .

A crash of shattering ceramic jolted her from her reveries. She gasped. Her doll's head, slammed too hard against the mirror, was cracked beyond repair. A single blue eye shot her a reproachful glance. Moaning, Meg hugged the wretched toy. Then she looked up in surprise.

The mirror was moving!

Meg stepped back, her knees trembling. She dropped

her doll and grasped the box, distantly aware that her chance was at hand, but suddenly terrified of the labyrinth beyond. She'd been there already, once, on the night Christine had been whisked away. She'd followed the others who'd pursued, to no avail, the Opera Ghost. Phantom that he was, he'd simply disappeared, leaving two murders unavenged and dancers, singers, stage crew hysterical and angry. But Meg had discovered what the others had not, and she'd taken quick advantage. She knew now where to find Christine's mysterious, wondrous tutor. She also had a payment in hand that he'd not refuse.

Stepping to the mirror, Meg sensed dark air beckoning, watching, aware.

"There is no Opera Ghost," her mother had told her. "It's a man, a clever magician. Oh, he knows how to use a mirror! He once made a hall of mirrors for the Shah of Persia!"

But Meg knew better. She'd seen the candleflame eyes, she'd heard the sublime, melodious voice in the walls during one of Christine's morning tutorials. He was more than just a man! He knew music better than anyone! Meg intended to surpass Christine's failing heart, to offer herself, body and soul, to this heavenly master.

Meg recalled how Christine had tried, jealously, to pinpoint a weakness in her: "What you fear is what you will become." It had proven to be Christine's own professional epitaph. It was *she* who'd fled the sacrifices of greatness, *she* who'd been unable to project her future from within herself. Meg was not surprised. It was, after all, the body rather than the voice which most fluidly and gracefully captured and expressed music. And she, Meg, was a dancer! Surely the great tutor would accept her as a pupil! She patted the box for reassurance, then stepped behind the mirror.

The inky passageway immediately descended into chiseled, spiraling stairs. There were five cellars below the Opera, and Meg had to find her way to the fifth, to the great lake below, where *his* house, not yet destroyed by the vengeful mob, sat like a sentry. But she had to hurry!

Wishing she'd brought a lantern, Meg felt along the damp, roughened walls. Scraping knuckles against stone, she felt, then tasted blood. Suddenly she remembered! Hand to the level of your eyes! The Punjab lasso! If the Phantom were about, if he did not realize her purpose, he might throttle her with the deadly rope that had already killed the scene-shifter, Buquet, and the singer, Piangi. A chilly tongue licked the hairs at the back of her neck as she raised one arm protectively. The passage before and behind was muffled to her vision as sound to plugged ears. The mirror had closed.

Pressing on, Meg sensed, tried to dismiss, then sensed again a pursuing shadow. She stopped, tensed.

"No one," Christine had whispered, and the dreadful, echoing image of no human face at all behind that Opera Ghost's mask dragged at Meg's resolve like sodden bread in day-old soup. She had no idea what he'd be like, cruel or kind, man or monster. Mentally she supplied him with darkly handsome, welcoming features.

Moist fingers caressed her cheek, then traveled light as a silken scarf across her neck and shoulders. She shivered, pressed against the clammy wall. It was not *he*—no, she'd see his gleaming yellow eyes. Perhaps just a breeze . . .

A scrabbling sound near her feet alerted her to a new danger so alarming as to crowd the Punjab lasso from her thoughts: rats! The sewers were nearby. There might be hundreds of rodents converging on her, tumbling, one over another, down the steps, perhaps sniffing that moment at her flimsy cloth shoes!

"If hungry enough," her mother had once warned, "rats will eat a living baby, right in its crib!"

With a rush of revulsion, Meg kicked out, caught a soft, squealing body, felt another rub over her leg, then fled down the stairs, one hand flapping to fend off further animal attacks. Out of breath, she passed the gaping red mouths of the boiler furnaces, realized she was to the third cellar, and used the psychological momentum to propel her feet faster, downward. She had to reach the lake!

Then she stumbled on an uneven stair and threw out her hands to catch herself. Something clattered for a moment, then was silent. The box! Desperate, Meg flung herself to her knees. She had to have that box, or all would be lost! If the Opera Ghost saw the box, if he guessed what was inside, then he'd certainly spare her, perhaps even be pleased to use her as a tool for his charismatic talents. She had to find that box!

Feeling along the dirt-strewn step, Meg discovered to her dismay that the staircase dropped off on the right. Her heart plugged her throat as she leaned against the single wall. If the box was gone. . . ! Urgently, she scrambled down the numbing, filthy steps, ignored the grimy clogs forming under her manicured nails. She sneezed twice, almost falling, then sent a silent petition to whatever god might listen in these last moments before she gave herself to another. She thought of going back for a light, remembered the rats, passed her hand to the next step. Her fingers encountered a satiny, squarish shape. She grasped the box, hugged it to her chest and drew in a dusty breath. It was several long moments before she rose, raised her hand to the level of her eyes, and continued.

Soon a damp chill alerted Meg to water. She saw bluish rippling light under brick-vaulted ceilings. The lake! Trotting down the last few steps, she flung herself into air thickened by the reek of stale water and mud. At the wharf, the boat still clung to its iron ring. Meg lost no time in pushing off, despite the clumsy, man-sized oars, her box clutched tight between her knees.

Drawn across the silent water as a fish reeled in by a fragile line, Meg's excitement ebbed gradually into haunting doubt. Did he know she was coming? Was he waiting eagerly for his willing pupil, or would he be angry at the uninvited intrusion, perhaps soured by Christine's traitorous flight? Was he, perhaps even there with her, an invisible ghost, watching as she gripped the splintered oars and pulled? Meg held up for a moment, uncertain. Then she remembered that she had not exactly gone unnoticed by this talented specter.

"The Opera Ghost made you leader of a dance line," her mother had declared one night, "went straight to the manager!"

He had predicted a bright future for her in a note to her mother. He could make it brighter still! Meg dipped the oars back into the water.

The lake seemed interminably wide. The girl's arms and back ached as she rowed against chafing palms. Her tight bodice choked her breath, and her cloying skirt, damp from sweat and sodden air, magnified the penetrating chill. In the bluish light, she thought she saw a shadow skim below the surface, thought she heard a curious, lethargic humming. She'd heard stories of bodies washed ashore, dragged down by a protecting Lorelei. But she set her mind on her goal, concentrating on her white arms moving in rhythm, dip and pull, dip and pull, taking her closer . . .

When Meg finally stepped out of the boat, she found herself in a dank drawing room, smelling of must and decay, and strewn with masses of wilted flowers, like an abandoned funeral parlor. Nervous, she pushed open a door, found a candle, lit it. Then she entered a small bedroom, appointed in Louis Philippe style. Someone lay on the bed. Meg approached, holding the candle high. She frowned. The sleeping figure was a woman, perhaps Christine. So she had not run off with the Vicomte de Chagny after all . . .

Meg jerked back her hand, almost dropped her candle, took a backward step. Breathing hard, her mouth sucked dry by adrenalized shock, she peered at cloudy blue eyes sunken, vacuous, into a waxen face.

Christine was dead!

"Christine!" Meg wailed, then clasped her mouth. She backed against a wall, frozen. Silent moments seeped by. Somewhere, water dripped into a tinkling puddle. Meg's candle sputtered.

Finally, more curious than afraid, the ballerina inched again toward the bed. Holding her breath, she raised her candle over the gaping face, then almost laughed out loud.

It was only a doll!—a wax figure, dressed for a wedding. But Meg's amusement bled into dismay then dread as she leaned closer. The once-beautiful replica of Christine Daaé had been violently disfigured. Someone—Christine?—had crushed the features from cheek to neck so that lips were smashed against nose and chin collapsed on ivory throat. Whatever fury had impelled such wanton destruction now sent a guarded shiver up Meg Giry's spine. She clasped her box. It was then that she heard the music.

At first she thought it had risen up in the room in which she stood, so close did it seem. Mournful, compelling tones caught at her throat, a lyrical Punjab lasso. Involuntarily, she raised her hand, then relaxed. She wanted to unfold her arms slowly over her head and weave herself into the warp of the contemplative notes which hung in the air, red bleeding hearts over a freshly dug grave. She filled her lungs with the rich, moist overture, losing herself in the image of a budding black orchid gently swaying on a fragile stem. The box fell from her hands and crashed to the floor.

Meg dropped into a crouch. *Her presence was known!* Nostrils flaring, she clutched the box and braced for those glowering, yellow eyes. Yet the music continued.

She rose, listening. For *this* she had come! Angel of Music, Christine had once called him, for good reason. Meg recognized from numerous rehearsals a compelling dance number from *Don Juan Triumphant*, authored by *him,* here in this darkness, then aborted on stage two days earlier by Christine's abrupt disappearance. Drawn toward the delightful strains, Meg wandered through the underground abode.

In an ebony-draped, gaslit room, Meg discovered him—the Opera Ghost, the Phantom, the man who spun the souls of mirrors. His back to her, he slumped dra-

matically over his melodic pipe organ. Cloaked in un-
dertaker black, cowl over his head, he moved, trancelike,
from right to left as he freed majestic notes from their
mechanical prison. Long, yellowed fingernails caressed
the keys.

Meg approached. She waited. The Master seemed
oblivious. She cleared her throat. The music stopped.
The melancholic organist stiffened. Curious to see his
face, Meg stepped closer. The cowl blocked her view.

"If you please, *monsieur*," she squeaked. She held out
the box. He'd have to turn her way, he'd *want* to see.
Still, he sat, his face in shadow.

Then a voice emerged, harsh and moaning as wind on
a swollen November day. "What do you want?"

Knees melting, Meg shook the box. She wanted him
to see her prize. With trembling fingers, desperate now
to find out if the face known only to Christine were handsome or horrible, she pried open the lid.

Before her startled eyes, the satin container exploded
into flame. Meg dropped it with a cry, flung herself
against a wall, and watched in horror as her secret trea-
sure, her tutorial wages, collapsed into sizzling ash.

A quiet, amused snort brought her eyes to the cloaked
form at the organ.

"If you wear a mask," came the sardonic hiss, "the
world will never find you."

Ominscent angel! How could he have known how she'd
retrieved his death's head mask, discarded in the confusion of flight and pursuit? And how could he perceive so
clearly what *she* wanted of him?

Fear and wonder converged into a cascade of pleas.
"Will you help me? I can do better than Christine! I can
be the expression of your music!"

The dark angel began to hum. Meg stepped closer.

"It is my deepest desire!"

She felt his scrutiny though she saw no face.

"Desire is only fear in disguise," was his stinging response. She heard a smile in those words, a challenge.

"I'm not afraid!"

A cloak-shielded hand came up. A skeletal finger emerged, pointing.

Meg hesitated. Her eyes followed the thin, leprous digit to a full-length mirror on the far wall. She understood. She was to look within herself, as she had watched Christine do, to see if she was, indeed, ready as she claimed. That was where Christine had failed.

Squaring her shoulders, Meg marched to the mirror, then realized her mistake. It was no mirror, but a doorway to a murky room. Inside, seated on a bed with her back to Meg, a young woman, faintly familiar, moaned and rocked, her face in her hands.

Christine!

Forgetting her former jealousy, seeing only how sweet Christine needed comfort, Meg took a step and bumped her nose abruptly against cold, impenetrable glass. Over her shoulder, mirrored in the unyielding pane were two bright yellow eyes, watching.

"He made mirrors for the Shah," her mother had said. It was a trick! Christine was not inside. The woman did not even resemble Christine, now that Meg really looked. It was a mirror which metamorphosed reflection into illusion. Nevertheless, Meg cried out, "Christine! Let me in, I can help!"

Soft laughter crept coldly up her back.

"Christine!"

The woman stopped rocking, began to raise her head. She turned slowly around. Her hands remained together on her lap, cradling something as if it were a fragile, holy relic. Meg kept her eyes on the woman's hands, she had to see what the woman held!

Standing now, the figure behind the glass began to walk in Meg's direction. She held out her possession toward the shivering girl. Meg saw, then realized too late how she'd misunderstood Christine's cryptic message:

"What you fear is what you will become!"

She had gotten it wrong, mixed it up, failed to hear the warning: she would *become* what she most *feared!*

She backed away, shaking her head, recalled how she'd

exposed, in Christine's mirrored room where an "angel"
had listened in, her darkest horror. What she feared, she
had confessed, was *to be ordinary* . . .

. . . her words returned to mock her as she lifted her
eyes, screaming, unaware of the phantom's hideous crescendo of glee, seeing only the hollowed, bloody form of
a once-beautiful face lying within those hands . . .

. . . *to be nameless* . . .

. . . and the thing which had torn itself, naked and
flayed from a mask of skin gouged off by the Phantom's
merciless nails, to show her the horror of what she would
become . . .

. . . *to be faceless!*

Behind her, angel of music, master of mirrors, rose
from his seat.

MARIAN'S SONG

by James Kisner

On our way back from Jupiter we ran into the creator of the universe and he played music for us.

It wasn't much at first, just a low-level buzz vibrating through the ship, almost subliminal, like the background hum of machinery in a factory. We checked for an equipment malfunction, but as the sound grew in intensity and became a hellish din, we discovered it was coming from out there. From space.

It was a terrible sound, a rasping, grating discordance that rubbed the nerves raw, like a thousand fingernails scraping a thousand blackboards. It came from everywhere at once. It boomed out of the stereo speakers in the crew's lounge, it buzzed out of every intercom, it trickled through our communications headphones, and it even talked out of our microphones. It permeated every moving membrane in the ship.

Just as the sound aproached the limits of our endurance, we found Jeff Morgan, down near the reactor, his ears torn off and his face frozen in a terrible grimace-smile of terror.

And the sound suddenly stopped.

My name is Richard Quint, and I was captain of the *Balboa*. My crew consisted of a dozen people, ten men, including myself, and two women. Our mission was to set test instruments down through the gaseous surface of

Jupiter and make observation videos of the massive planet.

It was a long, tiring mission and we were on our way back to the substation between the moon and the asteroid belt, where most of us would receive new assignments.

Jeff Morgan was a good man and I was sorry to lose him. When we found him, his arms were folded across his chest, and blood streamed from his hands, running down the front of his uniform. When the ship's medic forced Jeff's hands down, he discovered bloody wads of tissue clutched in each fist—his ears. Apparently, he had torn them off himself.

The medic didn't know quite what to make of it. He was a young man with only a few years in the service. He hadn't seen much of life—or death.

He judged that Jeff had suffered a heart attack, brought on by a failure to endure the noise from space. I knew better. I had seen faces like Jeff's before, and he looked like he had been scared to death.

At least, that was my first thought. But as I studied Jeff's face, a strange feeling came over me. There was something more terrible than fear etched in his face, something that made my whole body cringe. When I finally recognized it, I was mystified and not a little scared myself. His expression was one of joy, not horror. Maybe it was even more than that—it was ecstasy.

Jeff Morgan had died happy.

The sound returned within minutes, wracking the ship and my crew again. It now possessed a distinct rhythmic quality we hadn't noticed the first time.

Marian Cotter told me what it was.

"It's music," she said.

Marian was our computer officer. She had blonde hair, cropped in military fashion, and bright blue eyes. She was twenty-nine, and her uniform didn't disguise her sex very well. I confess a fondness for Marian that exceeded my responsibility as her commanding officer. Working closely with a young woman for months had worn on my

sensibilities. I had a wife and a son back home, but proximity often creates a semblance of love. Of course, there
were regulations against sexual involvement, especially
for a man in my position, so I had restrained myself. As
a result, I went out of my way to deny my affection for
her.

Thus I was perhaps unnecessarily gruff when I asked
her to repeat herself.

"You're crazy," I shouted back. "If this is music, it
must be coming from hell."

Marian had never given even the least indication she
might share my feelings. She remained pragmatic and
painfully respectful of our professional relationship.

"No, Captain Quint, but I do know where it's coming
from."

Again I was gruff, and somewhat skeptical. "Okay,
then. Where is it coming from?"

"Mars."

Marian was right, of course. The closer we came to
Mars, the louder the "music" grew. She was right about
that part too; the sound was a kind of music. Admittedly,
it was an awful, jarring cacophony, like all the bad tunes
ever played by every terrible high school band in the
world. But it was music nevertheless.

When we were within a few hundred kilometers of
Mars, the music ceased. This time there were no casu-
alties, at least no human ones, but all our observation
tapes of Jupiter were erased.

Marian was the bearer of that bad news.

"Are you sure?" My ears ached. I was beginning to
understand why Jeff had torn his own ears off, though I
still could not comprehend his final ecstasy.

"Absolutely. I checked the first one for damage and it
was clean. So are the others."

Her manner disturbed me. Instead of relating this disaster in a matter-of-fact military way, she seemed smug,
as if she expected it to happen.

"Goddamn it! You mean we have nothing to show for our mission? Nothing for all these months in space?"

Only some computer data. The floppies weren't damaged. The frequency of the music must have done it." When she said "music," I detected a lilt in her voice and a hint of satisfaction. I didn't know how to reprimand her for that, since even a captain can't control his crew's thoughts, but her attitude seemed wrong to me.

"That's a hell of a note."

I pondered this development for a few moments and turned to watch the data streaming across the CRT at my station. It suddenly occurred to me our view of the universe was composed of electronic blips, and that was a fragile view, indeed, one easily destroyed. I thought I heard someone whisper the word "music" behind me. I dismissed this as a residual sound—part of the aftereffects of the space music, like an echo.

I turned to address our radar man. "Farrell, did you get a fix on the source of the sound before it stopped?"

"Yeah. I didn't pinpoint it, but I'm close within a six kilometer radius. It quit before I could get any closer."

"Are there any missions scheduled for Mars? Any way there could be someone down there we don't know about?"

"No. I even tried communicating with the source, but there was no response."

"That's it, then. We're going down."

"But, Captain Quint—that's deviating from our course."

"We have to. We just blew a few billion dollars on research. If we don't find out what that noise was, we're taking a chance on future missions being sabotaged."

"Yes, sir."

I called aft to have the shuttle made ready, then I asked for volunteers to go down to Mars. Marian was the first to volunteer, and that bothered me. I considered denying her request to accompany us but didn't want to seem overprotective. Besides, I wouldn't mind her company in the cramped quarters of the shuttle.

But I would have felt much better about it, if Marian hadn't seemed quite so eager to go.

Two hours later, our shuttle had set down on an uncharted region of Mars in the northwest hemisphere where there was very little vegetation. This area was a vast plain of russet dust and rocks.

The starkness of the other planets in our solar system has always filled me with incredible sadness. It seems to affirm our utter aloneness in our corner of the universe. We seek to contact other intelligences and find nothing but algae and dust.

But the idea of music emanating from what we considered essentially a dead planet filled me with apprehensive hope. Music is not a random noise. If that sound coming from the red planet was music, as Marian said, then I secretly wished something intelligent was generating it.

Of course, I knew we might find a logical explanation. It could be a strange radio effect, or something else equally mundane, such as malfunctioning probe equipment. If it were one of those things, it would be something we could fix. If it was something else, I had no idea what we could do.

In addition to Marian and myself, there were three other crew members in the shuttle. There was little conversation during our descent to the planet, only the grim interchanges required to operate the instruments. I judged the taciturn mood was because of Morgan's death, or it could have been simple fear.

I was brooding myself. I didn't want any more deaths on my conscience.

We left a man behind to operate the shuttle radio, while the rest of us spread out on motortrikes to explore the terrain. We were fully-suited with helmets, and we each had a full instrument pack capable of detecting many possible sources for the music. Unless it was caused by mass hysteria, we were confident we would find its source.

I felt a pang as I watched Marian head out away from me. The dust raised by her trike's tires swirled around slowly, like fog in a dream, and I was suddenly melancholy. I set out east of the shuttle and rode for several moments, finding nothing.

It wasn't too long before one of the others, Gary Miller, contacted me.

"Captain, I've got something." His voice sounded tinny and harsh coming through the speaker in my helmet.

"What is it?"

"I don't know what to make of it. It's an entrance to the underground. Like a cave—it could be manmade."

'Anything else?"

"Yeah. The floor shows signs of being walked on recently."

"Where are you?"

"Six-point-two kilometers due north of the shuttle."

"I'll be right there."

Gary said he would wait for me outside the cave's entrance. I radioed my destination back to the shuttle.

After I signed off, the music started again, making the ground tremble. This time there seemed to be voices accompanying it, a million voices singing and screeching.

It was like a discordant opera.

On my way to meet Gary, my motortrike broke down and I had to walk the last kilometer. I tried contacting the others for help, but got only static on my radio. Approaching the point Gary had indicated, I saw two slabs of red sandstone jutting up from the surface of the planet, forming a triangular opening into a cave. Two motortrikes were parked outside and there was no sign of Gary. I was certain now that the strange opera was coming from the cave.

Almost unable to move now that I was so close to the source of the music, I trudged to the triangular entrance. Even though I had taken the precaution of packing extra ear protection in my helmet, the sound penetrated, shaking the bones in my head.

I stopped to examine the two trikes. One was Gary's. The other was Marian's. Had Gary and Marian gone in to explore the cave on their own?

I stepped inside cautiously, turning my lantern on and scanning the first few meters. Gary's instrument pack was lying on the cave floor; its liquid crystal display indicated a network of underground tunnels leading down from the cave's entrance. As far as I knew, no previous explorations of Mars had ever revealed the existence of such tunnels. We still had a lot to learn about the planet.

There was a surge in the music and the LCD display burst. Then the music ceased momentarily. I took a deep breath, trying to get my bearings.

"Gary? Marian? Where the hell are you?" The sound of my voice coming out of the helmet speaker was dampened inside the cave. There was still static on my radio when I tried to call back to the shuttle. I could take one of the trikes back, but I didn't think there was time. I decided to explore a little on my own, then go back if I needed help. I had two weapons with me, a stun pistol and a knife, but they didn't give me much confidence.

The cave floor formed an incline, slanting as it gradually led to a point where three tunnel openings converged. I checked my instrument pack and it was still functioning. I tried to get a fix on Marian and Gray. The LCD screen revealed someone standing just inside the middle tunnel.

"Gary?"

I found him about six meters in.

His body was standing against one wall, and his helmet was missing. His face mirrored the ghastly death repose of Jeff. His ears were gone, too; they had been sliced off neatly, flush with the side of his head. The knife was still in his hand.

A numbing sense of dread rippled through me. What if I discovered Marian that way? What if the rest of my crew were dead? I backed out of the tunnel and checked my instruments again. The screen indicated two figures moving deep into the lefthand tunnel. One had to be Marian, but the other was much taller and its movement was erratic, not like a man's.

The tunnel sloped down at an angle, taking me deeper and deeper into the planet. As I moved along, pausing every few seconds to look back, I noticed the walls were smooth and uniform, and arched in a perfect semicircle that indicated there was intelligence behind their creation.

After traveling a kilometer and a half into the tunnel, two things happened. First, the music began again. Second, my instrument pack fizzled out on me, and I had to continue with only my lantern and my senses to guide me.

The farther I descended, the louder the music became. I feared it would drive me crazy before I reached my destination.

Then the voices came again. Millions of them. Singing and screaming. It was meaningless to me, except for one particular voice that broke through the clamor. It was Marian's voice, speaking inside my head.

"Go back," she said. "Leave me here."

I forged ahead, convinced more than ever Marian needed rescuing, with no thoughts of my own safety.

The music grew more oppressive as the tunnel began to twist and turn. I was conscious of heat now. I guessed I must be at least two kilometers down.

I'm not a particularly religious man, but as the heat increased, the music hammered at my brain, and I was fast losing hope I would find Marian alive. I prayed to all the gods I knew.

"Go back!"

"No, I won't," I answered the voice in my mind. There was light spilling down the tunnel from just around the next curve, and I no longer needed my lantern. I

approached slowly, sweating profusely under my suit. I
was tempted to take it off—rip off my helmet, too—and
to hell with the consequences.

Around the curve was a vast cavern stretching half a
kilometer across. Its ceiling was so high I couldn't see
where it ended. Three walls were luminous, providing
light that was almost as bright as day; the fourth wall was
honeycombed with thousands of round deep holes filled
only with darkness. The music and the voices were coming from the holes.

And there was Marian. Her suit and helmet were gone
and she was strapped upright on a platform opposite the
honeycomb. Even though I was about ten meters away
from her, I could see blood trickling from her ears. Her
face was a portrait of absolute ecstasy, and she was
watching someone.

I turned to see who or what it was and saw a figure in
a red robe, maybe two and a half meters tall, stretching
its arms up and waving them frantically at the honeycombed wall, as if it were conducting the music. The
figure was vague, yet somehow substantial, a wraith, yet
real. Like a phantom.

Marian saw me then. Instead of the cry of recognition
I expected, she let forth a horrendous scream. I thought
it was a scream in protest of my presence, but her eyes
were looking not at me, but at the phantom figure.

It had twisted itself around. As the hands came down,
the music stopped abruptly.

The hood of its red robe had fallen away to reveal its
face. It's difficult to describe what I felt when I saw that
horrible countenance. Terror welled up in me, and fear,
and other tingling emotions that threatened to tear my
heart out. Its face was neither human nor beast, neither
man nor woman. It was a visage that seemed to bear all
the disfigurements of man. Running sores split its sallow
flesh. Pus drooled from its torn, flayed lips, above which
were were two open gashes instead of a nose. Its eyes
were watery gray-green orbs of fire. It had no hair on its
skull. And no ears.

It raised a hand at me and pointed. There was barely any flesh on its bony fingers, and one black fingernail dropped off. Its ravaged lips parted and the sound coming out was gibberish. Its breath wafting across the cavern smelled of sulfur and ozone.

I gagged, forced my eyes from the thing and approached Marian.

"Go back to the ship." Her features were twisted with anguish. "Leave me here!"

I kept coming, until I was halted by a stab of ice down my back. I wasn't hurt. It was the thing controlling me, compelling me to face it again.

The gibberish it had been spouting suddenly became clear. Its voice was deep and rumbling, almost a growl.

"I want only her. Go back to your—your ship—and you will be spared."

Foolishly, I raised my stun pistol. The thing crimped its nailless finger and the gun evaporated in my grip.

"What the hell is this?" I looked back and forth between Marian and the monster. "You can't kidnap my crew members." I felt puny, making demands of the thing.

"She came of her own free will."

"I doubt that."

Marian's face had relaxed. Despite her bonds, she seemed comfortable in her captivity. "It's true. I—I erased the Jupiter tapes myself—so I could get closer to the music."

"You're talking out of your head. I'm taking you out of here." I glanced at the imposing figure. Overcoming it was a dubious prospect. "Somehow."

It was so hot in the cavern, I found it difficult to breathe. I tried to buy time, so I could think.

"Who are you?" I questioned the figure.

"Demiurge."

"What? Marian. . . ?"

"He's Demiurge, just as he says."

"And who the hell is that?"

"The creator of the universe."

I gave Marian a look that said she was crazy, but it didn't register. "Marian, don't talk nonsense."

"It's not nonsense. It's the truth. I know it in my soul; I knew it from the first time I heard his music. You should be thankful you're so fortunate—to see the being who created . . ."

"Come on, Marian. Be sensible." Her expression was earnest, and I felt sorry for her. "It's that damn music— if that's what you want to call it. It drove Jeff and Gary out of their minds—and maybe some of the others. It's getting to you, too, filling your head with delusion. Can't you see that?"

She looked away from me, and I felt abandoned. The figure stirred, getting my attention.

"I *am* Demiurge." He moved his arms while speaking, and each gesture was complemented by a soft rush of music and voices emanating from the honeycomb. "I created the universe, the world, and all of you—everything you see, touch, and feel. I know everything about you, including all your languages, for they came from me. I have been in exile for centuries, for eons, on this barren world—rejected by my creations while they worship the wrong gods and ignore my songs."

Watching him, listening to his growling voice, I shook with fear and awe. I couldn't control myself; I felt like I was seeing the face of something really beyond my ken. Whatever this thing was, it believed it had created the universe. I couldn't digest the basic idea, though. There was nothing in my experience or anything I ever learned in my life that could convince me this being was nothing more than a deranged monster. Yet, in the act of confronting it, letting its words penetrate my awareness, where they reached into hidden corners of my mind that doubted the reality I had grown to accept without question, all the gods I knew suddenly seemed insufficient, either as a defense or as an argument.

I spoke more to appease it than to understand it, hoping to find the chink in its armor that would show me a way to rescue Marian and save myself. "Your songs?" I whispered.

"My songs are everywhere, but humans do not recognize them. I sing in the vapors of being, in the fabric of your awareness. I'm there, animating your every breath. My music spins the world and causes the sidereal machinery to work ceaselessly to keep mankind going. But my beautiful music has been controverted to evil, while the lesser music of your punier gods is exalted."

By this time Demiurge had lost me, though I found myself somehow soothed by the rough poetry of his speech. For a fleeting moment I thought I understood what he was saying. It was on the bare edge of my awareness—an idea, a thought, an all-encompassing concept of the world that minimized my tiny, self-centered view of things. I reached for that total understanding—reached— and missed it. But the scariest thing was that I almost understood the ecstasy in embracing its music, in accepting what its music was supposed to say, and what the monster wanted from humanity. In a way, it was tantamount to meeting God, and *knowing* him.

But even God might be denied in some circumstances, and ultimately, I realized I only felt pity for the thing. It was a pathetic creature, deluded by a grandiose vision that dwarfed the most audacious Napoleon.

I tried to bring the conversation back to reality and gestured at Marian. "Why do you want her?"

Demiurge growled. "I became impatient, waiting for humans to recognize me. I vowed to destroy it all—all my creation—unless I found one human being who could love me without question, one person who could listen to my compositions and know me. I composed this opera of the universe, for the universe, for mankind, to give you a final chance. I sent my music out into the spheres, among the stars, hoping it would reach someone who would know, understand, and love it. It contains my sorrows and all of mankind's traits, including all that is good and evil." He pointed to the honeycomb, which responded with a brief measure of music. "That is why it has driven some of you mad. It is *all*."

"All?"

"All—the entirety—the beginning and end of time, the being and nothingness of all existence. This will show mankind I'm worthy of their worship, and will topple God from his supremacy."

"But what does Marian have to do with it?"

"I needed only one person to know me—one person, and I would let the universe continue. Marian is that human being, the one I'd hoped to find." He emitted a noise that sounded like a broken sigh. "That is enough. Take this knowledge with you and go back." He turned away from me then and raised his arms, ready to resume conducting.

I looked at Demiurge, then Marian. I considered what had to be done.

"Let's go, Marian."

She strained against her bonds briefly, then lay back. The smile that crossed her lips chilled me. "I won't go back."

"You'll die."

"I don't care. The joy I'm feeling is more important than living or dying. It's beyond either."

Demiurge's arms came down and the music rose, resonating through the cavern, building to an awful crescendo that shook the whole planet. I realized this was Demiurge's last performance and Mars was his instrument.

"Don't you understand?" Marian screamed at me, tears of joy rolling down her cheeks. "Demiurge wrote this opera—just for *me*."

"I can't leave you here! It's not right."

"I can't hear you." Her smile stretched until it split her face. Her uniform burst into flame, then evaporated, exposing her whole body to the opera. Every muscle writhed in time to its relentless rhythms, every fiber of her being straining not to absorb the music, but, as I understood too late, to become it.

Pieces of the walls began dropping all around us. The ground beneath me swayed. I ran toward Marian, reached out for her, and grabbed air. Then I fell down, tumbling over and over, and slid back toward the tunnel.

My head was filled with a wonderful music and a brief flash of joy. Then it was filled with blackness and I dove into the void.

It was an eerie journey, traveling with the dead, but somehow I managed to pilot my ghost ship back to the substation. I had a difficult time with my superiors. They dismissed my story as the ravings of a madman. I expected that, I suppose. After all, I couldn't explain why every speaker in my ship was destroyed. Nor could I really explain why most of my crew was dead, or why two of them were missing, or how I was the only survivor. At least, I couldn't explain these things in terms anyone would understand.

The investigators found nothing on Mars, of course. No cave. No tunnels. No trace of Marian or Gary.

Later, once I figured out how to spell it, I looked up "Demiurge" in the encyclopedia in the prison library. There was a Demiurge in the arcane lore of some forgotten religion, so people did believe in him at one time. Maybe they will again. Maybe they should. I think that's why I was spared and why the music didn't drive me to suicide, so I could tell people about Demiurge.

Of course, I'm not sure I believe in him myself. I don't know what he was or where he came from. I don't even have a theory—unless there *is* other life in our solar system. Maybe we aren't so alone.

I do know that somewhere out there Marian may still be alive, listening to the music of a phantom that says it's the creator of the universe. Whatever it is, it's powerful, and somebody should listen to it. I also know this now— that the universe is more than a bunch of electronic blips—and we should show it more respect. The explosion that destroyed Mars should tell us something, if we only have ears to listen.

At the moment, I'm waiting for the day they'll let me out of prison. It's something to hope for, even if life will never be the same for me. I'm a lot older now, and I have no family and no job.

I have no ears either, and I still can't get Marian's song out of my head.

THE LIGHT
OF HER SMILE

by Karen Haber

The scars. She was not prepared for them; long, incised lines, livid against the pale flesh of his cheek, like ritual tattoos. Or razor tracks.

Christine saw them as he raised his dark glasses. He smiled thinly as she froze in recoil.

"Shocked?"

"Startled," she said, managing an even tone of voice. "Do they hurt?"

"No. Smile, please. Lower your right shoulder. Good." The dark glasses descended into place. The shutter clicked. From hidden speakers in the gloom of the studio, a tenor protested his love—or something—in throbbing Italian arpeggios.

She'd been warned, of course, but no words could have prepared her for the actual sight of his scars, any more than the magazine articles she'd studied could have provided more than superficial understanding of the man who stood behind the camera. Erik, the legend. The ghost—the Phantom, they called him in the modeling studios, behind the clothing racks in the salons, around the editorial offices of the slick fashion magazines, and all along Seventh Avenue. The Phantom.

He'd photographed the legendary, the celebrated and the merely great. Frozen them forever, at their peak, on glossy paper. Icons for posterity. Garbo. Dietrich. Taylor. Lana Turner and Jacqueline Onassis. And now he'd summoned her.

Christine was two years out of Texas—the accent was already fading, taking on the gloss of late night dinners at 21, days spent at shoots in showrooms, fawned over by makeup artists and production assistants on location in Ibiza.

"Turn, please. Ah, just so. Hold that."

She turned, long dark hair swinging into place, back arched. The yellow silk dress slithered against her tawny skin. She froze. The music swelled. The shutter clicked. "Good."

He was much younger than she'd expected, or much younger looking. Black hair shading toward gray at the temples, caught in a small ponytail in back. A strong face, broad forehead, impassive. Powerful body clad in black turtleneck sweater, wool slacks, leather boots. The color of his eyes was difficult to make out when he'd removed his glasses, but they were dark. His teeth were white, uniform. Only his voice, a foreign lilt when he spoke, betrayed exotic origins.

"The red dress now, yes?" He turned away, reaching for another camera.

Christine hurried toward the dressing area, stomach clamoring for food, nerves screaming for champagne. It was past midnight. Christine had considered bringing some coke, but this was the test shoot. She liked to be fresh, at least the first time.

She shrugged out of the silk and reached for the red strapless leather sheath. The music pouring from the huge speakers changed to something harsher, a strident soprano singing in German. She tried to shut it out and pondered the accessories. Different shoes? Hose? Christine wasn't accustomed to working alone like this. He'd applied her makeup, selected the garments. She knew he preferred to do things his own way, but it made her nervous. The late hour, the studio, dark save for the island of light in front of his camera. The passionate, brooding music. Phantom or no, she'd be relieved when this shoot was over.

She emerged from behind the screen. Saw him perched

on a stool, arms folded, smoke from a cigarette leaving sinuous trails around him. Behind him, the singer declaimed: "Ich will vor ihr mich niederwerfen und die Fusse ihr kussen . . ."

"What's that music?"

He smiled, tight lipped. "*Elektra,* by Richard Strauss. With the diva, Nilsson. The definitive interpretation, I think. Splendid, isn't it?"

"I guess." The opera cascaded over her like a physical assault. Her heart pounded.

"Ready? Good."

Christine took her place before him. He stepped up to the camera, dark glasses in place. How could he see?

"Now, my dear, I want boldness. That's it. Chin out. Shoulders back. Fists. Listen to Nilsson. Let her guide you. Yes. Fine. Don't breathe."

Click.

"Allein! Weh, ganz allein. Der vater fort, hinabgescheucht in seine kalten Klufte . . ." the soprano sang. Christine's breathing slowed. She began to relax, to stop fighting the pulsing, overwhelming music.

"Turn your head to the side. Eyes closed. Lovely."

Click.

"Look directly at me. Now, give me passion."

Christine turned toward him, licked her lips, gave him a provocative smile.

"No, no, not teasing. Passion. Wildness."

She tried again, eyes half-lidded, mouth pouty. No longer could she lean into the music—suddenly, Nilsson sounded discordant, frenzied.

"No. This will not do." Erik sighed, walked from behind the camera and faced her. She was tall, but he was taller still. She could almost feel the heat emanating from his body, he was so close. "Do you know what I mean by passion?"

"I think so."

He moved behind her. Behind him, the orchestra moaned from the massive speakers. "You must live it.

This is not a fiction we are making here. Your body, your soul must be for the camera.''

Delicate butterfly touches, his hands, moved over her shoulders and up, to her neck. Tingling. "We must feel you living, breathing. Can you think?''

"Of course.'' She felt dizzy. Were those his fingers or the composer's notes dancing over her skin?

"Your imagination. Your heart. Use it.'' His breath was warm on her cheek. He gripped her hair, pulling her head back. She stared at her reflection in his dark glasses. A startled stranger stared back.

"Think of your first fight,'' he whispered, stroking her hair. "Your first love. Your first orgasm.'' He released her. Walked back to the camera and peered through the lensfinder. Nilsson, voice dark as night, serenaded them.

"And now. Passion! Yes, head back like that. Good.''

Her heart hammered. Christine took a deep breath. She blazed at him, hair flying, arms raised. Elektra, yes! She would be Elektra.

"Turn.''

She spun on her heel.

"Frown.''

She glowered.

"Was willst du? Rede, sprich, ergiesse dich . . .''

"Lovely. Excellent.'' The shutter clicked in approval.

She changed into a pink gown in which she was demure and flirtatious, then a blue velvet cocktail dress in which she was sophisticated, world-weary. She lost track of time, of who she was, of everything except for the music and what was required by the man in black behind the camera.

Hours or days later, Erik looked at his watch, a somber, gunmetal Rolex.

"And that is sufficient, I think. We did some good work, my dear. I will talk to you soon. My driver will take you home. Rest now.''

He nodded toward a door at the far wall of the studio and was gone, disappearing back into the gloom. The stereo was silent. The opera had ended.

Christine dressed in her street clothes, suddenly chilled and hungry. When she opened the door, a short man in a dark uniform was waiting beyond it.

"Miss Day? I'm Roger. Mr. Erik has asked me to take you home." He opened another door, and she saw an alleyway, wet pavement glinting in the purple, pre-dawn light. An ink-toned, high-grilled Rolls Royce was parked at the curb. He held the door open for her as she climbed into the cushioned recesses of the back seat.

"Roger?"

"Yes, Miss?"

"Do you think we could stop and get something to eat?"

"You'll find a fully-stocked refrigerator and microwave oven in back, Miss. To your left."

Christine sighed. Sure enough, there was enough food here to feed three of her. Hardly what she had in mind—if she'd wanted a picnic, she'd have brought her own barbecue. But this was the end of a shoot. She wanted to relax, have a drink, party. She hesitated.

"I'd really prefer to stop someplace, Roger."

"I'm sorry, Miss. Mr. Erik told me to bring you home."

They rolled past two of her favorite after-hours clubs. Christine almost cursed as she recognized Johnny E.'s silver Mercedes coupe outside of Gwen's. She chewed angrily on a carrot stick and waited for the ride to end.

Roger saw her into the lobby of her apartment building. She waved, watched him drive off, then punched the elevator button for the garage. Gleefully, she climbed into her red MG. It was almost five—she could be at Gwen's in fifteen minutes.

The package was waiting for her at the reception desk of Marks'. Jilly, Mr. Marks' niece and the agency receptionist, looked up and smiled. Christine noticed that her hair, what was left of it after her latest cut, was bright green. Last week it had been pink.

"Great hair, Jilly."

"Oh, thanks. Are those your Phantom pictures, Christine? Can I see them?" She sounded eager.

Christine shrugged. "Sure." She opened the package. And gasped. Jilly looked, eyes huge.

"I don't believe it. Quick, show my uncle."

"See if he's in."

"Oh, he's in. Must have had a bad night." Jilly rolled her eyes. "Just go on. I'll tell him you're coming."

Christine clutched the portfolio under her arm and strode down the hall. Leonard Marks' plush office was at the end, next to his wife Sylvia's plush office. She was in Spain. Christine had expected Leonard to be off sampling the agency's stable as he always did in his wife's absence. The only reason he hadn't hit on her yet, she supposed, was because she was half a foot taller than he was. Whatever the reason, she was grateful.

She saw Marks sitting at his desk in a cloud of cigar smoke, nodding as he spoke into the phone. He put the receiver down as she walked in. The overhead light glinted on his bald head.

"Chris, Jilly tells me you've got something I need to see." His voice was nasal, the accent pure Brooklyn.

"The proofs from the Phantom shoot," she said, spreading them across the desk.

He stubbed out his cigar in the Waterford ashtray and flipped through the sheets. He paused, stared, flipped through them again. Then he sat back, studying her with sharp, vulture eyes.

"They're fantastic. You've never looked so good."

"That's what I thought."

"My god, Christine, what's his secret?"

"What do you mean?"

"C'mon, you tell me. I always thought you were this ice maiden from Corpus Christi. What did this guy do, shtup you? That shot in the red leather is hot enough for the cover of Cosmo. I might just call Helen. Or maybe Hef."

Christine was accustomed to Marks' style. A year ago, she would have walked away from his crude comments in tears. Now, she just shrugged. "They don't call him the Phantom for nothing."

Marks smiled an ugly smile. "Too bad Sylvia is coming back today. I'm beginning to see possibilities in you I hadn't thought of." He relit his cigar. Shrugged. "These shots are good. So good, I'm going to move you to our A-list. Bergdorf's, all the Federated accounts. Maybe Tiffany's. Let's see what we can do."

"But I thought Erik only takes the accounts he wants."

"Of course. But we can use these to promote you. The Phantom won't mind as long as he gets paid. And who knows, maybe we can convince him to take on some other accounts." There was a gloating tone to Marks' voice that Christine didn't like. She left him the proof sheets and excused herself. She had a Macy's shoot in an hour at Trump Tower.

When she got home at seven, there was a package in her mailbox and two messages on her machine.

"Miss Day, I'm pleased by the photos, as I hope you are. We will work well together. Roger will come for you at seven tomorrow evening. Until then."

The nerve of him! Christine had a full day of work tomorrow, and there was a reception at the Russian Tea Room for Baryshnikov at ten. Erik might be the Phantom, but he had another thought coming if he believed he could dictate her schedule as if she were some little toy.

The second message was from Johnny E. "Christine, my dream. I can't make it tonight. Something, as they say, came up. See you tomorrow at Gwen's? Kiss kiss."

Shit. He was probably off with his backup singer again. She'd have to dig up an escort for that Baryshnikov thing now. Well, she'd worry about it after she'd taken a bath.

Strewing clothing behind her in a trail, Christine walked into the bathroom. Put the package down on the counter and turned on the water. She'd left the champagne in the kitchen. Damn. She retrieved it, opened the bottle. Poured it, golden, sparkling, into a graceful crystal flute and savored the first sip. The second.

The package caught her eye. It was from the Phantom. More photos, she wondered? She tore it open. A gift box with a note. "To my dearest Elektra, a memento of our first time together. Erik." The box contained the red leather dress and a smaller box which yielded a pair of golden earrings in the form of elaborate sunbursts. In the center of each was a glittering diamond.

Well, he certainly knows how to give gifts, Christine thought.

She left the dress on her bed, caressing it once to feel its yielding softness. She put on the earrings, pinned up her hair, and got into the bathtub. She took a deep breath and leaned back into the steaming, fragrant water, admiring the prismatic reflections of the gems on the ivory tiles. The hot water began to unknot her back. She reached for her glass and took another sip of champagne, toying with an earring.

"Do you know what I mean by passion?" he'd asked her. She could feel his hands on her skin, on her hair, stroking. His breath on her cheek. She could almost hear Nilsson agonizing in the background. Was he Svengali? A madman? Who knew? She hit the jets and let the bubbles distract her.

Roger was waiting by her apartment at seven the next evening. Christine ignored him, got into a cab, and went to the Russian Tea Room alone. When she left, Roger was waiting by the curb. She'd hitched a ride to Gwen's, only to discover that Johnny E. had stood her up. Again. Piqued, she left early, at midnight. Roger was waiting outside, the dark Rolls purring like some big jungle cat.

She looked down the street. Deserted. She'd never find a cab now. She sighed and walked toward the car. Roger hopped out to assist her.

"Good evening, Miss."

"Good morning, Roger."

She'd half expected him to take her home. But the car moved quickly, silently, toward SoHo, and in twenty minutes Roger was handing her out of the back seat at the entrance to the Phantom's studio. The front door was unlocked.

"Ah, my dear Elektra. So good to see you." Erik appeared from the back of the darkened studio in the same garb he'd worn two nights ago. Opera pulsed from the speakers at the back of the room. "Quickly now, change so we can begin."

Christine felt like stamping her feet in frustration. "I've been working all day. I've been out all night. How can you expect me to work now? I need sleep. And why do you keep calling me Elektra? You know my name is Christine."

"I call you Elektra because that is who you will be. Who you are meant to be. As for sleep, you will have it. Later. You look beautiful. This is exactly the combination of beauty and vulnerability that I require this evening. Come."

He took her hand, led her toward the opalescent screen that guarded the changing area. In the background, Christine heard the music surging, harsh, dramatic. She sighed and gave in.

The shoot was similar to the first, save that he moved more quickly and she responded as though she knew what he would ask next. It was a complicated pas de deux, punctuated by the click of the camera's shutter and the rustle of silk, enfolded in each throbbing aria.

Erik only approached her once. Taking her by the shoulders, he turned her face toward the mirror at her left. He grasped her hair and twisted it to the side.

"You must have this cut, yes?"

Christine shook her head. "Oh, Erik, my hair is fine the way it is."

"Fine . . . the others can settle for fine." He said scornfully, releasing her. "That is not what we are doing here. We attain perfection here. That is why the hair, the name must change. Will change." There was steel in his voice, behind the silky intonation. Christine wondered why she was agreeing with him, but she nodded as he indicated how she should cut her hair, and promised to have it done tomorrow.

"I'll probably lose some jobs because of this," she said, giggling nervously.

He shrugged. "That will not be important. You will see."

She awoke late, rushed to her first appointment, and sleep-walked through it. She found a message from her service indicating that she had a two o'clock appointment with Van Salent, the hottest haircutter on Madison Avenue. She knew Erik had arranged it. And probably programmed Salent as well.

Roger was waiting outside the shoot to take her.

"So you're Erik's latest discovery," Salent said in acid tones. A short man with thinning blond hair, he looked as if he could have worked in a bank. He combed her hair thoughtfully. Stepped back, hand on hip, eyeing her critically. "Hmmm. Yes, I can see what he's talking about. We'll cut here, and here."

"Are you sure this will work?" Christine was suddenly panicked at the thought of making the wrong cut, losing jobs. A bad haircut could be fatal in this field. She gazed into the mirrors encircling her. Multiple green-tinged Christines stared back.

"Relax, sweetie. Erik usually knows what he's doing. And I always do."

Christine leaned against the chair's cushion, closed her eyes, and allowed herself to be lulled by the rhythmic snip of the scissors, the tinkling Mozart sonata in the background, the glass of white wine supplied by Salent's assistant.

"So have you seen his scars yet?"

Christine opened her eyes. "Yes. Where did he get them?"

Salent shook his head. "Nobody knows for sure. The rumor is that he and Dietrich were lovers, until she clawed him in a jealous fit." He smiled. "Erik's certainly good at picking 'em. But not as good at keeping them.''

Christine stared at him. "What do you mean?"

Salent spun her around in the chair to work on the back of her head. "I mean that he's made a habit of building up these models into superstars, and then they leave him to marry princes or move to Hollywood. But they never look as good. Nobody can make them look as good as he does. He's magic. Evil." He spun her around again. "There. Not bad."

She fought the urge to gasp. The cut was severe, asymmetrical, the bangs sweeping only partway across her forehead, the left side swept back in severe layers, the right forward. It was completely contrary to everything that was being done in hair at the moment. And brilliant. She knew it. She could see Salent knew it. He nodded, lips compressed in a tight, begrudging smile. Squeezed her shoulder.

"Good luck."

The proofs from the second photo session with the Phantom were waiting for her at Marks' front desk the next morning. They were better than the first set. Sylvia Marks crowed to her husband as she looked them over with a hawk's precision.

"Oh, these are fabulous. F-a-a-bulous. Honey, we knew you were special. We always knew it, didn't we, Lennie?"

"Sure. Sure." He said swathed in a cloud of cigar smoke, eyes lidded, snakelike. "You gonna send these to Givenchy?"

"You bet I am. And Blass. It's time to move her up to the big names. And honey, the hair is fab-u-lous. Inspired."

"Thanks." Christine sat placidly, feeling like a hunk of meat being discussed—shall we roast or saute her? She told herself it was part of the job, and concentrated on the names of the designers. They promised much more money.

Within a week, she was taking better assignments than she'd had since she got to New York. The proofsheets were causing a sensation. Everybody wanted her.

She couldn't walk into a shoot without the photographer coming to greet her personally. The news of the Phantom's interest in her had spread throughout Seventh Avenue and beyond. Everybody asked her about Erik: What was he like? How did he work? She enjoyed the sense of power it gave her as world-famous photographers turned into gasping sycophants at the mention of the Phantom.

Even Johnny E. pestered her with questions.

"Can I meet him? Would he photograph me?"

"Johnny, I think he just does women."

"Why?"

She'd sweet-talked him out of a sulk, but she knew he was curious, and even a bit envious.

On the Friday of that busy week, she found three messages waiting on her phone machine when she returned to her apartment. The first, from Johnny E., reminded her of their date that evening. He'd become much more attentive since he'd seen those proofs, she thought. Good.

The second reminded her of the shoot tomorrow night at the Heldstrom flagship store on Madison.

The third was a wrong number, apparently. No message.

As she stood there, pondering, the phone rang. She grabbed the blue receiver.

"Hello?"

The long-distance hiss set the hair on the back of her head standing on end. A man's voice, deep, with a southern twang, cursed her.

"Lazy bitch. That check ain't here yet."

No, Christine thought. Not him!

She saw his face again, ruddy skin, broad cheekbones, bristling blond crewcut looming over her . . .

She fought for self-control. "Let me speak to my mother."

He chuckled. "I'd hate to have to come up there to that shit hole city and pick up that money personally."

Christine hated his voice, hated that threatening, gloating tone. She'd heard it in a hundred nightmares, too many memories. It had pursued her throughout her childhood, all the way across the country, and into an expensive therapist's office. He'd always sounded that way before he'd started to touch her.

"Put my mother on or I'll hang up," she said, voice cracking. She heard bouncing sounds of the phone receiver flung down, followed by fumbling noises.

"Honey, is that you?" Her mother's tentative quaver.

"Yeah. Listen, you know I don't want to speak to him. I don't ever want to speak to him. After what he's done. We had an agreement."

"Dollface, I didn't know he'd called. I'm sorry. Of course I know your check is comin'. I never question it."

"If he calls me again, I'll change my number."

"Chrissy, he's my husband. What can I do?" Her mother sounded pathetic. Christine hated it when she sounded that way.

"Yeah, well, I'm your daughter. "She softened her tone. "Are you taking your medicine?"

"Sure thing."

"Did you get those sweaters I sent?"

"Uh, yeah, they were lovely." Christine knew she'd probably never received them. Her stepfather had probably found them first and given them to one of his girlfriends.

"Well, good. Uh, mama, I've got to go. I mailed that check two days ago. You let me know if it doesn't arrive."

"Sure, honey. Sure." The line went dead.

Christine replaced the receiver in its cradle, and leaned her head against the wall, fighting back tears. How far could she go to outrun her childhood and that man? Paris? Russia? She'd hoped that New York would be far enough.

The phone rang again. She let the answering machine

take it, then realized the call was from Erik. She grabbed
at the phone.

"Erik? I'm sorry, I just walked in . . ."

"Ah, Elektra. You are pleased with the haircut, yes?"

"It's wonderful."

"Good. Tomorrow we will work again."

"Oh, uh, Erik, I can't. I've got a shoot tomorrow at
the Heldstrom store."

A pause.

"Cancel it."

"I can't. Oh, Erik, this is the first time they've asked
for me. It's a marvelous opportunity."

"I see you do not yet understand what we are about."
The phone clicked. Christine listened to the dial tone.
He'd rung off.

Furious, she slammed the receiver down. Damn the
man. He didn't control her. The Heldstrom shoot was a
golden opportunity—the kind of job she'd been waiting
for. If he couldn't understand that, perhaps there was
something wrong with him.

The music was loud, electronic, rhythmic. It bounced
off the cherrywood panels that lined the store's walls.
Christine pulled on a purple denim jumpsuit over her
high-necked Victorian blouse. She tied the laces of her
Italian hiking boots and rejoined the shoot. It was gruel-
ing. They'd assembled at seven, started at eight. Now it
was one in the morning but they were only halfway
through. Christine felt the tightness in her shoulders and
neck that signaled exhaustion. She had to keep going.
She thought about the little vial of coke in her purse,
antique silver, a birthday gift from Johnny. She could just
pop into the bathroom . . .

A flash of light, a few muffled screams, then a crash
that sounded like a thousand bottles breaking as the room
went dark.

"What was that? What's happened?" Christine called,
clinging to a handrail by the stairs. For answer, she heard
sobbing, quiet murmurs, and the sound of glass being

crunched underfoot. A dim light bobbed, weaving toward her.

"Stay calm, people. We'll get lights up in a minute. Just stay where you are." Christine recognized the voice as belonging to Amelia, the production assistant. Around the room, desk lamps flickered to life.

"Everybody all right?" Amelia held a flashlight like a torch, casting it around the room. Christine walked toward her, feeling glass grit beneath her shoes. She saw huddled shapes on the floor which could have been clothing. Or models.

"What happened?"

Amelia wiped her forehead. "The big chandelier, crystal one, at the front of the store, came down."

"My God! Did it hit anybody?"

"No, but a couple of the girls got cut by flying glass."

"Jesus!" Christine touched her own face.

Amelia shook her head. "Can you find your way out of here okay? We're sending everybody home. We'll collect the clothes tomorrow."

"Yeah, sure." She picked her way amidst the broken glass and crying girls, pushed out the double doors and was in the cool air of Madison. The street was deserted, but she thought she saw a big, dark shape turn down an alley to her left. Could it have been the Rolls? She thought of the huge chandelier swaying, crashing down upon her friends and fellow workers. A chill crept up her back, isolating each vertebra, each hair on her head with its cold caress.

Christine stumbled toward Fifth and Madison, hoping to find a cab there. She wanted to go home and lock her doors.

The next evening, Erik greeted her as though there had never been any coldness, any disagreement. Again, Nilsson spun through *Elektra*. The shoot was flawless. Christine could see that Erik was satisfied, and she felt a certain pleasure in that knowledge—he'd done so much for her career, and for no personal reward that she could see. She didn't mind if he wanted to call her Elektra. She was getting used to it.

She put on her street clothes. Erik waited for her by the door.

"You've been so good to me, Erik. I'm very grateful . . ."

He held up his hand to stop her mid-sentence.

"Talent must be valued, developed. I'm merely the means, the medium, my dear."

"My bookings are twice as big, all the coutourier houses are calling . . ."

Erik smiled. "They are just the beginning. Once you're living here with me, we will be able to concentrate solely on your career."

Christine tried not to gasp. "Wait a minute, Erik. Who said anything about my living here?"

"But it is the most convenient arrangement, yes? You will not pay rent. All your earnings will be your own, to do with as you please. And Roger will be available to you. I will oversee all your assignments."

Christine wanted to tell him to go to hell, to forget it. Behind her, mockingly, it seemed, a soprano sang "Sie werfen dich in einen Turm, wo du von Sonn' und Mond das Licht nicht sehen wirst . . ."

Then, a scene, unbidden, shaped itself in her mind, of her arriving at Chanel chauffeured by Roger, tutored by Erik. In the space of a month, his influence had brought her into the inner circle at the agency. Released from the agency, with Erik's help, she would be unstoppable.

"But my contract with Marks' . . ."

"A mere formality. I will purchase it in the morning. They may continue to refer clients, of course—for a fee which I will negotiate."

Christine watched his sunglasses sparkle in the studio lights. She nodded, feeling a little giddy. Erik would take care of her. And as for the price she assumed she would have to pay, well, she'd deal with that when she had to.

Within a week, her apartment had been sublet, her red MG securely sheltered under a dropcloth in the studio's cavernous garage, and Christine had been installed in the most luxurious rooms she'd ever seen.

Her suite included a small kitchen kept immaculate by Erik's maid, a bedroom, dressing room, bath with jacuzzi, sauna and shower, living room, and den. Her closet was stocked with new clothing which Erik had selected. The white pile carpet was dense as the hide of a wild animal, the furniture overstuffed, upholstered in pale yellow velvet, subdued gray silk.

"If the colors are displeasing, the clothing, you must tell me immediately, dear Elektra. Your comfort, your pleasure, are my primary concerns."

The first night, she'd taken dinner with Erik in his suite, serenaded by lush, passionate music from the elaborate stereo that occupied one wall of his dining room.

After port and cheese, he'd escorted her back to her rooms. Christine had found the evening exciting, his worldliness and sophistication appealing. She was tremendously aware of his body as he walked beside her toward her apartment. She'd dressed in his favorite colors, rose and gold, even down to the seductive lingerie which she hoped would please him. Heart pounding, she prepared to invite him in.

When he put his hands upon her shoulders, she closed her eyes, hardly daring to breathe. Then he kissed her gently on the forehead.

"A pleasant evening, my dear. Thank you."

He turned and walked back into the darkness toward his apartment. Christine watched him disappear. She felt disappointed. And relieved.

Of course the agency squawked over releasing her, but Erik prevailed. True to his word, he began to establish her in the rarefield levels of modeling to which she'd never dared aspire before.

She was interviewed, photographed, cited as "the celebrated Elektra, the fabulous Phantom's latest discovery." She was invited to opera openings, to attend museum fundraisers, to appear in commercials. One month she was on the cover of Vogue, Life, and Cosmopolitan. Her billboard in Times Square became a landmark as the light of her smile shone down upon the theatergoers and cabdrivers, the executives and beggars and messengers and stockbrokers, casting its benign radiance from ten stories up, from an electronic angel named Elektra. His angel.

When the calls came from Hollywood, Christine expected that Erik would nod and select the best offers, as he'd done before with all the magazines, the interviews, and the fancy invitations. Instead, thin-lipped, he'd crumpled the notes, erased the message tape.

"Not Hollywood. You're not ready."

"But Erik, can't we meet with them, at least?" she'd cried.

"No meetings."

And no amount of pleading could change his mind.

Christine had pouted for a week, then decided that Erik usually knew best, didn't he? Still, she began to feel just a bit, well, oversupervised.

A few days later, as she prepared for the Balenciaga retrospective shoot, she pondered her choices for the party afterward. Erik would probably recommend the rose silk sashed at the hip. But it was so dressy. Besides, he wouldn't be there. He never attended parties or shoots. Just sent his recommendations. And regrets.

She looked at the black leather jumpsuit at the back of the closet. Erik had told her, lip curling, that it made her look "mannish." Well, why not? Rebelliously, she tossed her Taxco silver necklace and earrings into her bag and a pair of high heeled black boots with silver studs.

After the shoot she had about two hours before Roger would collect her at eleven. She gazed around the room and saw Johnny E. at a table near the back.

"Chrissy—I mean, Elektra!!" He blew her a kiss and waved her over. She threw her arms around him.

"Oh, please, don't you start that Elektra crap with me," she said. "Let's get out of here, boy!" Casting a quick eye for Roger, she ran toward the back door of the restaurant. Johnny followed.

"Where's your car?"

"In the alley."

Giggling, she jumped into the passenger's seat. With a loud whoop, Johnny gunned the motor and the silver Mercedes coupe sped away into the night.

Christine awoke the next morning in a pool of sunlight, confused. Where was she? Morning light never reached her bedroom. For a moment, she didn't recognize the head of bronze curls on the pillow beside her. Then memory flooded back. Stretching luxuriously, she turned on her side. The bedside clock read ten o'clock.

Ten o'clock?

Erik would be furious. She felt a pang of guilt. He often waited for her return at night, to conduct a party post-mortem, to give her a chaste good night kiss that she hoped—and feared—would someday lead to more. What right did she have to treat him like this?

Christine looked at Johnny and sighed. Even in profile, he was seductive. And many women would gladly sell their parents, brothers, and sisters for the chance to lie beside him. Why shouldn't she enjoy herself? The Phantom couldn't dictate her life. She tried to ignore the needle prick of guilt that told her otherwise.

She nudged Johnny and slithered out of bed.

"Wake up. I've got to get back."

"Huh? Why?" He blinked rapidly, his blue eyes hazy with sleep.

"Erik will be worried."

"So? What is he, your father? Your lover?" Johnny sat up in bed.

"No and no. Come on, Johnny, don't be jealous. I've explained this to you already. He's sort of my mentor. I don't want to upset him. I owe him a lot. Now come on. I've got to get going!" She couldn't really explain her feelings about Erik to Johnny, or anyone else. And she didn't want to try.

She managed to get Johnny dressed and into the car in half an hour. As they approached the studio, she saw the big Rolls pull away from the curb. Telling Johnny to wait, she went inside alone.

"Erik?"

No answer.

The stereo was silent.

She walked toward his rooms, footsteps echoing in the gloom, trailed by the steady, trickling sound of an underground stream. Had she ever heard that before?

His apartment was unlocked. Uninhabited. How odd, she thought. Eric never went anywhere, especially during the day. And at night, only to the opera. Christine felt uneasy. Where was he?

"Weird place."

"Johnny!" She jumped. "I told you to wait in the car."

"The coast looked clear to me." He shrugged and walked toward the stereo. "So this is where he casts his spells. Hmmm. *Elektra. Tristan and Isolde.* Strong stuff. If music makes the man, I wouldn't want to tangle with him."

Christine tried to ignore her growing sense of unease. If only Johnny had stayed outside. He didn't belong here. swaggering through the Phantom's sanctum. Erik would be enraged if he knew.

"You can wait for me in my rooms while I shower and change," she said, voice quavering. "Since he's not here, we can go out and get something to eat."

Johnny leaned against the doorframe, hands on his hips. "Oh, you don't share a room? Good. I was beginning to think of him as your keeper."

When she emerged, freshly clothed, Johnny was nowhere to be seen. She could hear the distant strains of music—some aria from Erik's suite.

Christine strode into his rooms.

"Erik?"

There was no one there. The compact disc player serenaded ghosts and empty spaces.

"Wenn einer auf mich sieht, muss er den Tod empfangen oder muss vergenhen vor Lust . . ."

She left the music playing and walked out into the corridor, nerves jumping. To her left, she saw light seeping from beneath a door, from rooms where she'd never been.

"Johnny?"

No answer. Her voice echoed down the hall to mix with Nilsson's vengeful recital.

These rooms were always locked. She'd assumed they were storage rooms where Erik kept his files. But the door opened now. Johnny walked out clutching an envelope, his face pale.

"Johnny. What were you doing in there? How did you get in? I told you to stay in my room!" She was furious. How dare he violate this precious, private place?

"I found a key. Come on. Let's go." He started to walk down the hall.

"Give me that folder." She pulled it out of his hands. "I told you not to touch anything!"

Christine darted into the room and put the folder down on a table by the door. She turned to leave, then a prickle of curiosity stopped her. She looked around. It seemed like a regular storage area with file cabinets, darkroom equipment, and what appeared to be straps hanging from the wall. The tan envelope she'd held contained proof sheets. Well, maybe she'd look at these before she left. Were they Grable? Garbo? She pulled the sheets out and scanned them. Her throat closed.

No. Not movie stars nor celebrities. The sheets were filled with photographs of young girls and boys, naked, limbs glistening. The photographs had been shot in the studio, unmistakably. But when? How long ago? The children looked confused, drugged. And the man pictured with them—was that Erik? A muscular middle-aged man wearing a loin cloth in some photos, and not in others . . . Yes, the face was scarred. Erik. With all those naked children. She shoved the photos back into their folder, stomach churning.

Erik, no. No. Not you, too.

"No wonder he kept that place locked up." Johnny said hoarsely. He stood in the doorway, watching her.

Christine fought for air. She'd thought she was safe, finally, with a man who loved her and would take care of her. But it was her stepfather all over again.

Erik, how could you? I trusted you.

She looked at the proof sheet again. She wanted to tear it up. Or hide it, burying it safely behind locked doors where nobody else would ever see it. Pretend that nothing had happened. Nothing really had happened to her, had it?

Then a mental picture formed, a man with ruddy features, broad cheekbones, blond hair. And scars. Standing over her bed. No. No. This time she would stop him. She would punish him. Them. All of them.

When she mailed the proofsheets to the police, Christine included Erik's address, but not her own. She didn't want to be involved in what was to come.

She'd been tempted again to dispose of the photos. After all, Erik hadn't done anything to her, had he? But then the dreams had started, dreams in which she was very small, very young, and a man with blond hair and scars across broad cheekbones had pursued her through dark rooms as she screamed.

The day after she mailed the package to the police, Christine left for the West Coast with Johnny and his band.

The test shots at Paramount seemed a bit, well, pale, when she saw them. Erik would have changed the lighting, she thought. And the angle of the camera. She'd have to talk to them about it later.

She picked up some freelance work with Chanel, did the cover of Vogue, and a photo spread to accompany an interview she agreed to for Time. When the reporter showed her the proofs from the shoot, Christine winced. The lighting was all wrong. And how could she have let them talk her into wearing green? But she wouldn't complain now, the reporter was sitting there, ready to begin her questions.

"Miss Day, what's your reaction to the Phantom's murder in jail?"

She tried not to flinch. "I didn't know."

"They found him yesterday."

Christine turned away, her eyes stinging. The last time she'd seen Erik, he'd been in a photograph on the front page of the New York Times under large headlines. She'd crumpled the page and thrown it away. She closed her eyes, and, for a moment, heard the ghostly echo of an impassioned operatic lament.

"Miss Day? Are you all right?" The reporter sounded nervous.

Christine snapped back around to face her. "I'm fine. And call me Elektra. My name is Elektra."

TIME-TRACKER

by Barry N. Malzberg

Oh, Mesdames & Monsieurs, bien attendu s'il vous plait: this is the story of Obedient Participant, Observative Partner, Original Partaker, listen if you will please and note his subservience, his pleasure, his ordinary and chaste submission—

Crouched in the anteroom, in his hiding place, Ossie Publick listens to the final rehearsals of *Carmen,* Bizet's masterpiece and make no mistake about it, a message to posterity from the composer who all unaware of the great success to come will die within days of the premiere, convinced of his failure, his obliteration. *Merde!* says Ossie Publick to the partitions surrounding him and similar expletives and scatological explanations of which we need have no further knowledge. He is a short bitter man with a short bitter scar slashed across his features, a high and dreaming aspect to half-concealed eyes staring wistfully below an enormous forehead, limbs of some disproportion meant to scuttle. Looking at these wizened atrocities, thinking of the strange and winding events which have brought him here, Ossie Publick is overwhelmed by the weight of time, the shadow of his mortality which twists his features ever further into a simulacrum of malevolence. The Flower Aria quests three levels below. Publick sighs, sighs again, tries to find better purchase for his position, thinks of the inglorious and tubercular Bizet (1837–1875) who could learn a thing or

two about counterpoint from his inferiors if he were a
more humble man.

Publick has not always been in this condition, he re-
members a better time, but then again, like the luckless
Don Jose he seems to exist in a gray and spavined place
circumscribed only by desire. "Oh Georges, oh
Georges," he mutters as if Bizet were within range of
his voice and he could somehow appeal to the luckless
composer over the ridge of the centuries but there is of
course no possibility of reply; no one knows of the secret
place Publick occupies except those who will do nothing
to save him. "Georges—" Publick mutters again. He is
looking for the proper words, looking for some aspect of
confrontation or knowledge, but (and this is an old problem) he does not quite know what to do.

In the chorus, Olive Partness, a small sinister woman
with tight and sinister features, the arc of a rose stem
slashed across her cheekbones, tries to blend in with Escamillo's troubadors as she allows the wave of movement
to carry her from stage left to stage right. Her scuttling
motions are ungraceful, even ridiculous and the mask
clamped like a veil to the scarred side of her face seems
to constrict her breathing. Breath is life, life is that which
stirs within me, she thinks and does what she can to meet
the requirements of melody but it is difficult, it is very
difficult in such circumstances to carry on in that debo-
nair and casual fashion affected by the choristers. She
wants to reach out, clutch them, turn her face greedily
unto them and expostulate upon her problem, she wants
to make her situation evident but of course that cannot
be managed under the circumstances, not without addi-
tional difficulty. Staggering here and there, trying to balance off the needs of gravitation against her desperate
impulse to run, to leave the stage, to take the consequences whatever they might be and bring an end to this
she casts her eyes up, up, looking for Ossie Publick's
secret place which it has been promised will eventually
become her own cubicle.

She loathes *Carmen*. Ersatz music, ersatz emotion, all of it cobbled from the ill knowledge of a self-indulgent, silly man. It had not been meant for her to end in this fashion. Moving left to right, right to left, she catches her heel on Escamillo's cape as it extends on the floor for a flourish, feels herself beginning to topple, suspects, as if for the first time, her ultimate doom. Falling into that dense and misbegotten part of hers. Knowing that the disaster will leave her unmasked, without response, open to the last elements of her exposure.

At this point, sur la pointe, the legend takes a different turn; poised as if on a knife-edge of extinction, Obervant Participant is exposed to yet another trick of fate, a whimsy of circumstance which relocates the perimeters of his necessity—

Opaul Pauling, a lovely young singer of lovely young dimensions, sunk into her young and lovely life yet at the same time filled with a sensitivity which makes her yearn for something more, something different, something outside of the simple and conterminous bleakness of her eager and superficial life, this very same Opaul Pauling with luminescent breasts half-beating above the heart of her extravagant gown finds the secret place of Ossie Publick and blunders through the door, shocked by the meagerness and disorder of his quarters, shocked too by the vivid stain of his features, yet moved as well by the kind and stricken eyes which he raises to her. "Oh, mademoiselle," Publick says to the strains of Carmen's final screams of defiance, "oh, mademoiselle, you have come to strange quarters," and his hands twitch with necessities which he can barely define as slowly, slowly he begins to circle Opaul Pauling.

She is not experienced; the panels of her beauty, if they were to be pried open, would disclose a loving but simple personality, the kind of personality which can be manipulated in almost any direction, even against itself, so tentatively has it been formed and this is something that

Publick senses; if he were in a position to open those panels almost anything could happen . . . but he cannot judge yet the depths of his own desire. Perhaps he merely seeks companionship. "Oh, my dear," he says in his low voice, fighting for control, "come and sit with me, we shall listen to this jewel of *Carmen* together, I will tell you of Bizet's tragic fate—"

"I must have come to the wrong room," Opaul Pauling says. She is a gentle spirit, unformed and capable of tragic difficulties but she is not totally without cunning and in Ossie Publick's gray and bloated features she can detect real threat. "I'll just be on my way," she says, "if you will forgive—" She turns toward the passageway which gave her entrance and for a perilous moment Publick thinks that she is lost to him, but then her heel slips, catches some detritus and twists wildly and as her knees buckle, as she fights for purchase, Publick is upon her, seizing her along the plane of her being, tilting her lips, the lovely extended line of her sudden throat drawing him in—

Through the sewers and festivals, the stinking public bars and the lost places of Paris, Oliver Private, captain of the gendarmes, has pursued the notorious Ossie Publick, seeking knowledge of his whereabouts, trying to bring him to that justice which awaits. Private is a sinister man with bitter features, a bitter man with sinister intent, but he thinks of himself as a servant, as a man committed only to the exaction of justice and who is to quarrel with him? He is a splendid figure in his full uniform and even when in mufti casts a certain and determined light. In and out of the public and private houses of this twinkling city, Oliver Private has stalked Ossie Publick, knowing that his mission is of terrible and urgent importance. Lately the rumors have coalesced, Private has obtained certain knowledge from informants, burglars who owe him favors, prostitutes who have their own reasons for confidence have told him that Ossie Publick is somewhere in the Opera, has secreted himself there, has been

there perhaps for years in rooms of his own devising,
poisoning the corridors with his own brand of corruption
and casting curses upon all of the productions which
come in. Private has felt the rising blood of the chase,
the movement which precedes entrapment, now, entering
from the rear, coming in through a stage manager's entrance of which few are aware, he feels that he can scent
Ossie Publick; the familiar, cloying odor of the felon
seems to assault him as it did in the years long past when
they were in the Outer Port together. The policeman's
clarity upon him, the mingled lust and horror which he
knows so well bearing him along, Private is carried
through the corridors of the opera house as if on a tide
of being. Sinister and bitter, bitter and sinister, he allows
the waves of compunction to take him along.

*Ah, this is the most suspenseful and burdensome part
of the tale and yet it is not as you expected; bien attendu
yet further as the slow and clamorous climax comes upon
us—*

Olive Partness hears the sudden squalling as if it were
external, as if it were coming from the orchestra, roaring
over the stage in splashes and shudders of sound. But it
is only her inner function which is attending; she has
heard Opaul Pauling scream. Opaul and Olive are the
closest of friends, closer than sisters, even though Opaul
is a splendid and promising young singer and Olive
trapped in the back rows of the chorus, still they respond
to one another with a sympathy and adoration which is
absolute and it is her sister, her sister who is calling for
help through all the layers of distance and obfuscation.
"Ah succors!" she thinks she hears Opaul shriek and
then, even as the wretched Don Jose lifts the knife to
show Carmen the measure of his love, Olive is running,
she is running toward that place from which she hears
the screaming. I must save Opaul! she cries to herself,
Opaul needs me! and in an utter and luminescent dark
she is running—

* * *

Ossie Publick finds himself on the verge of a kind of consummation; not since the ballet scene in Verdi's *Macbeth*—which Verdi was forced to insert against his wishes because Ossie Publick himself, the spirit of the Opera house made his insistences well known, fought for the public taste—and perhaps not even then has he found himself so pleased. Opaul Pauling lies swooning and exposed before him, she is at his knees, in just another moment he will be able to swoop her into his grasp and then, *then,* there is no way of telling but in that poised moment before he will touch her some hesitancy, some infusion of reluctance strikes him and Publick is frozen in that post, his hands clawed above the exposed bosom of the lovely young singer, the room filled with the cries of the dying Carmen—

—And he thinks, this has happened before! Some well of familiarity seems to open underneath him, in his mind he is returned to a place he has known before and there is a vast and spilling confusion—

Too late, too late Oliver Private knows, and yet he keeps on running, he has already lost but the gendarmerie never quits, there is neither reason nor point to what he does and yet he will do it, finding himself unutterably drawn to that place at which rumor and intimation together tells him Publick must be located, Private's sinister consciousness is riven as if by a knife and he comes to understand that this is perhaps not the first time that he has made this gesture, that it has happened many times before and yet what can he do? he must carry on, he must attend to the villainous and brutal Publick, he must—

Is it not a splendid tale? It does not say what it seems to say, it has much to convey other than what is conveyed, one can in the understanding of this tale perhaps grasp the nettle of the higher, the finer plot which otherwise fully exposed would sting—

* * *

"It is you!" Olive Partness says, bursting into the room, recognizing Publick, seeing the arched and clawing shape of his grasp. "It is you, it was you all of this time!" Her tone is bitter, her features strained, her eyes sinister and bitter in the cold and bitter light of the hiding place. "I should have known—"

"You," Publick says, seeing Partness, recognizing her, too, in that shocking instance and suddenly, as he turns toward her, Opaul Pauling at his feet becomes contemptible, becomes of no interest, he turns from her as if realizing for the first time the true measure of what has occurred. It is Partness who possesses him, Partness who draws him in as he turns toward her, but on the verge of that awful collision impending, Private, the police, hurls his bulk at the two of them, having propelled himself through the door with speed and desperation. He slams against Publick, moves him away from Olive Partness and the prostrate Opaul Pauling, grasps the sinister and suddenly chaotic Ossie Publick by the lapels and hurls him against the wall several times. There are hollow thuds, sounds of crumbling. "At last!" Private shouts, "at last I have you—"

There is a clatter in the distance: the knife has fallen from Don Jose's hand. Bleeding, he scuttles on the floor, looking for Carmen's rose but the crowd has returned, the crowd—without Olive—has surrounded him.

And so the tale has reached its proper ending, a tale of heroism, malevolence, cowardice, linkage and blood. And yet, and yet as in all of our legends, there is not so much surcease as impulsion. Attend, please, and consider—

Crouched in the anteroom, in his hiding place, Oliver Private listens to the final rehearsals of Gounod's stinking *Faust*, that loathsome opera stolen from Berlioz's *Damnation* which will yet live and live as (he knows) *Damnation* cannot. *Merde!*, Oliver Private says, a sinister and bitter man, rapt with need for Opaul Pauling, desperate through all these months for the touch and scent of her, trapped by his own bestial necessity while out in the distance, in the sewers and festivals, the stinking public bars and the lost worlds of Paris, Ossie Publick patiently tracks him, while Opaul Pauling, hopeful little chorister watches Marguerite ascend, while Olive Partness, Marguerite herself rises—

They rise and rise. Nor do they sink. Watch what he has contrived, then, for our endless diversion, merciful captivator of us all—

DARK ANGEL

by Gary Alan Ruse

Caroline looked out on West 44th Street from the window of the theater manager's office on the first floor of the Majestic. She could see steam rising from storm drains and gutters, floating like ghosts in the chill autumn air outside. She watched a river of yellow taxicabs flowing through the gray, unfeeling canyons of the city, and the hustle and bustle of pedestrians oblivious to all but their own private journeys. It was an afternoon like any other, and yet now, strangely chilling.

"Terrorists . . . here, in New York?" Caroline said softly. She turned away from the window and faced the men gathered in the office. "I'm not sure I believe that . . . not sure I want to."

Besides her husband Lawrence, and the theater manager himself, there were only these two disturbingly polite men in their gray suits and ties. Their FBI credentials were in order and there was no reason to mistrust them. It was only their message that was alarming.

"We can't be certain, of course," replied Agent Kimball, a middle-aged man with kind eyes and a face that spoke of authority and hard work. "But the State Department has alerted us to the possibility, and we must proceed on that basis. It would be folly not to warn you."

Lawrence leaned forward on the leather sofa, his arms braced upon his knees in what would look a casual pose, were not his fingers so tightly interlaced that his knuckles had turned white. "What exactly do they know?"

"Not much, I'm afraid," said Agent Resnick, the other FBI man. "They intercepted a radio message sent by a fanatical splinter group in the Middle East. It was incomplete . . . there was data missing . . . but it made clear reference to a terrorist strike within the United States. Specifically it mentioned Broadway, a musical, and international celebrities. With what's playing on Broadway this season, that pretty much narrows it down to this production of yours."

"But it's crazy," Caroline protested, pacing nervously about the room. "Terrorists always strike at . . . at political targets, or airports, or plane flights, or . . . or . . ."

"Or anything that will get them the kind of news coverage they seek," added Kimball. "You all have been in the headlines a lot already. You're the darlings of the media. That makes you very powerful targets, for kidnapping, or worse. Especially in an election year."

"What can we do?" asked Lawrence. "We can't just suspend the run."

Kimball shook his head. "No. We're not asking that. Not yet, anyway. But we must ask you to be careful . . . take some basic precautions . . . be especially alert to who and what is going on around you. We will, of course, do everything in our power to head off any trouble before it reaches you."

"How reassuring," Lawrence said softly, eyes downcast. He quickly rose from his seat as the FBI men prepared to leave. "Forgive me . . . it's just that we've had quite enough to worry about just getting this revival of the *Phantom* ready and past the problems. Now with this burden . . ."

"Should we tell the others?" asked Caroline. "The rest of the cast, I mean. If they're in danger as well—?"

"No," replied Agent Kimball. "We would rather you didn't do that, just yet. The more people that know about it, the more likely the information will leak out, and that could cause problems of its own. Please let us handle that part of it."

They shook the agents' hands at the door. Lawrence told them, "All right, then. As you wish. Thanks for letting us know. We do appreciate whatever help you can give."

After the government men had gone, their footsteps fading down the hall, the three remaining exchanged looks and nervous sighs. Lawrence gave his wife a reassuring hug, and then put a question to her.

"Are you sure you're going to be up to it tonight, after all this?"

Caroline set her chin resolutely. "Yes, of course. Don't be silly. Takes more than vague warnings to frighten me. Now . . . I'd better go and start getting ready. There's only three hours before the performance, and we must give the audience their money's worth, mustn't we . . ."

That evening, Caroline stood in the wings, waiting for her cue to go on. The ominous chords of the pipe organ reverberated through the theater until they seemed to make her vibrate with their power. As she stood there, trying desperately to concentrate on her performance, she could not help scanning the dark recesses of the wings, the catwalks, the shadows cast by the movable set pieces, even the dark sea of faces that made up the audience. She imagined weapon toting fanatics lurking in every pool of murk, waiting to spring from every alcove, every crevice. The musical they were about to perform was a fantasy, its horror a mere entertainment. The potential horror conjured up by the FBI men was quite another matter.

But at last the magic of the production, the romance and power of it, caught her up and made her forget such thoughts. The notes of the score poured pure and bell-like from her throat, captivating the audience for yet another night.

Caroline felt drained when the show was over. After the last curtain call she walked slowly back to her dressing room, eager to get out of her makeup and into her street clothes. She wanted nothing more than to join her husband, get something to eat, and retire to their hotel room.

Oddly, Lawrence was not waiting in her dressing room as she entered. There was only her dresser, Corinne, putting away the costumes and checking to see if any of them needed repairs before the next evening's performance.

"I'll be out of your way in a moment," said Corinne, glancing up from her duties as Caroline entered. She quickly moved to help the performer out of her wedding costume, then hung the garment up carefully with the rest. "Is there anything else I can do for you before I go?"

"Thanks, no. You're a dear for asking." Caroline reached for a tissue to apply cleansing cream to her face. Her hand halted abruptly. Looking closely at her makeup table for the first time since entering the room, she saw a perfect red rose lying there, near the mirror. Its blossom rested upon an envelope of purest white. "Corinne—wait. Did my husband leave this?"

"The rose? Oh, no, ma'am. At least, I don't think so. I only had a glimpse of him as he was leaving, just as I got here myself, but I assumed it was Robert, with the cloak and the hat and all."

"Well, I don't see how. He left the stage when I did. I would have seen him myself if he came here."

Corinne frowned. "You think it was some imposter? I'm sure security wouldn't let anyone backstage who shouldn't be here."

Caroline picked up the rose and smelled it. Its perfume was rich, almost hypnotic. She closed her eyes as she savored it. "Yes, I'm sure you're right. Perhaps it was my husband after all, having his little joke on me. Thank you, Corinne."

"Good evening, ma'am," said the dresser, closing the door behind her. "See you tomorrow."

Caroline sat on the bench before her table and picked up the envelope. Both it and the folded note inside were on expensive stationery. But it was not her husband's handwriting that greeted her as she opened it. Written in an elegant hand with what surely must have been a fountain pen were the words:

> To Caroline,
> the perfect "Christine,"
> from a devoted fan
> and patron of the arts.

There was no signature. No name or return address. There was only an embossed initial upon the surface of the note and the envelope, visible when the light struck it right: the letter E in a bold script style, elegant and impressive. It was all quite beautiful, but the sight of it sent an odd chill down her spine. Her gaze shifted from the card to the rose, then from the exquisite beauty of the blossom to the sharp thorns of the stem.

There was an abrupt sound behind her, startling for the moment that it took to recognize it. It was a rhythmic knock, Lawrence's knock, at the door, and as he poked his head into the dressing room with a wry grin, he said, "Are we decent?"

"Nearly so." Caroline smiled back, but her expression was troubled.

Lawrence closed the door behind him and walked to her side, his look now one of concern. "What is it?"

"You didn't send this, did you?" she asked, holding the rose for him to see.

"I have before, and certainly I should like to often," he told her. "But no, I did not send that one. Have I a rival?"

Caroline extended the card to him. "You tell me."

With a puzzled frown, Lawrence read over the note, examining it thoughtfully. At last, he said, "Well, it must have come from someone in the cast or crew."

"That's what Corinne thought. But what of the initial?"

"The E? But of course it must be a joke. Don't you see? E for Erik, the opera ghost, the Phantom. . . ?"

Caroline's mouth twisted into a skeptical smile. "How clever. I suppose it's a well-intentioned prank, whoever did it, but frankly, I'm in no mood for whimsy right now."

"I know, I know." Lawrence kissed her tenderly on the cheek. "You sang beautifully tonight, as always. I'm proud of you. Now, let's get you ready, then we'll have a spot of supper and call it a night."

"You'll get no arguments from me."

"Oh, and I've been . . . making some special arrangements, which is why I was a bit late tonight."

"Arrangements?"

"Yes, from now on, coming and going, we'll have a special limo with some built-in safeguards, and a driver with security training."

"Do you really think it's necessary?"

Her husband gave a sober shrug. "One hopes not, but we may as well play it safe. . . ."

Two weeks passed without incident, and the daily routine, the constant press of performances, the challenge of keeping the show fresh and vital, all these things helped keep Caroline from being unduly preoccupied with the possible threat to their lives and safety. In fact, things were otherwise so normal that it was hard to believe anything was wrong. Then, on the morning of the fifteenth day, events brought the matter sharply into focus once more.

Cold sunlight streamed in through the windows of their hotel suite, filtered by the New York haze and by the sheer curtains drawn across the glass. A room service cart gave off the delectable aroma of breakfast and the sounds of the shower competed with the *Today* show as Lawrence finished dressing in the living room. The news was on, with its predictable litany of world events and natural disasters, when suddenly one of the items caught Lawrence's attention and brought his head sharply up while he was in the midst of tying his shoes. With one set of laces still undone, he leapt to his feet and started toward the bedroom.

"Caroline! Caroline—come and hear this!"

With eyes and ears still straining toward the television as he moved, he reached the door to the bath and rapped quickly upon the heavily painted wooden panel. "Caroline—" he said once more, then before he could knock again his wife pulled open the door and peered out in alarm, dripping wet and bundled in a terry robe.

"What is it?"

"Come on—" Lawrence said, pulling her into the living room "—it's on the news just now."

Caroline combed her fingers through the wet strands of hair that had fallen across her face, staring at the images parading across the television screen. They were all nighttime shots of a street and a reporter with a handful of onlookers in the background. There were police cars parked in front of some innocuous house in the suburbs, their lights whirling ominously as three swarthy young men were escorted out in handcuffs. The gray-suited men who guided them to a waiting police security wagon seemed as reluctant to be photographed as their captives.

"What's going on?" demanded Caroline.

Lawrence pointed at the screen just as the camera grabbed a closer angle on the trio. Then the scene cut immediately to shots of weapons stored within the house.

"They're terrorists," Lawrence told her. "I didn't hear it all, but the FBI and police caught a cell of terrorists in New Jersey last night, just over the river from Manhattan."

Caroline's hand went unconsciously to her throat. "My word! Do you think they could be the ones Agent Kimball warned us about?"

"I don't know. But I intend to find out." Lawrence went to the desk and hastily searched the contents of the top drawer. He found a business card there and read it quickly before getting an outside line on the phone and dialing the number. There was a long pause as the phone at the other end rang repeatedly, then there came a click and a response. Lawrence said, "I'd like to speak with Agent Kimball, please."

Caroline hurried to his side and put her ear next to the phone handset. Her husband tilted it so that both of them could hear.

"This is Agent Kimball," came a reply from the other end.

Lawrence identified himself and asked about the news item.

"Yes, sir, it's true," said Kimball. "I've been involved with this thing all night. I intended to call you later this morning, once we were sure of the facts, but it would seem that you can relax now."

"Then you think they were targeting us for . . . something dastardly?"

"Well, we still aren't sure whether it was you or some other target, but we tracked their movements from the Middle East to Greece and then to Miami, where they entered the country with forged student visas. Then they traveled to New Jersey using various means of transportation. The house they ended up at was already under surveillance by the local police for suspected criminal activity, and the weapons confiscated there remove any doubt that they were up to no good. They're in the custody of federal marshals now, and I can assure you those three won't be bothering anyone for a long time."

"That's certainly good news," Lawrence told him. "Good news indeed. Thank you so much, Mr. Kimball."

"Our pleasure, sir. We'll be in touch if we learn anything else."

Lawrence hung up the phone and turned to his wife with a look of relief. "You heard?"

"Yes! What wonderful news. I hope they got them all. I hope there aren't others lurking about."

He gave her a reassuring squeeze. "I'm sure they must have, and even if not, then I'm sure the others were sent packing. They couldn't be foolish enough to try anything now."

Caroline kissed him quickly and started back for a towel. "I'd better get dried off. Suddenly I have an appetite for breakfast!"

"The merry prankster strikes again," observed Lawrence, with less amusement than his words suggested. It was a short while after lunch and they had returned to the theater.

Caroline came through the door to her dressing room a short distance behind her husband, peering around him to look at her makeup table. "What . . . more flowers?"

"And another note." He picked up the elegantly addressed envelope. "But this one's for both of us. I suppose I can't feel jealous this time."

Caroline watched as he turned over the envelope and broke the wax seal on the back. The card inside was the same as the one before, bearing an elaborately embossed letter E, and the handwriting within was immediately recognizable. She looked closer as Lawrence held it for her to read. The words in their elegant script stated:

My Dear Sir & Madam,
  I would greatly enjoy meeting you, at a time convenient to your schedule, to discuss your marvelous production. You have but to say the word. I know everything which transpires within the Majestic, and your reply is all that I most humbly ask.
                                          Your Devoted Fan

Caroline arched a lovely eyebrow and gave her head a shake "*Who* is doing this?"

Lawrence slipped the note back within its envelope and laid it beside the vase of flowers. "My money's on Syd. This sort of thing would appeal to his sense of humor."

"But didn't you ask him before . . . the first time?"

"Of course. I spoke to everyone in the cast and crew about it. Guilt was roundly denied by them all. But then, what would you expect?" Lawrence gave a wry chuckle. "All right, then, Mr. Devoted Fan. Let's end this charade. If all we need do is say the word, then I accept your invitation. Let's make it tonight. We can all go to dinner after the performance and have a good chat.''

Caroline gave him a nudge that was half playful, half cautionary. "Really, Lawrence," she said teasingly. "Do you think that wise?"

"What, do you really expect him to hear me?" He flashed a bemused smile. "Well, perhaps the walls do have ears. This is an old building. But if Syd, or whomever our mysterious friend is, does show up, then at least we will have resolved our little puzzle. Now—I shall leave you to your preparations and tend to a few errands I need to do before the show. Bye, Love—"

"Be careful, Dear."

"Always," Lawrence told her at the door. "But I'm feeling much easier since Agent Kimball's news this morning. Much easier, indeed . . ."

The closing strains of the music had long since died away and the audience departed, as had most of the cast and crew. Caroline had already changed to her street clothes. She turned off the lights on her makeup table, glanced around to be sure everything was in order, then rose and joined her husband by the door.

"Well," said she, "I took my time getting ready, as you suggested, and still no visitors."

Lawrence opened the door and looked up and down the corridor. He shrugged. "Disappointed?"

Her lips pulled up in a wry twist of a smile. "Hmmm. Perhaps a bit. Your theory about Syd must go untested a while longer."

Lawrence thrust a confident finger in the air. "You shall see I'm right. Mark my words! Now, let's go. I'm sure our security limo is waiting."

"Didn't you cancel it? Surely we don't need it now."

He made an expansive gesture with his hands. "It's paid up through the end of the week. We may as well enjoy it."

They turned out the lights and closed the door behind

them. The stage door was a relatively short walk down
the corridor, around several corners and past the wings.
The guard watching the door nodded a cheery greeting
as they approached. He held the door open for them and
gave a tip of his cap.

A cold breeze gusted in through the open door and
stirred the curtains in the wings, seeming to carry some
of the autumn night's darkness and gloom with it. Waiting at the curb on 45th Street, glistening dully in the
streetlight, was the silver-gray limousine that had been
transporting them for the past few weeks.

As the couple approached, walking side by side, the
car's driver quickly got out and moved to open the rear
door for them. Lawrence noticed at once that it was not
their usual driver, nor his regular replacement for nights
off.

"Where's Coulter?" he asked the new man.

"He's sick tonight," replied the driver, waiting for
them to enter the limo's dark interior.

Something about the man's voice, his stance, his very
look, make Lawrence hesitate. There was a nervous energy underlying the man's calm. Lawrence tightened his
grip on Caroline's arm, holding her where she was without seeming to, staying her entry into that car. He stole
a quick glance down the street and saw that although
there was the normal departing traffic for this hour, there
was also a dark car parked by the curb a short distance
back from their limo. He was certain he could see the
shadowy figures of several men within, their intent gaze
directed his way.

"Drat! I knew I was going to forget something," said
Lawrence abruptly, snapping his fingers as if in sudden
recollection, and wishing he had acquired more training
in the field of acting. "Caroline, that . . . that parcel I
bought this afternoon is still sitting in your dressing
room. I really *do* need it tonight." To the driver he added,
"Sorry to keep you waiting—we'll be back in a moment."

Before the man could respond, Lawrence was steering

his wife back toward the stage door. And judging from the lack of resistance on her part, she had sensed something was wrong as well. They had almost reached that door, opening for them as the guard within peered out through the small pane of glass set in the panel, when the sounds of car doors flying open and feet running on pavement came from behind them.

Alarming images came frighteningly fast—the guard leaning out with his weight, holding the door open for them, frowning past them at danger beyond—a backward glimpse of men darting toward them from the second car, machine pistols in their hands—another armed man, swarthy like the rest, emerging from the back seat of the limo itself.

"Run, Caroline!" Lawrence snapped.

In the next second there were several dull pops of sound they recognized as silenced gunfire. A slug tore through Lawrence's overcoat sleeve, narrowly missing his arm. Another caught the guard in the chest and the man sagged to the ground just as the couple darted past him into the theater.

"My God," Caroline blurted out, her terror-filled eyes lingering on the crumpled guard. "They've killed Rudy! And they must have killed our driver."

"Don't know," her husband said, propelling her onward. "We've got to reach a phone—got to get help."

"They'll never get here in time!"

There was a phone on the stage manager's desk not far from the door, and they started toward that. But even as they did, the terrorists were entering behind them and would quickly close the gap if they stopped to call.

"Here—this way," Caroline gasped, urgently directing her husband toward the darkened rear of the stage where the flats and pieces of the set offered some shelter from the line of fire.

There were only a few stagehands still working, straightening up after the performance. They looked up in surprise at the sudden invasion, and as more shots were abruptly fired, they dropped what they were doing and dove for cover.

Caroline led her husband past the play's grand staircase, which looked nowhere near so grand now that it was folded flat against the theater's back wall. They ran, nearly stumbling in their haste, working their way around to the far side where the wings were crowded with props and pieces of sets, and movable banks of candleholders stood waiting for the next performance.

There were more pops of sound, followed by an outcry from one of the stagehands, apparently struck by a shot. A few work lights had been left on, casting their glow upon portions of the stage, but there were still pools of deep shadow here and there, and it was through these bits of murk that Lawrence and Caroline scurried.

"Should we try for the outside?" Caroline gasped softly as they paused for a moment, huddled behind the base of a false theater box facade in the left wings.

Lawrence's nervous breathing was close at her ear. "The front doors are locked by now, I'll wager. If we could get to it, there's a gun in the manager's office."

"Against these odds? You can't be serious." Caroline jerked slightly to her left as a faint click of sound came from behind her. "What's that?"

Lawrence peered into the shadows in the direction of the sound, but saw nothing. Yet in the next moment the answer to her question made itself apparent. A wave of foglike mist now came rolling in across the floor of the stage, created by machines in the wings. It was an effect well-employed during each performance, but its appearance now was bizarre and unexpected. Tendrils of the chemically produced mist coiled about their ankles and began to rise toward their knees, obscuring the floor and lending an eerie aspect to the stage.

Another sound caught their attention, this time from the right. Standing centerstage, near the front and the orchestra pit, one of the terrorists was revealed in a pool of light. He stood there, brashly poised with feet apart and his machine pistol raised to do battle. The man's eyes

were ablaze with fanatical fervor, and those eyes alertly
scanned the stage, seeking the couple as his compatriots
did from other directions.

"You cannot hide from us forever," the terrorist
abruptly shouted. "Reveal yourselves! Do you wish to be
responsible for more innocent people being harmed?"

As if to punctuate his threat, the man pointed his
weapon higher and fired a burst of rounds skyward, tearing holes in the curtains and chipping plaster and wood
from the proscenium. A rain of fragments and tattered
shreds of cloth came down, to disappear within the mist.

"You are in our power now!" shouted the man. "Do
not resist."

There was a brief moment of silence, heavy and tense
after the gunfire. Then another voice was heard, a voice
strong and confident, deeply resonant, unearthly in its
tone. It seemed to come from just behind the young terrorist, and from nowhere.

"Impertinent fool . . ."

The man whirled in his place, nervously firing a few
rounds toward the back of the theater. His eyes jerked
first one way, then the other, as he desperately sought the
source of the mysterious voice.

"Looking for me?" said the disembodied voice, seemingly at his elbow. "Perhaps I am here . . ." The voice
shifted now, appearing to come from behind him once
more. "Or here . . ." Now the voice haunted his right
side, teasingly near, yet still with no visible source. "Or
perhaps . . . *here!*"

The terrorist whirled again, then jerked his head upward as a wrenching sound came from above. The great
chandelier, built and wired to mimic a fall in each performance, just as in the classic Leroux novel, that great
chandelier now crashed down upon the stage in precisely
the spot where stood the transfixed terrorist. It was over
in a moment, with nothing of him visible save for a protruding arm, his fingers still tightly clutching his weapon.
The rest of his body lay hidden beneath three-quarters of
a ton of decorative metalwork, lighting, and beads.

Caroline let out a gasp from her place of hiding, then gasped sharply again as a hand touched her arm on the side opposite where her husband crouched. She looked up into the eyeless gaze of a silhouette. A man, or something like a man, bent over her, cloaked in darkness, his face shrouded in shadow from a broad-brimmed hat. After working so much with Robert in this production, anyone wearing a cloak made her think of him. But somehow, intangible as the feeling was, Caroline was emphatically, chillingly, certain that this was *not* Robert.

"Quickly—" said the specter in a commanding whisper "—this way if you wish to escape."

There was something so compelling in his words, and in the strong grip of his clawlike hands, that the couple found themselves being drawn with him, back, back through the shadows of the stage to a space between two flats. It seemed a poor exit, this route the stranger led them. Yet there upon the floor, in the mists that coiled and eddied, was a faint glow of light, ebbing up from below.

The stranger boldly stepped into that glow, descending silently from view, leaving only a beckoning hand visible above the mist. Lawrence swallowed hard and followed, fumbling within the opening of a stage trapdoor he had not known was there. As his feet found the rungs of a ladder, he cautiously lowered himself, then reached up to guide Caroline's uncertain descent.

Some of the mist was spilling, cloudlike, through the opening as they emerged below stage. A small battery lamp hung on a support brace was the source of the ghostly glow. From somewhere above came what sounded like cursing and barked orders in a foreign tongue.

"Get down!" the stranger whispered harshly. "I must close the trap before they see it."

As they cleared the last steps of the ladder and set foot upon the floor, the couple stood aside, watching as their seeming benefactor climbed a few rungs upward and threw a lever which slid the door back into place. He quickly rejoined them, but not to pause, for the sound of heavy footsteps reverberated through the stage flooring, heading in their direction.

"This way!" snapped the cloaked man, snatching up his lamp. "I fear they have seen the glow."

They ran, hurrying through the odd network of braces and passageways that honeycombed the space beneath the stage, with dust and cobwebs assailing them, and with only the bouncing, wavering glow of the battery light to show their way. Though the Majestic was a large theater, the space beneath the stage was not vast, and they quickly found themselves along the back wall, where stairs led to a basement.

Once more they descended, through the basement storage area and then still deeper into the old building's sub-basement, hurried on by the urgings of their mysterious benefactor and by the sounds of the trapdoor above being blasted open by gunfire. The terrorists were pursuing, more determined than ever, their flame of fanaticism being fanned by righteous anger.

As they rushed onward, Lawrence gasped, "Please—who are you? Tell us!"

"A friend," came the reply. "For now, that is all you need to know."

There were sounds behind them, above them, footsteps on the stairs, in the level they had just left. The terrorists were not far behind.

Caroline lost track of direction. She knew that they were many feet below the street level of the city, but she could not guess whether she now faced north or south, east or west. Suddenly a wall loomed before them, solid and gray and dusty, a barrier that seemed to seal their doom. "What now—?" she gasped.

"Here," said the stranger, directing them to a portion of the wall where two squarish columns rose from floor to ceiling. Dust on the floor showed signs of recent movement there, and as the stranger pressed heavily against the narrow portion of wall between the columns, it gave way, pivoting to reveal an opening. He directed them through, and quickly closed it after them.

They now passed through a thick section of wall, part of the very foundation of the building, and entered a passageway which bore ancient looking waterpipes. Electrical conduits overlaid old gas lines, and everywhere was the look of long neglect. A musty odor permeated the still air. The passageway covered no more than forty or fifty feet, then ended abruptly in a dead end of bricks and mortar and plaster. An opening had been made at one side of this odd wall, and it was through this that the specter now led them.

"This chamber is the terminus of an old private subway train," he told them. "In the late 1800s, it was converted from an abandoned public line by a wealthy speculator and financier who used it to visit the theater district. We are very near the subway lines of Times Square Station. In fact, that locked door over there gives me access to it, though it appears sealed from their side. I had not planned for our first meeting to come about under quite these circumstances, but the transportation shall serve our needs nonetheless."

"Subway. . . ?" breathed Caroline, but she saw in the next moment that his words were true. At the edge of the platform upon which they stood, a very old looking and beautifully crafted train car sat at the end of tracks leading off into a narrow tunnel. Smaller than a modern train, it clearly was not meant to transport more than a half dozen or so people. On a nearby siding sat a smaller maintenance car, open-air and functional looking. Electric lights in ornamental fixtures dimly illuminated the chamber, and dotted the length of the tunnel at regular intervals.

The cloaked stranger stood poised before the private subway car, his gloved hand extended toward it, his face still hidden in the shadow of his hat. "Will you join me?"

Lawrence and Caroline exchanged nervous glances. Lawrence asked, "Why can't we just go through that door you mentioned—the one into Times Square Station. There are police there."

The stranger gave a shrugging gesture. "You may if

you wish. I leave the choice up to you. But I can assure you that what few police are there will be no match against terrorists armed with automatic weapons. I cannot guarantee your safety up there, as I can at our destination.'' His voice, that powerful yet sophisticated voice, took on a cajoling tone. ''Besides, with your sense of drama, with your flair for the exotic, *how can you resist. . . ?*''

The couple considered a moment longer, then their ears pricked up as distant scrapes of sound reminded them of their pursuers. With a sigh of sudden resolve, they started for the subway car.

They quickly boarded. The luxurious old car had rich walnut paneling throughout, and the window glass was etched with floral borders in the Victorian style. Velvet upholstered seats, blood-red in hue, showed signs of age, but were still quite comfortable. As an added touch, ribboned sachets hung from the lamp fixtures, giving off a scent of violets.

Taking the forward seat, the cloaked man inserted a golden key into the small control panel, flipped a switch and turned a throttle crank. The car rolled away from the platform as its electric motors hummed to life, then shot into the tunnel with increasing speed. The amber glow within the car, and from the tunnel lamps whizzing by, seemed of another age, as if the very light itself had yellowed with the passage of decades. Caroline cast a fearful glance backward and thought she glimpsed the terrorists running onto the platform behind her, but then the car rounded a slight curve and they were lost from sight.

With a rumbling, grumbling roar, the tiny subway car sped along tracks that occasionally wavered from a straight route, but that never curved more than a few degrees without soon recovering. Its passengers and its bizarre conductor remained silent, and in a matter of a few minutes the car slowed under the man's ever watchful control. Finally, it pulled to a halt at another platform, the tunnel having broadened into a small underground chamber similar to the first.

"We are here," said the man, and the words, while not truly ominous, were not particularly reassuring, either.

Caroline looked around as they emerged from the car. "And where exactly *is* here?"

"Home," replied the man, then he said no more as he led them to an antique elevator with glass walls, surrounded by a wrought iron grille. He bade them enter, and closed the gate and door behind them.

Ascending several hundred feet from the subterranean chamber, the elevator brought them to what appeared to be the ground floor of a private home. Once more their spectral companion used his special key, this time to twist in the elevator control box before opening the glass door and wrought iron gate. He escorted them out into his home. The place was clearly a mansion of more than modest proportions. The furniture and fixtures, even the wallpaper, all were Victorian in style. Gas lights cast a subdued but warm glow over all, and rich brocaded curtains were drawn across the windows, against the night. It would be easy to imagine that this house had not changed in over a century.

"We are in West Manhattan, near Morningside Park," their strange host told them as he led them through the parlor and toward another room. "I welcome you to my home. But I do not welcome the world at large, and I must take steps now to insure my privacy is maintained."

"You think the terrorists will follow us here?" asked Caroline.

"I am certain of it. But their fate is already sealed. It is the police who concern me. If they find my private subway the press will get wind of it, and through them, the public. That is something I do not wish."

The room to which he led them appeared to be a study, decorated with an odd mixture of elements. Shelves filled with rare books lined two walls, while the third wall was dominated by a pipe organ and a smaller, modern, electronic organ. There were also tape decks and stereo equipment, and in the center of the room stood an ornate antique desk cluttered with papers.

Yet it was objects arranged along the fourth wall that caught their attention and held it. A large French Provincial cabinet's shelves held computer equipment and a half dozen television monitors, each of which displayed a different image. A panel below the monitors bore switches and dials of unknown purpose. Filling the space beside the cabinet was a long table, one end of which was outfitted as a makeup stand, with mirror, jars, and accessories.

Caroline felt a chill, her gaze riveted upon the other end of that table, for there stood a row of heads staring back at her with empty eyes and gaping mouths. It took a moment for her to recover from her initial shock and realize that these bizarre objects were not heads at all, but merely latex masks resting atop the sort of stands that wigs are commonly displayed upon. Each mask was different, fashioned with surprising realism, and disconcertingly empty, as if someone's face had been peeled off and draped over the stand. There was also a variety of wigs in different colors and styles, arranged in a row behind the masks on a slightly higher tier. Caroline found herself thinking that, with her theater background, this all should seem quite familiar and ordinary. Yet it did not, *could* not, and the shudder which coursed along her spine was ample proof of the strangeness.

"My God, Lawrence," Caroline said in a tense whisper. "What have we gotten ourselves into?"

Her husband's only response was an awestruck look and a raised eyebrow. He squeezed her hand, but his reassurance was halfhearted.

"It is as I feared," said the imposing, darkly cloaked figure ahead of them, his face still turned away from their curious gaze. "The vipers have left my secret door open."

His words brought their attention to one of the monitor screens, where a high angled view was displayed of the door that had been their exit from the Majestic's sub-basement. The secret panel was indeed standing open, revealed in the scarlet glow of infrared light. The strange man quickly flipped a series of switches upon the panel beneath the monitors, watching the screen intently as his actions caused remote mechanisms to close the door, and hydraulic pistons to thrust a literal wall of bricks forward against the back of the door, forbidding entrance to the hidden domain.

In their hasty escape and the poor light, neither Lawrence nor Caroline had noticed the camera that gave them this view, but it was clear it was not the only one covering their path. Another monitor showed the first subway station chamber they had entered. It was empty. *Truly* empty, for in addition to the antique subway car which had brought them here, the maintenance tram was now also gone. The switch leading from the siding to the main tracks had been thrown. Two of the other monitors showed the private subway tunnel itself, and the first of these revealed an alarming fact, growing larger as it neared the camera's point of view.

Five men now rode the maintenance tram. Grim-faced, swarthy men, eyes ablaze with fury and fanatical determination. Their weapons glistened in the tunnel's amber glow, poised and ready to do their deadly work.

"They *are* coming after us," said Caroline, her tone flat and horror-filled.

Lawrence took due note of the situation, but his frowning gaze shifted to the enigmatic man who seemed to hold their destiny in his clawlike, gloved hands. Finally, he voiced the question that he had asked before—the question that even now he was half afraid to ask. "Really, sir, we are grateful for your help, but . . . but, we still do not know who you are. Will you not tell us? If we are to face death together—"

"I am surprised," came the swift response. "I should have thought you might have guessed. In fact . . . *I think you already have. . . .*"

"The cards and flowers—" Caroline said abruptly, "—you sent them?"

The stranger gave a slight turn of his head. "Yes."

Caroline took a step closer toward their mysterious benefactor, driven to know, almost against her own better judgment. "And . . . and are we to understand, then, that the initial on the card stands for . . . your name?"

Another slight turn of his head. "Yes."

"Your name . . ." murmured Caroline, her spine suddenly seized by a shuddery chill at the thought of what she was saying, ". . . is Erik?"

"Yes." The man's face was turned enough so that a faint glimmer of light from his left eye could be seen. A golden, haunted glimmer, deep within shadows. "Do you see now why I had to contact you? Both of you? I was so moved by your music. Unlike the others, I thought surely *you* could understand . . . and accept."

Lawrence's mouth worked soundlessly for a moment as he struggled with the idea. "No . . . no, you can't be serious. The legend is a work of fiction, invented by Gaston Leroux, the novelist."

"Leroux was a *journalist,* who turned to writing novels. I came to know him well, after he discovered the facts behind what happened at the Paris Opera House in the 1880s. I told him everything. He presented it all as a novel, a deception I willingly encouraged, for it suited my purpose to remain hidden. But with his odd sense of humor he could not resist planting clues to his deception. He repeatedly referred to his tale as *veracious*—true and accurate. Even so, everyone assumed that was merely a writer's ploy, and that the Phantom was no more than a figment of his fertile imagination."

"This is impossible," Lawrence protested weakly. "That would make you . . . nearly one hundred and fifty years old."

"One hundred fifty-eight," he corrected. "But age is meaningless for one such as I. I am a freak of nature . . . a cruel and capricious prank of the gods. I was born with the look of death upon me, and though I do not claim immortality, I swear that I do not seem to age. Do you still disbelieve? Do you? Then look, if you must have proof, upon the face of reality . . .''

The one who called himself Erik now turned, slowly, fully facing them, even as he removed his hat and cloak and threw them aside. Revealed in the gaslight's glow, his features elicited a startled gasp from Caroline.

The face! So like Leroux's description, yet even so it caught them off guard. The gaunt and skull-like features, the yellowed skin stretched tautly over bone, the flattened nose, the eyes—the haunted eyes—sunken within their dark sockets, and peering out with a look that was at once both frightening and pleading. He wore a modern tuxedo of rich velvet and satin, a ruffled shirt and dress tie. The stark black and white of them made all the more terrible his funereal look.

"Please—do not fear me," said Erik, seeing their reaction. "I have only admiration and respect for you, and hope you will grant me yours in return."

A voice came from behind them, startling and unexpected. A feminine voice, light and musical. "Erik— what is it? Have we guests?"

Framed in the door to the study, a young woman stood. Her long hair cascaded around a lovely face that beamed with sweet innocence, and with her pale complexion and long white dress she seemed almost ghostlike.

She caught Erik's attention immediately. "Lydia, I am here by the monitors. And yes, our friends from the theater have joined us. But we are in danger—a murderous band of men attacked our friends at the Majestic, and they pursue us even now."

The young woman addressed as Lydia gave a small gasp, then hurried forward with a soft rustle of cloth. She moved straight for Erik unerringly, but something about her movements and the way her gaze seemed locked upon some distant point suggested she was blind.

Erik reached out to take her hand as she reached him. He took it tenderly in both his gloved hands and let it linger there a moment, then conveyed it to the hand of each of his guests as he hastily introduced them. "This is Caroline . . . and her husband, Lawrence. I hope you will forgive our abrupt arrival."

They greeted the young woman as best they could, but Caroline could not keep her eyes from returning to the bank of monitor screens that held her fear-gripped attention. As she glanced at them once more, she was alarmed to see that the maintenance tram and its deadly passengers had disappeared from the first tunnel monitor and were now looming large in the monitor which showed the nearer end of the private subway tube. "Look—they're nearly here!"

Erik turned back to his control panel and studied the monitor image—the faces of the men so eager to wreak destruction, and the weapons that had already killed, and would do so again. With a deep and angry sigh, he flipped several switches upon the panel and said, "Their fate is in their own hands, now."

Caroline turned to Lawrence with fresh alarm as the sound of the elevator started up in the hall beyond. The car was departing the ground floor, returning down its rock-lined path to the chamber below. With an urgent look to Erik, she said, "Can't you do something? You said we would be safe here."

The Phantom said only, "You are." Then he strode past them to the organ which dominated the first wall. Seemingly oblivious to the imminent danger which faced them, he turned the organ on and took his seat upon the broad and ornate bench. Eric removed his gloves, revealing bony, almost skeletal hands with the same jaundiced flesh as his face, and then he began to play. The composition was strange, driven, as complex as a Bach toccata, yet more somber and tortured, almost maniacal in its raw power. The music filled the room and made the walls reverberate with its energy.

Caroline was aghast. The music, for all its frightening beauty, seemed no more than an escape from the reality that was drawing ever nearer. She looked to the monitors once again. There, on the fifth screen, was a view of the chamber so far below the house, where the subway terminated. The camera clearly showed the base of the elevator shaft with its fancy ornamental grille. The car was just arriving, sent down by Erik's command to greet the terrorists.

Worse yet, the maintenance tram now entered the picture, pulling to an abrupt halt at the end of the tracks as the man at the controls jerked the lever back. Leaping out onto the platform, the five men scuttled toward the elevator car, looking about rapidly, warily, covering each other's backs and checking their weapons' readiness. It was an eerie dance they did, choreographed by their military training, and accompanied by Erik's nightmarish score. They threw open the door to the elevator and entered.

Caroline gasped as the sixth monitor, which displayed the interior of the elevator, now gave her a close-up view of the terrorists. She saw them close the gate, and work the controls that would send the car up. It was like watching some horrid television drama unfold, but the image she saw was of deadly reality, closing in on her.

She turned away from it, seeking support from wherever she could find it. At his organ, Erik still played with all-consuming concentration. The young woman, Lydia, for whom the monitors were quite useless, had taken a chair, sitting quietly with her hands clasped before her, lost in thought or in prayer, swept up in the Phantom's music and seeming to sense something dreadful in its melancholy power.

Caroline grasped her husband's sleeve. "Lawrence," she whispered imperatively. "Lawrence—!"

He seemed not to hear her for a moment, listening with rapt attention to the music and seemingly frozen where he stood. "What?"

"Lawrence, is he crazy? Are we? Part of me wants to leave, to run out into the street, screaming. But it's as if I've lost the will to move." Her eyes darted back to the monitor screen. "They're coming for us! The elevator is rising. They'll be here any moment."

Her words seemed to rally him. 'Yes . . . yes, you're quite right. But if we just run outside, they'll follow us. We must have something to fight with.'' He went to the door and closed it, turning the latch, his actions ignored by Erik and the girl. Next he went to the desk and pulled open a drawer. ''See if you can find a gun, Caroline. Anything!''

They both began to search, but had barely started when the elevator whined to a halt down the hall. The terrorists had arrived. The monitor with the view of the elevator's interior showed them leveling their weapons, reaching for the door handle. All that separated them from their prey now was that decorative glass panel, the iron gate just beyond, and a short stretch of hallway.

Caroline stared at the monitor, frightened by its image, yet unable to take her eyes from it. She hoped for an instant that the elevator door would not open . . . that it had to be unlocked to gain entry to the house, as Erik had done with his golden key upon their own arrival. But even that vain hope was dashed as she saw the leader of the terrorists take hold of the lever and pull it over into the open position, without the use of Erik's key. The glass door swung open a crack as they peered out cautiously, their machine pistols pointing through the opening.

''My God,'' she breathed.

At that moment, several things happened simultaneously. Erik's music reached a peak, holding on strident, heavy chords. The handle on the glass elevator door pulled free from its mounting, still clenched in the terrorist's hand. And servos clicked at key points within the gilt frame of the elevator car.

With startling abruptness, the entire floor of the elevator swung down, pivoting upon hinges at the rear of the car and slamming open. There was nothing beneath it . . . nothing but the gaping chasm of the elevator shaft, stretching down, down, down into the depths. There was only a brief instant, seemingly frozen in time, during which the five killers clawed desperately at the smooth glass walls of the elevator car, trying to take hold of anything to prevent their fall, but it was in vain.

The terrorists plummeted into the shaft, their silent screams visible on the monitor as they receded into the darkness and were lost from sight. Whether the shaft stopped at the floor of the subway chamber or reached deeper into the bowels of the Earth was uncertain. The only thing that was certain was that the threat from these killers was over.

So, too, was Erik's music. The Phantom rose from his organ bench, his intricate, compelling melodies finished, his energies spent. He moved to Lydia's side, helped her to her feet, then rejoined his shaken guests.

"We are safe, now," he told them, taking hold of their hands. "You are trembling. Let me get you both a brandy to calm your nerves." Erik went to a stand where his brandy decanter stood, and returned in a moment with two glasses, which he gave his guests. "You must let the authorities know you are all right. Lydia and I will drive you to your hotel. You have endured too much to enjoy the evening I had hoped for, but please, promise that you will both come back, under better circumstances. There is so much we could talk about. My wife and I have so few friends."

"Lydia is your wife?" said Carolina.

"Forgive me, I neglected a proper introduction," Erik said as the young woman came to him and stood close by his side. He looked at her fondly, and a softness came over his haunted features. Looking back to his guests, he continued. "I know what you're thinking, but Lydia knows who I am . . . what I am. She knows everything, and accepts me, anyway. She has her handicap, and I have mine, but together we have found peace."

Lawrence nodded with understanding. "What shall we say to the police and FBI?"

"For the sake of my privacy, I would prefer you told them only that you escaped the terrorists, and eluded them in the streets until you could contact the authorities. May I ask that favor of you?"

"You've saved our lives," Caroline told him. "It's the very least we can do. . . ."

The following week, on the night there was no scheduled performance, the couple found themselves once more within the brooding old mansion on Morningside Drive, not far from the cathedral of St. John the Divine. They were moved as much by curiosity as by gratitude, enough so to overcome their own remaining fears and doubts. And so now they were gathered in the parlor, with Erik having donned one of his realistic latex masks so that he might appear more normal for his guests.

The conversation had covered many topics, music being foremost among them, and when Erik mentioned that his wife sang, Lawrence insisted that she demonstrate for them. With some prodding, Lydia complied, exhibiting a voice that was pure and clear and sweetly melodic.

Caroline was quite taken with the performance. "You sing beautifully, Lydia."

Erik took hold of his wife's hand. "She has a natural talent for it."

"It is your training that deserves the credit, Erik," she insisted. "His own singing puts mine to shame."

Caroline's eyes roamed the Victorian parlor in which they sat, marveling at its detail and splendor. "I still think it a perfect twist of fate, that you should have come to live here, in Manhattan."

"I left Europe in 1937," Erik said, "when Hitler's threat became clear. I came to New York and found work in the design, construction, and renovation of theaters. I invested my money, with great success, as it turned out, and became quite wealthy. So much so that for years I have been not only an anonymous patron of the Metropolitan Opera, but also a principal theatrical financial backer, or "angel" as they are known on Broadway. In fact, one of the productions I have backed is *yours*."

"Our 'Angel of Music,' " Caroline murmured. "I love it!"

There was an awkward silence for a long moment, during which Lawrence stroked his chin and frowned in thought. At last, he spoke up. "Tell, me, Lydia, we've had ample proof of your singing skill, but I wonder . . . if the moves were carefully blocked out for you, do you think you could find your way around a stage?"

"Why . . . why, yes," replied Lydia. "I suppose I could."

"What are you thinking?" Caroline inquired of her husband, her lovely eyebrow raised.

"Yes," said Erik, a protective tone in his rich and resonant voice. "What, indeed?"

"Merely an idea I'm suddenly toying with," said Lawrence. "You may think me quite mad for suggesting it, but I can't resist the thought. You see, there is a special performance of the musical coming up, at which neither my wife nor Robert, our male lead, will be able to perform. Assuming I could protect your true identities, and your privacy, would you at least consider the possibility of you and your wife singing the parts of Erik and Christine?"

There was a moment of awestruck silence, and then the Phantom tilted back his head and roared with laughter that seemed to echo and reverberate through the room. When at last he looked at them again, there was a merry sparkle in those haunted eyes.

"The Phantom, playing the Phantom, eh? What a pretty puzzle that would make. No . . . I thank you for your kind offer, but I think we had better keep to ourselves, and leave the performing to the professionals." There was another pause as Erik turned to gaze at Lydia. "Still . . . I must confess . . . I find the idea *deliciously intriguing. . .*"

THE UNMASKING

by *Steve Rasnic Tem*

"I've had that poster a very long time, Chelsea," Andrew said to the young woman in bed. Lon Chaney as the Phantom, right after the moment of unmasking, when he'd stepped away from the appalled Christine Daaé. The Phantom's face had been the perfect revealation— Andrew was more convinced of that now than ever. The eyes were the only thing alive in that skull face. "See the resemblance?" He grinned as widely as he could, showing his perfectly cared-for teeth.

"Don't be ridiculous, Andrew," she said in a sleepy voice. "You look nothing like that."

Andrew held his huge smile a few seconds, then closed it up, shut it down. She didn't understand now, but she would.

The poster had yellowed over the years. With every one of his many moves, more damage had been done. The countless tears mended carefully with Scotch tape, then later transparent tape when that went on the market. Now, at last, in the home of his dead parents, perhaps his precious poster could remain on the wall.

"Can I get you anything?" he asked.

"A new mother, a new father, and a father for this baby." She laughed mirthlessly.

Andrew didn't return the laughter. "You know I would if I could," he said.

"I know, Andrew."

"You know I'd do anything."

"I know, Andrew. Now let me sleep." She rolled over to the wall. Andrew stepped softly to the kitchen, thinking to have some food ready for her when she woke up.

She'd been with him a week. He'd taken every precaution; there seemed little chance anyone would trace her there. He'd had the house to himself since his mother died; most of the neighbors were new, and none had ever paid much attention to him. When Chelsea wanted air, he insisted she use the back balcony with its solid sidewalls and the surrounding high trees.

They might hear her singing, he mused. Small chance. His was a silent bird. He'd even suggested that a good song now and then might make her feel better. She'd stared at him as if he were mad.

Perhaps she did think he was crazy. Surely she must. He knew he had enough quirks. He knew there could be few people more obsessive than he. But she needed him, so she didn't call him crazy. To his face. What she didn't know was that he wouldn't have taken offense.

He scratched at the scab on his cheek. It was beginning to itch. He thought there might be a scar there, eventually. If he permitted it to heal. The scab was crescent-shaped, to match a fingernail, and the tissue seemed slightly warped where the fingernail had gone in. A definite possibility of a scar. He pictured himself with a scar and felt his smile come on, as if his teeth were visibly growing and spreading his lips apart as the crowns expanded.

He was careful making the omelet. He threw out the first attempt because it stuck to the pan. The second because the color wasn't quite right. After all, he was making this omelet for Chelsea. It would be passing her beautiful lips, dropping down her pale throat to exquisite belly and then to all her secret places, providing nourishment for both her and her unborn child. This could not be an ordinary omelet.

He heard a soft padding behind him and turned.

Christine Daaé stood silhouetted in the kitchen doorway, her hair glowing under the dim, flashing fluorescents. And then it was Chelsea, rubbing at her eyes, her expanded belly pushing her nightgown out, stretching the cloth to a sheerness that mapped every mole, crevice, and contour.

"Smells good," she said. Andrew reached up and lightly rubbed the scab on his face, imagining the skin ripping open. "Does it hurt?" she asked.

"Not at all. It didn't even hurt while it was happening."

Chelsea made a shuddering motion. "Ugh! I *hate* blood."

"Warm blood makes us human," he said. "That's what we want out of a kiss, a close embrace. That's all. We want another human's warmth."

She smiled and walked toward the kitchen table. "You're a poet, Andrew."

"Oh. Far more than that."

She stopped and turned to him with a puzzled expression. But she did not ask.

Her parents didn't want anything to do with her. They'd called her a "tramp," she said. Andrew thought that was a curiously old-fashioned term. Like "dishonor." *You have dishonored our family name.* He imagined her parents were very much like his own. *I can no longer cover up for your little infatuations. I can no longer protect you from the police. Why can't you stop bothering these young women?* They could not accept her for who she was. They could not appreciate her free ways. Well, he could.

"Coffee?" He held the pot up close to his face, where he could feel the heat through his tender skin. He imagined all his features, his personality, the small lies of appearance melting away.

"No, I've had enough. Makes me pee too much."

Andrew turned away, a small disgust playing with his lips.

"Andrew, I'd like to go out today."

He gripped the pot so firmly it tipped. Tiny splashes steamed off the stove top. He slowly returned the pot to the counter. "Why? You have everything you need here. What I don't have now, I can get for you."

"I just need to get out. Staying cooped up like this in the same place all the time . . . a person's *bound* to go crazy."

He turned and faced her. He could feel his teeth making him smile again. "I stay here all the time," he said. "I almost never go out. Are you saying that I'm . . ."

"Of course not! Andrew watched as she took a deep breath. A perfect breath, judging from the way the thin material over her breasts rose and fell without wrinkling. She was composing herself. Andrew had noticed how good she was at composing herself. "I'm just not as strong as you, I guess," she said. "I need to get out, see other people."

"No, you're not strong, Chelsea. You're going to have a baby soon. That means you need your rest."

"But I *need* to get out!"

Andrew could feel his smile stretching, pulling the skin around his scab so that it began to itch again. "See, you're upsetting yourself. And that's not good for you or your unborn child. I'll just run out and get you some ice cream. Strawberry, your favorite flavor. And nuts . . . I'll get nuts. And cherries and whip cream and butterscotch. I know how much you like sundaes. Remember? I first met you at the ice cream parlor. I was working behind the counter?"

"I remember, Andrew," she said quietly.

"I'll just run down there and fix you a strawberry sundae and bring it right back up."

"You quit that job, remember?"

He began looking for his coat. He finally tried the inside of the broom closet door and there it was. He turned and looked at her while slipping the coat on. It required three attempts to get his right arm into the sleeve. "I *remember*," he said. "I had to take care of you, didn't I? Not that I minded. I didn't need that job anyway. I'll get the ingredients at the grocery store and make the sundae here, on the kitchen table. You'll *love* it."

"Andrew . . ." He almost ran to the door. "Andrew, please." He jerked it open and slammed it after him. "Andrew, I *need* to get out!" she screamed from the other side of the door. He locked the door, pocketing the key.

He went down the staircase into the old entranceway. It was the only way to the apartment upstairs; there was no outside entrance. After all those years of failed relationships, after he'd been forced out of so many apartments because of complaints he was "bothering" the young women there, making them "uncomfortable," he'd had nowhere to go but his parents' house. And since moving back he'd always lived in the apartment upstairs. It had always been sufficiently large for him, and even with both parents dead he could see no reason to expand his living space into the rest of the house. All the furniture in the ground floor was kept covered with sheets and plastic, and years of dust. The telephone sat by the front door—he'd used it as a doorstop while carrying some of Chelsea's things in. It hadn't been connected in years. He'd also flipped off the circuit breakers that controlled this part of the house, and shut off the heating vents, so that these rooms were always cold and dark. He liked to think of them as a protective barrier of cold and dark between the outside world and his living quarters upstairs. This was his no-man's-land, his dark lands. He'd informed the post office no one lived here anymore. No one would guess someone still lived here.

He felt strange in the fresh air, the bright sunshine. Chelsea had come to him on a rainy, dreary day, virtually without warning, although he'd known she'd been having trouble at home for some time. She talked about it every day at the Ice Cream Shop.

"They're going to kick me out, I just know it," she said, jabbing the plastic spoon forcefully into her sundae.

Andrew leaned over, supported by his broom. Leaned over her, gauging the smoothness of her cheeks, noting the contrast between her oh-so-black hair and the paleness of her skin, observing where the paleness grew pinker, where warm blood—excited by nerves—welled closer to the surface. He glanced at the door to the back room, saw Mr. Carter's face there, watching. Andrew had been warned repeatedly about young female customers. Not to stare at them, lean over them, to stop bothering them. "Why in the world would they do that?" he finally asked.

Chelsea looked down and gently patted her stomach. "I'm preggie, and the daddy is long gone. My folks'll have a fit."

Andrew had blushed slightly at her casual reference to pregnancy. So far, it had been the only flaw he'd found in Chelsea: her vulgarity, her too-easy familiarity. But he had been sure he could teach her how to overcome that. "I have a large house. If the worst should happen, you could stay with me."

Chelsea had looked at him with a smirk. "You hitting on me, Andrew?"

Andrew had felt his face burn, even though he knew this was her way of kidding, her way of maintaining control. He could train her to overcome that, as well. Still, the feeling of heat in his face would not go away. He imagined it highlighting all his imperfections. "I'm offering as a friend. You know that. And really, it's a very large house."

Chelsea's smile had faded a little, her skin paling. Vanilla ice cream, he thought. "Thanks, Andrew. I'll keep that in mind."

He had seen the calculation in the way she said that, the evidence of planning in her features. Like so many young women before her, wondering what they could get out of loyal Andrew. And Andrew didn't mind. *Thank you, Andrew. You're a true friend. I don't know what I would have done without you, Andrew.*

Now, he stared into the Ice Cream Shop window. His replacement was working behind the counter. The shiny glass mirrored Andrew's features, yet hid the secret imperfections. It always amazed him how mirrors could lie.

He continued his trip to the grocer's. Then Chelsea's brother pulled up in his car.

"Hey, Andrew! I'd like to talk to you a minute!"

Andrew kept walking as if he hadn't heard anything. He made his face as stiff as possible, thinking as he had since high school that if he just made his face into a mask no one would notice him. And for a very long time it had worked. People rarely, if ever, noticed him.

But not this time. "Come on, Andrew! You know where she is, don't you?"

He turned and stared at the crewcut protruding from the open driver's-side window. "I don't know who you're talking about."

"Chelsea! Come on, I'm on her side. Mom and Dad are ready to take her back in. They know they overreacted and they want to help her out."

"Well, I'm certainly glad they've come to their senses. But honestly, I have no idea where she is."

The crewcut looked confused a minute. "I thought she would have told you," he said. "Could you call me if you hear from her?"

"Of course. I'd be more than happy to."

The crewcut did something with his hands, then handed a slip of paper out the window. "Here's my number."

Andrew waved him away. "I already have it."

Again, the crewcut looked confused. After a minute he waved back and drove away.

On the next block two young girls were getting onto a bus. They were perfect, unspoiled, their skin scrubbed clean, their hair lustrous and natural. One of them turned and looked at Andrew, then nudged her friend. They both laughed.

Anger flared, consuming Andrew, burning his face before he could stop it. He reached up and tore the scab off his face. "You simply haven't looked closely enough!" he shouted at them. He poked his finger into the fresh wound and began tugging on the skin to widen it. It felt blood-warm. It didn't hurt at all. "You have to look beneath the mask! Maybe you'll understand that some day!

Maybe I'll even be your teacher!'' The warmth ran down his finger onto his hand. He brought another finger up with its untrimmed nail and started working on the other cheek.

The girls screamed and leapt onto the bus. The other passengers stared out their windows at Andrew. When the bus driver stepped down, Andrew ran away.

When he was a teenager, Andrew's mother used to tell him that there was someone for everyone. And he'd believed that. Later, he'd believed that there were probably hundreds of possible matches for every one of us. You just had to find people attracted to your particular mask, or perhaps you could alter your mask if it didn't seem suitable to enough people. After all, no one knew what you really were inside. No one could truly see beyond the mask. This was both a curse and a blessing.

He looked down. Blood was spotting his shirt. He ran behind a store and dipped his face and hands into a rain-filled metal barrel he found there, then splashed some of the water on his clothing.

He made his way down the alley until he reached a parked car. He leaned over and peered into the rear view mirror. The mirror had a wide-angle lens mounted on it, which distorted his face, made his wide smile even wider, and exaggerated the extent of his wounds. He blinked several times, fascinated as his lids raised and lowered over burning, blazing eyes. There was a world within those eyes, if people only bothered to look. His skin was ghastly pale in the alley's dim light. The blood running from his cheeks stood out like thick theatrical makeup. His nose had receded into shadow, so as to appear virtually nonexistent.

Behind him, flashing red and yellow lights traveled the street that intersected the alley. Andrew ran down to the corner, his left foot dragging a bit. He must have hurt it in his flight.

A patrol car had stopped across the street. An officer was talking to the two young girls from the bus.

He had always hated the police. *What were you doing*

with that girl? They all thought they knew what he was
about. *What were you thinking about doing with that girl?*
They were always stopping him, questioning him, watching him, waiting to catch him. *Why don't you stop bothering them? We'll have to run you in if you don't stop
bothering them.*

Andrew turned and ran back down the alley. He had
leapt and caught the lower bar of a fire escape when he
heard a car turning into the alley behind him. He made
his way to the roof of the building, and then he heard the
shouting below.

Andrew ran across the line of roofs, leaping the man-
ageable gaps with wild, animal abandon, tearing at his
cheeks, tearing at his hair, feeling the blood grow thicker
on his face, warm layers of it supplanting the layers that
had gone cold. Now and then he heard more shouting,
but he was far too swift for them, far too clever. The
wind caressed his scars. He felt like singing, full of this
new-found freedom.

He would have liked being like other people. Always,
that had been his goal. He would have liked having a
wife, children, a home where friends and neighbors might
visit. But his appearance put him apart from other human
beings. Not the appearance that everyone saw—that was
merely the mask. It was the appearance that lay beneath
the mask that would have terrified, that would have left
everyone he met shaken and appalled.

*There is some music that is so terrible that it consumes
all those who approach it.* The Phantom had known it all
too well.

It was dark by the time he got home. He was faint with
exhaustion, but exhilarated.

The apartment key was slick with his blood. He
dropped it twice, then held it with two shaking hands and
jammed it into the lock. The doorknob was slippery. He
pulled out one corner of his shirt to grip and turn it.

The kitchen was dark. He could see the dim glow of
the bedside light through a crack in her door. He passed
the couch, and noted that she had tidied his bedclothes.

He either bled, or sweat, profusely. It drenched him as he walked through the darkness. He stopped outside the bedroom door, where she wouldn't be able to see him. But he could see his Phantom poster on the bedroom wall.

Only now did Andrew understand his fascination with the expression in the Chaney-Phantom's blazing white eyes. The overwhelming, animal emotion. Looking into those eyes now, Andrew could not understand how he could have missed it all those years. The fear. The raw, animal fear.

The Phantom had been terrified of Christine Daaé. Terrified of her beauty, and terrified of what she must think of him. Terrified that she would soon discover that even his hideous skull-face was a mask, and that there were more masks to be discovered underneath. He would have had her think that he was a romantic poet trapped beneath that hideous mask. That if not for that mask he would be her perfect lover. But he was far more than poet or lover. And it was those other selves he was terrified she might see.

He knocked softly. He could hear the bedclothes rustle softly on the other side of the door. "Andrew, is that you?"

"Yes. It's Andrew. You remember Andrew. I'm sorry, but I couldn't get your sundae." *The beauty and power of his voice.*

"Don't worry about it. You can come on in—I'm decent."

"Decent" seemed like such an old-fashioned word. "I can't."

"Can't? Come on, Andrew. Stop playing games. We have to talk."

"We can talk through the door. I don't feel well. I'd rather you not see me just now."

She didn't say anything at first, but Andrew could hear her breathing. He imagined the way her chest rose and fell. He imagined the way her nightgown must look on her. He imagined her pale skin and her so dark hair. He imagined her as he had imagined every other woman who had obsessed him, who had seemed like the only woman possible for him, even though he knew hundreds were possible, if he just wore the right mask. He imagined her loving him even after seeing his one true face. He imagined who she *must* be, and yet never was. "But I need something to drink, Andrew. My throat's so dry. Can't you get me something to drink?"

"Of course, Chelsea. I'll have it to you in just a moment." He went into the kitchen and poured her a glass of orange juice. Vitamin C. It would be good for her as well as for the baby. The paring knife was on the counter. He picked it up with his other hand.

He stopped in the shadows just outside the bedroom door. From here he could see a crescent portion—a selected slice—of her face, and the poster on the wall behind her. He studied the planes of the Phantom's cheeks, the line of jaw. "Here it is, Chelsea. Come to the door, but no farther. I'll hand it in to you."

"Andrew, this is *silly*. I've lived here with you for a week."

"I've kept things very proper. I've remained the old-fashioned gentleman. Humor me, please. Just do as I requested."

He heard her get out of bed, the soft pad of her feet toward the door. Soon he could feel the warmth of her blood near him. He reached his hand through the open door.

"Andrew! What's happened to you?"

"Just take the glass. A minor nosebleed, nothing more. Foolishly I tried to stop it with my hand."

He could feel the cool glass leave his hand. Then her warm hand touching his. "But your nails are all torn," she said.

"I told you I was foolish. Now get back into the bed."

He could hear her doing as he instructed. Once she was in bed, he heard her take a deep breath. "I want to leave tomorrow." He gripped the paring knife tightly. He weaved slightly, leaning into the light. "Andrew! There's blood on your face!"

"I told you I had a nosebleed. There's really no point in your leaving. You have no place to go. I'll take care of you. Who else could take care of you as well as I?" He stepped farther back into the shadows, where he was sure she would be unable to see him. He raised the knife and slipped it into the edge of one of his open cheek wounds. Then he pushed the blade toward his nose. He was thankful for the blade's sharpness. He felt faint, his stomach lurched, but it was surprisingly painless. His head floated.

"I have to face my parents sometime. Maybe they'll take me back now that they've thought about it awhile."

He ran the blade into his other cheek and permitted it to dance through his flesh. "I saw your brother today. He said you're not welcome." The blade hit something hard and he pulled it back. He dipped it in again and began to write.

"Joey? You saw Joey and he said that? I don't believe you."

"He said you were 'preggie.' You've shamed them." The blade hit nerve after nerve and Andrew's flesh quivered electrically. He could hardly see. He didn't know how much longer he could stand. "I'd do *anything* for you. You know that."

"Then let me go! You locked me in today! That's not taking care of me, Andrew. That's making me your *prisoner!*"

"I just need you to understand!" He could feel the tissues giving, pieces of his face dropping to the floor with small, wet sounds. "I need you to see me as I am!"

"I *want* to understand. I'll do anything I can to help you. But first you have to let me *go!*"

"Okay!" he shouted, pulling the knife out of his face. "But *first* you have to *see* me!" He flung open the bedroom door and pushed his ruined face into the light. Her cry was a high, inarticulate shudder. He couldn't see her, but he could still hear her breathing. He held the knife out in the direction of her chalk-white skin, her terrible black hair, her warm blood reddening lips and cheeks. "Take it, Christine! Help me *finish*. *Unmask* me! Then you can *see* who I *really* am!"

THE GROTTO

by Thomas Millstead

"Extraordinary," Clayton breathed, flinging out an arm in a typically grandiose gesture. "Those radiant colors—as vivid as if they'd been painted last week!"

"Careful," Wrenfeld muttered. "The footing's tricky."

The two men inched their way along the cave's narrow passageway, casting the beams of their flashlights along the walls.

"Incredible!" Clayton marveled, focusing on the huge form of a woolly mammoth, powerfully depicted in red ocher, its shiny tusks sweeping upward, its snakelike trunk raised in defiance.

Trembling, Clayton threw the light farther ahead and three colossal, galloping bison sprang into sight. Beyond them were several large aurochs, forelegs upraised, locked eternally in violent movement.

"Majestic!" said Clayton. "The sheer artistry! To think these were created forty thousand years ago!"

He shook Wrenfeld by the shoulder excitedly. "These are more magnificent than the caves of Lascaux or Font-de-Gaume or Altamira! Hermetically preserved for all these millennia!"

Wrenfeld wriggled free of Clayton's grip. "Unquestionably, a major discovery. I congratulate you."

Wrenfeld had been ready to give it up weeks ago, to return to the museum and to assessing Cro-Magnon artifacts dug up by others. After all, after the excavations of the past century, it appeared unlikely that there were more of those hidden Ice Age caverns still to be uncovered here in these lonely foothills of the Pyrennes so close to the Spanish border.

He and Clayton had haunted the other caves whose discovery in the late nineteenth century and earlier in this century had so dramatically altered science's perception of early mankind. They had exhaustively studied the beautifully crafted cave friezes. But always Clayton had insisted there must be yet another such cavern that had escaped detection, and he had paced the rugged terrain endlessly, obsessively.

Until he'd stepped into the small cleft beneath the scrub brush and dropped down into this world of wonders.

"Come on!" he called, plunging forward.

Wrenfeld lumbered along behind. He was large and awkward and had never liked archaeological field work. He much preferred the tidy certainty of his small office during the day and the predictable comforts of good food and wine and his beloved classical record collection in the evening.

But now he followed Clayton eagerly. This would make their reputations, he realized. This was a find that would stun their colleagues, that would attract global attention.

The gallery of life-sized animals continued on, every turn of the dank, clammy corridor a new surprise. They were animals now extinct but shimmering in the semi-darkness, seeming to move and paw and toss their heads.

Clayton stopped abruptly and gasped.

"Wrenfeld, look!"

Both trained their flashes on the creature hovering above them. It was humanlike, but it wore a stag mask surmounted by spreading antlers and it was draped in thick animal skin. The upper body was bent, as if dancing, and the eyes were round and unblinking, staring directly at them.

"The shaman," Clayton said at last. "The wizard. The tribal sorcerer. A self-portrait from the dawn of our race."

Suddenly, resonating distinctly in the still, chilled air, was the sound of a voice.

A high voice, lilting, sweet, excruciatingly pure.

Wrenfeld shook his head, certain this was some neurological, inner-ear quirk.

But the melody flowed on, floating in and out, echoing everywhere.

Clayton stood stock still, head cocked, listening.

"My God," Wrenfeld murmured. "Who. . . ?"

"This way!" Clayton shouted, darting deeper into the cave.

Wrenfeld followed, swinging his light dizzily from the limestone floor to the passageway ahead. The labyrinthian path descended in treacherous zigzags, and he stumbled several times. They rounded a corner and entered a sprawling clearing. Wrenfeld heard scuttling nearby, as of some startled rodent.

Clayton was far ahead of him now, loping along smoothly.

The intensity of the voice grew stronger, bouncing off the walls to the unseen ceiling. In the dancing shadows, a shifting tracery of white fluttered in and out of visibility. It was a trailing luminescence, as of some flowing garment, and, above, the pale smudge of a face. The gliding soprano notes arched upward in a flawless, heart-swelling crescendo.

Then the object melted away, out of the great hall. Clayton disappeared into the same patch of gloom.

Panting, Wrenfeld pounded after him. Still the voice trilled, somewhere ahead. The cavern roof was low here, and he had to stoop.

"Clayton!" he cried. "Wait!"

There was a jagged switchback to his left, Far in the distance, the beam of Clayton's light splashed frantically from side to side.

For an instant it caught the figure in white: her creamy gown, the bared and satiny shoulders, the soft oval of her face, the imperious cheekbones, the tawny sheen of her chestnut hair.

In that moment she peered at Clayton, eyes wide and glistening, lips parted as her voice sank to a tremulous diminuendo. She extended her arms toward him as if in supplication.

But it was only for a pulse-beat, and the vision dissipated.

Dimly, Wrenfeld heard Clayton call to her, and then he, too, was swallowed up in darkness.

Wrenfeld tripped and crashed headlong to the floor. The flashlight flew from his hand. Desperately, he snatched for it, but the light somehow spiraled away from him, twinkling into nothingness.

From a vast distance came the gentle plash of something hitting water.

Wrenfeld groaned. He had badly twisted his leg and the fiery pain shot through his entire body. With one hand, he groped over the pebble-strewn floor until his fingers were waggling in midair.

A precipice! He began shivering uncontrollably. Only a few feet beyond him. And, to judge from the time it took the flashlight to fall, it was a horrifying drop.

The singing had faded, reverberating hollowly until it died. Blackness and silence engulfed him. It was blackness and silence such as he'd never endured before. He thought of yelling for Clayton, but he feared even to hear the rattling frailty of his own voice.

Time passed, but he could not begin to measure it because all that was real for him was the fear and the pain.

Still there was utter silence, so that when fingers tightened on his arm his body recoiled in a spasm of terror, jerking him closer to the edge of the abyss.

"Clayton?" he croaked.

"Please?"

She said it softly. Her fingers slid down to touch his hand. He felt her breath against his ear, smelling ever so slightly of fresh cloves and jasmine.

"You!"

"Please?"

"What?"

"Help me!"

"How?"

"Help me to leave him! Please!"

"Leave who?"

She paused, fingernails digging anxiously into his wrist. "The master. You know of him? At the Opera House in Paris? You have heard of him?"

"*Him?* Here?"

"He fled. He found this refuge. He forced me to join him."

The rich soprano voice quickened with urgency. "Now I must leave him! But he will not permit it! He is hunting me even now! Through these chambers, these passages. He knows them all. Please!"

She pulled Wrenfeld to his feet.

"I'm not sure," he faltered. "Which way, I mean. I've lost my bearings. And it's pitch dark . . ."

"I know!" She put an arm around him. "I know this place almost as well as he. Please come! Please help! I know he is close behind!"

Hobbling, he leaned heavily against her. They made their way laboriously, weaving through serpentine twists, bumping occasionally into solid rock, feeling their way past sharpened outcroppings.

At last Wrenfeld halted, sagging against a damp wall, fighting to regain his breath.

"No, we must hurry!" she persisted. "He may be anywhere! Do you know what he will do to me?"

"You are Giselle Marchant?" Wrenfeld asked.

"You know me!"

"You have been singing 'Ritorna vincitor.' I recognized your voice at once. I have your performance of *Aida* on record. I play it often."

"Yes? But now we must go—"

"But then you left the stage. It was something of a mystery."

"*He* brought me here. I told you! To sing for him! Please come away! The danger is great! Oh, *mon Dieu!*"

The silence broke open suddenly, exploding, before closing about them once again.

It was Clayton. Wrenfeld could not tell how close he was because of the distorted and muffled acoustics.

But it was Clayton. He shrieked once. There was a ratcheting clatter and a loud splash. No more.

"Quickly!"

Giselle tugged Wrenfeld forward. Staggering, he clung to her hand as she steered them up what he sensed was a slippery, curving ramp.

He heard her grunt, pushing against some barrier.

Then he was propelled into a center of dazzling, leaping firelight that blinded him momentarily.

Wrenfeld blinked, trying to adjust. When he did, he gave a whimpering bleat and crumpled to his knees.

Torches flared throughout the circular, vaulted enclosure. And standing above him was the incarnation of that shaman, that sorcerer, painted four hundred centuries before.

The man was towering, face hidden behind the mask of some black-horned creature that could have existed only far back in the mists of time. His huge body was cloaked in rough, mottled fur. The eyes were deeply set, like unfathomable, subterranean pools.

"This," he boomed, "is the Grotto. "Here were conducted the earliest rites of our most distant progenitors. This place is sacred. For it was here, in this Grotto, that they created art. Here, in their ceremonies and rituals. True art, genuine art. Language. Painting. Music. This place is hallowed. And I have made it my own!"

He jabbed a finger at Wrenfeld. "In Paris they drove me from what was most precious to me. From what was the very essence of my soul. The fools!"

His laughter was a harsh, ringing bellow. "But I have regained my soul! You see what I've found here? It was here that brutish beasts struggled up from the slime and were transmuted into beings of sensitivity, of imagination, of creativity. It happened here. I can feel it in this ancient sanctuary! I absorb the emanations! You see, I have become as one with those magicians of genius who gave birth to all that is noble in our species—all that distinguishes us from lesser breeds. To culture, to art! And do you know why I've done so?''

Wrenfeld shook his bowed head, unable to look up.

"Because I am composing a work unprecedented in scope. An opera that captures this birth of the human spirit. A work that penetrates to the heart of humanity's primeval beginnings and its transcendence from bestiality to splendor. Is that not so, Giselle?''

In the fierce, crackling light of the torches, Wrenfeld saw that her luminous eyes were glowing with pride and adoration and madness. Her gaze was fixed steadily on the Phantom, and her lips stretched into a thin, vulpine smile.

"It will be a masterpiece! From the grandest master the world has know! *My* master!''

"I don't understand . . .'' Wrenfeld choked out the words. "Why you've done this . . . Why Clayton . . .''

"He knew nothing of great music.'' Giselle shrugged. "He was tested and found wanting. But *you* . . . Ah! You have an ear!''

"This opera!'' Passion filled the Phantom's voice. "It is all I exist for! But works surpassing genius take time. They emerge with a few notes here, a chord there. Painstakingly blended together. Discarded. Replaced. It builds. But slowly, slowly. Over the years. Over many, many years.''

He strode to a large boulder, rolling it in front of the entranceway, sealing them in.

"It may take a lifetime to complete. But what better way to invest my remaining years? It is of no matter that I'm unable to leave here. That merely enables me to concentrate on my composition during all my waking hours. And, fortunately, Giselle is able to use her voice as an instrument to bring to life my ideas, my chords, my arias.''

Still on his knees, his inflamed leg throbbing in agony, Wrenfeld whispered: "But what . . . of me?"

"The absolute essential that we have lacked to this point," the Phantom replied, "has been an appreciative audience."

COMFORT THE LONELY LIGHT

by Gary A. Braunbeck

"Comfort the lonely light and the sun in its
  sorrow,
Come like the night, for terrible is the sun
As truth, and the dying light shows only the
  skeleton's hunger
For peace, under the flesh like the summer rose."
—Edith Sitwell
"Street Song"

I

Andy could hear the longing in the old woman's voice as
she sang; it pulled up in his chest until it became a tight
ball of pressure that made him ache. God, how sweetly
she sang! Yet for her tortured efforts only a few of the
passing people tossed coins into her hat.

Tuppence, he thought, remembering the old lady in
Mary Poppins who fed the pigeons. Like that old pigeon
lady, the woman who stood a few yards away exuded
loneliness, and loneliness was something Andy could
never turn away from.

He blinked as a passing stranger bumped his shoulder
and mumbled low obscenities on his way. The hurry of
dawn's somber crowd. The old woman was invisible to
them. It seemed a pity.

Her singing seemed to grow all the sweeter now. He

stepped closer, ignoring the impatient stir of those around
him, drawn by the sound of her voice.

The beauty of her singing denied her situation. Bag
ladies were supposed to be crazed, howling travesties of
womanhood, decaying representations of a luster that
might have been if only drink or brutality or drugs or
poverty hadn't grabbed them by the throat and pulled
down. Her clothes were old and shabby, but Andy could
tell that in her own eyes she wore the grandest and most
glittering of gowns as she took the stage. It made him
shiver: the astounding loveliness of that voice laid no
claim to her appearance or surroundings. He listened as
she sang:

> "Holy angel, in Heaven blessed,
>   My soul longs with thee to rest!"

He recognized it; one of Margarita's arias from *Faust*,
his mother's favorite opera. He smiled to himself.
Even the most accomplished of the world's sopranos
would shrink in envy were they to hear this old woman.

His smile widened. For just a moment he'd had an
image of his mother, God bless her, sitting in her rocking
chair in the nursing home listening to her opera records.
Her head was tilted back, her eyes were closed, and she
was lost in her favorite dream: that of being an opera
singer. The image was a touch bittersweet for Andy; his
mother had died in that nursing home, never getting the
chance to try out her dream in the outside world, and she
should have been able to, just once. Everyone should
know a moment like that, just once; a dream fulfilled,
no matter how small the dream or how brief the fulfill-
ment.

Andy shook himself back to the present as he reached
into his pocket for some money. The old woman deserved it; if not for her music, then for enabling him to
remember his mother without guilt or regret. He tried to
keep the smile on his face as he offered the five dollar
bill. He didn't want the old woman to think he pitied her.

Just once, he thought.

The old woman stopped singing. She turned, looked straight into his eyes, and clasped two strong hands around his wrist. She was much stronger than her thin frame suggested.

"Is something the matter?" said Andy.

"Raoul," she whispered, looking deeper into his eyes. Fear mixed with the ache in Andy's chest. He knew that many street people were only half sane, some maybe less, but he'd never imagined himself being this close to a loony—if that's what she was. Looking into her eyes of the softest blue he'd ever seen, he wondered if madness could eventually fold in on itself and appear as benevolence—for that's what stared back at him. Kindness. Lovingness. And emptiness.

"I beg your pardon?" he said.

She giggled and released his hand. "I'm sorry. You just reminded me of someone."

"Raoul?"

"M. le Vicomte Raoul de Chagny, to be exact," she replied. "He was a . . . friend of mine. It was a long time ago." She looked in her hand and saw the money. "Why so much?" she said.

It took him a moment to come up with an answer.

"You sing very well."

"Honey, I been singing like that all morning and ain't no one give me more than fifty cents a pop." Her gaze drilled deeper. "You don't look to be the high roller type, no offense meant."

"None taken," he said, relaxed by the woman's candor. A high roller he wasn't, though he sometimes wished he could tell people he was. Andy often wished he could boast of great accomplishments to people, display for them his many talents and regale them with stories of his grand triumphs, but the truth was this: there were no great accomplishments or grand triumphs, only a small, private handful of precious boyhood fantasies that kept him company, for Andy possessed no creative talents whatsoever—though he very much wanted to. Painting, poetry, acting, writing, music; he'd tried his hand at them all, failing in due succession and carrying the memories of those failures with him. But he did not harp on such things anymore. He was just a night janitor. No shame in that, but no glory either.

"Well," he said, pulling his hand away, "thank you very much."

"You still ain't told me what I did to deserve this."

"You sang beautifully."

"Bullshit."

"All right. You reminded me of my mother. *And* you sang beautifully."

"Really? Ha! Ain't that something. Tell me about your mom." He did, though he couldn't understand why. He told her about his mother, her dreams of the opera, how she'd wanted to be something more than she was, something she'd believe was special. But she was special to him, yet he could never convince her that there was no shame in just being a loving parent who made him proud. He spoke of the nursing home and how his mother insisted she be put there after his father died. He spoke of his regret and how he tried to fight it off whenever it showed up. Somehow all of his memories seemed so much finer as the old woman smiled and listened. She seemed to be as enraptured by his words as he was by her singing. He felt as if he were introducing this old woman to his mother and watching as they became quick old friends. When he finished he put his hands in his pockets and shrugged, thinking he should have felt awkward; he didn't.

"You seem like a sweet young man," said the old woman. "What's your name?"

"Andy."

"You seem very sweet, Andy, and I wanna thank you for the money. I can surely use it." She reached into a pocket of her coat and pulled something out. "I want you to take this," she said, shoving the object into his hand. "A little token of my gratitude."

Andy looked down; in his hand there lay a simple but lovely gold ring.

"I can't take this," he said.

"Sure you can," she replied. "I been waiting a long time to give that to someone special. Someone like you. We're a lot alike, you and me. I've been fighting regret all my life, too."

"You want to . . . get a cup of coffee or something?" It just came out. He almost withdrew the invitation, but he suddenly realized he'd made a friend of this old woman. Yes. He liked her a lot.

"Can't," she said. "I got me at least six more hours of good trade here." She punched his arm playfully and smiled through perfect teeth. "You maybe come back here tomorrow and try me again. Promise?"

"Promise," he said. It was Friday and he had the weekend off. Saturdays were usually reserved for reading or watching rented videos, a routine that had become stale years ago; not so much *boring,* but he'd been without companionship long enough that they now lacked a certain sparkle.

"I still can't accept this," he said, offering back the ring.

She rolled her eyes in good-humored impatience. "Just wear it for the rest of the day." She leaned toward him, her voice a mock conspiratorial whisper. "It's got magic powers."

"Right."

She pulled back, seeming a little huffed. "Why would I lie about it? Just wear it. If I'm crazy, then nothing will happen." She winked at him. "But if I'm telling the truth, well, then you've got a lot to look forward to, huh?" How could he resist that smile?

"Okay," he said. "But I'll still bring it back." He started to walk away when something occurred to him. He turned back. "What's *your* name?"

"People just call me Chris," she said. "Be seein' you tomorrow, Andy."

"Count on it." He was already looking forward to

seeing her again. He was about twenty yards away when he heard her call: "Have yourself an interesting evening!"

He waved at her without looking back. Then, just for the hell of it, he slipped the ring onto the wedding finger of his left hand. It fit perfectly. He smiled his surprise and turned to show Chris.

She was gone.

But the sound of her singing echoed back to him over the heads of those who chose not to hear.

II

Old furniture with handmade covers. A dusty piano his mother played when no one else was home. Books, many of them thrice read, crammed into every available space. A small record collection, mostly jazz, but he kept his mother's opera recordings to remember her by. Pictures of the family. A lazy cat that only stirred to eat and use the litter box. A television, a VCR, a collection of classic movies on videotape.

Home.

Everything about the house said: *Here is a son, the sum of his family's parts. This is not a great man, but a good one. He is not a poet, a leader or a visionary, but you will find yourself decently treated in this place, for it belongs to a decent man.*

Now he stood in front of the bathroom mirror. The reflection did not show him the man the boy often dreamed of becoming. He couldn't understand it. Since coming home this morning he'd found a great disquiet rising up in him. He knew it was because of the ring.

The ring. It lay on the basin, shining brightly under the light.

Why had she given it to him? Had it been some cheap gold-plated ring you could buy at Kmart for eight dollars he would not have felt so uneasy, but it wasn't cheap, not at all.

On a whim he'd stopped into a jewelry store to get the

ring appraised. He stood before the counter with his mouth dropping open as the jeweler explained about a special smelting process which originated in Paris during the late 1800s, a process used in the making of the ring. He pointed out the almost imperceptible details on the ring; the tiny engravings of musical notes. But the most surprising thing—and the most unnerving—was the name inscribed on the *inside* of the ring: Christine.

And next to the name, a date: 1891.

The jeweler said there was no easy way to affix a price, for the workmanship was so rare as to make the ring almost one of a kind, but he finally admitted it might be worth one, possibly two thousand dollars. Maybe even more.

Andy put down his razor, wiped the shaving cream off his face, and picked up the ring.

Two thousand dollars. Maybe more.

And she sang for pennies to buy food.

Tuppence, why have you no friends?

He examined the ring again, noting the beauty of the detail work. He wondered if Chris was related to the woman in the inscription. Perhaps the ring was a family heirloom or something. There was no question: tomorrow he would return it to her and tell her what the jeweler said. She could sell it and not have to beg for her meals. She could have a nice place to sleep, a place with a roof and a bed.

The ring glistened under the light, beckoning for him to put it back on. He slipped it back on his finger. He wouldn't lose it this way. It still mystified him that it fit so well; almost as if it had been designed with him in mind.

Still, there was the disquiet. Why had he been so ill at ease since waking up? He shook his head, touched the ring, looked up—

—and nearly lost his balance from the shock. Good God! The face that looked back at him! In the mirror there was now a death's head mask: eyes that stared out from blackened sockets, eyes of the deepest and most fiery red, skin shriveled and graying like that of a corpse, a mouth hideously twisted out of shape to resemble nothing human, and . . . his nose.

He stared, unbelieving.

His nose looked to have been bitten off, leaving only the two tearlike openings in the front of his skull. He could almost swear the bone was sticking through. With a shaking hand he reached up to touch the face of the monster. The lights flickered, casting the slightest of shadows on the terrible features, and in that flickering of shadows he watched as the face began to burn itself, an exposed film negative dissolving forever into the light. He could see the color of his own skin surfacing, the slight blush of his cheeks, his thin lips, his own eyes. The image of the monster was gone.

The flickering stopped and he was looking at his own face again.

He sat down hard on the toilet and tried to calm down, catch his breath. Tired, he was just tired, that was all, he needed to get out more, do more things, not spend so much time alone and—

He snapped his head up, smiling.

Jesus! Of course! He knew the face well enough. Lon Chaney. The good old Phantom himself. Why, he'd watched the movie on tape yesterday before going to work. That explained it. Man, how the mind played the damndest tricks on you at times.

But something in the back of his brain told him that yes, the face was *like* the one fashioned by Chaney for the classic scare film, but it was not *exactly* the same.

A knock at his front door forced the thought down before he could dwell on it too much. When he answered he was pleased to see Susan, his next door neighbor, standing there. A red-haired young woman who shimmered in his eyes, she always seemed to be busy, either with groups of friends or going out with the countless young men who came calling; but she always got home at a decent hour, never staying out all night or inviting her young men to spend the night with her. When she'd moved in, Andy helped her with some of the heavier furniture. She confided to him that she liked the neighborhood because it seemed to her an old-fashioned one, and she considered herself an old-fashioned gal. Andy never worked up the nerve to ask her for a date. She ran with a talented crowd, actors and musicians and writers and such, and he had nothing to offer her in those areas. Sure, he read a lot and liked to listen to music, but why should she spend her time with one who admired such things when she could be with those who *created* them? There was no bitterness in Andy's admission of this; it was simply the way things were.

"Hi," he said, feeling self-conscious.

"Sorry to bother you," she said, "but I was wondering if, well . . . this is sort of embarrassing . . ." Her hair was soaked and she held a blow dryer in one hand. "Did you just get a power surge? Did your lights flicker?"

"Yes." God, she was beautiful!

"Mine did, too," she said. "My power went off. I tried everything, but it won't come back on. You see, I have a date in about forty minutes and I was wondering if . . . well . . ."

He smiled and pulled open the door for her. "Sure. Come on in."

"Ah, my knight in shining denim," she said as she passed, touching his cheek and blowing a kiss. She went toward the bathroom, shaking her head and laughing. Andy smiled as the smell of her perfume enfolded him. This had happened before—four times, in fact—and each time he was more than happy to let her finish getting ready here. He liked the fact that he got to see her before her date. Sometimes she would ask how she looked and he would make suggestions, she—more often than not—would agree with them, and by the time her date pulled up she and Andy had turned her beauty up to full light. He liked that a lot. She thought of him, he knew, as a good friend and neighbor, nothing more. Damnit.

"So, where you off to?" he called to her over the roar of the blow dryer.

"The theater. Some group is doing *Macbeth* in Kabuki dress. Can you believe that? It'll be a scream." He stood off to the side, watching her. She leaned from one side to the other as the hot blasting air of the dryer blew her hair in every direction. He could well imagine what she would look like standing before a bonfire on some beach at night, the wind making her hair dance in the glow; perhaps she'd shiver a bit from the chilly breeze, toss her head to get some hair out of her eyes, then she'd smile and gesture for him to come over, and he'd come over, he'd get his ass over there like a thunderclap, but he wouldn't look desperate or anything like that. He'd be cool. Then they'd stand there snuggling and she'd turn to kiss him—and then someone would drop the Bomb or he'd get a call telling him he'd just won twenty skillion dollars or he'd wake up and find the cat licking his chin, demanding to be fed. He laughed at himself, then walked into the kitchen and poured the two traditional glasses of Pepsi they always drank before she left. Soon the dryer stopped and she called to him. She'd be right out.

He sat at the table, glasses of soda at the ready, his chin resting in the palm of his hand. She came out. She looked stunning; so what else was new?

"How do I look?"

"Stunning."

"I *know* that, the question is will my stunningness compare to that of a Kabuki Lady Macbeth?"

"Probably not, but you've got a better disposition." She crossed to the table, sat, downed her Pepsi in three gulps. Then she belched.

"You bring such dignity into my life," he said.

"Can I have another?"

"Take mine, I haven't touched it."

"You had all your shots?" He just smiled back. He never tried to get into bouts of verbal fencing with her; she was too quick. He imagined her surrounded by friends, all of them turning up the wit, trying to outdo each other. It must be something.

He found himself rubbing the ring as if for luck.

"I really look okay?"

"You really look okay." And then something shot forward in his head, latched onto his tongue, and forced him to open his mouth. "No, I take that back. You look incredible." Where was this suddenly coming from? "I think you are the most beautiful, exciting, attractive woman I have ever known." God, was this really coming out of *his* mouth? "If I could pull the image of my most perfect fantasy from my mind and give it life, it would be you." He felt his jaw drop. Oh, *Christ!*

It took a moment for her shock to wear off.

"My, my," she said. "That's quite an answer."

He fumbled for a way out. "Uh . . . I didn't mean . . . well, yes I did . . . but not . . ."

"Methinks you've said more than you intended, good sir."

"I . . . uh . . . haven't been up long. It takes my brain a little while to catch on. Now, if you'll excuse me, I'm going to go swallow lye." He rose and walked into the front room, cursing himself. *Nice shot, dumbass!* Spill your guts often? Oh, Lord, what was he supposed to do now?

He paced back and forth, feeling a hot surge of embarrassment turn his face red. Why in hell had he let that slip? Now she knew, ohgod, she knew and she was sitting right there in the kitchen and he—

"Everything all right?" she called.

"Yeah, just . . . checking something."

"Like what?" He froze. What was he supposed to say to that? Oh, brother. If the world had ended at that very moment, Andy might well have cheered.

My fantasy. What a yutz you are, Andy.

He looked down at his hands. God! They were shaking. And they *hurt!* They felt on fire.

How you gonna get yourself out of this, pal?

The fingers on both hands flexed involuntarily. He felt

dizzy. Thought the lights flickered again. The dizziness passed and he found himself sitting at the piano with his hands on the keys and he was, Jesus, he was *playing* and he knew it must sound horrible because the only thing he knew was "Chopsticks" and he'd played that so badly Mom found it hard not to laugh, but there was nothing he could do, he couldn't stop, couldn't lift his hands off the keys and now, ohgod, now Susan was standing in the doorway watching him, her eyes wide, she looked surprised but beyond that he couldn't tell anything but it didn't matter because he was just plain scared now as he watched his hands dance over the keys; he heard the notes but not the tune, he didn't know what it sounded like, but his hands wouldn't STOP he just wanted them to STOP and HOLD ON and KNOCK IT THE HELL OFF but no good, no go, they just kept playing and she kept watching as his fingers pressed down and the notes came out of the walls as he felt the sweat trickling off his forehead, dripping into his eyes, making him feel stupid, but the music kept coming as quickly as his breaths, the muscles in his arms were screaming as the music went on and on and on, so lovely, it must be lovely because she was smiling until, at last, his hands seemed to know it was time to finish: they made a grand flourish up and down the keyboard, then up again, cramping into the shape of spiders as they pounded out the last few chords then played out a soft closing measure.

He fell back, leaning against the wall, trying to breathe. Susan stood in the doorway, silent and staring.

He looked up at her. "I'm sorry," he said.

"What the hell for?" she whispered. "My God. I've never heard anyone play Rachmaninoff so beautifully."

"W-what?"

She came over and sat next to him on the bench. "Why didn't you ever tell me you played so well?"

He couldn't find an answer. He only knew that his hands wanted to play again.

She put an arm around his shoulders and kissed his

cheek. "You're just full of surprises tonight, aren't you? It's always the quiet ones."

He looked at her, his hands suspended in air above the keyboard. "I don't understand."

"Yes, you do. I always thought you were too shy for your own good." She kissed his cheek again. "You got a phone?"

He pointed to where it sat on the stand. Without a word she crossed over, made a call, came back.

"I'm all yours," she said.

"Huh?"

"I canceled my date. He wasn't understanding."

"But . . . why? Kabuki, and all that."

She sat down next to him and took his hands in hers. "Just listen to me, all right? Don't say a thing." She took a breath and smiled at him. "I have always been fond of you, Andy, but you never . . . did anything, you know? You were always the perfect gentlemen. Half the time I was worried that I was scaring you without meaning to. You never told me how you felt until tonight. God, I hope this doesn't sound silly. Yes, I could go to the theater with my date, but I'd rather not. All the guys I know are just so damn smooth. It's like they're going through this well-oiled routine on a date. They're not exactly putting on an act, but it lacks a certain amount of honesty. Not at all like you." She placed the palm of her hand against his cheek. "Why didn't you tell me how you felt? Why didn't you ever play for me before?"

"Just afraid . . . I guess. I've never been good at . . . social situations." He was getting dizzy again. God, what was happening?

She turned his face into hers and kissed him squarely on the mouth. He felt the blood rushing through him. She tasted so sweet, felt so good next to him.

She put her arms around him. "Well," she said, "thank God for power failures, huh?" He didn't know what to say, so he didn't say anything. It all seemed so absurd, so wonderfully absurd, and he decided that if he was hallucinating, he'd be content to stay this way.

"Play for me," she said. "Just for me." She sat in a chair a few feet away from him and smiled. He placed his hands on the keys.

It began again. As his hands flew up and down the length of the keyboard, the gold of Chris' magical ring caught the light and shone it back to him like the happiest of smiles. He felt strong now, and in Susan's gaze he felt proud. If this was what falling in love felt like, he wanted more. He wanted this never to end.

III

He woke on the sofa the next morning with Susan's scent all over him. It was the most pleasant waking he'd had in quite some time. They hadn't made love, but it didn't matter; the glowing feeling of her affection was within him. He laughed, noticing she'd forgotten her hair dryer. Maybe she'd come back over for it and have some coffee.

Just once, he thought, looking at the ring. He smiled at its golden shine, its lovely etchings, its—

Blood. He felt his heart skip a beat.

There was blood on both his hands. He stared at them, dumbfounded, looking for a cut of some kind; there was none. He rose quickly and went into the bathroom to wash.

He could not take the ring off. His hands would not respond to the command from his brain. He tried several times, but could not remove it.

He poured himself a cup of coffee and sat listening to the radio. He was lost in thought when the news came on. Then he lifted his head, very attentive.

Four people had been strangled to death last night, all victims of the same killer. Some historian described the type of lasso used in the killings, even gave its odd name, but Andy didn't hear it quite right.

He did, however, hear what the lasso had been made from.

Piano wire.

A terrible taste was in his mouth. His hands shook. He

wanted to tell himself there was nothing to it, but he knew differently, as surely as he knew Susan had kissed him endlessly last night before leaving.

He gulped down the coffee, ignoring the searing pain of the heat in his throat. He turned the radio off. Walked into the living room and stood next to the piano. Waited for something to happen.

So? Lift the lid, dummy! Simple enough: lift it up and look at all the wires, secure in their place with none missing. He reached out and grabbed the lid.

For a moment his hands refused to grip.

He bit his lower lip, concentrating.

Please, Tuppence Lady, he thought. *If this ring is magic, let it help me.*

He raised the lid. Looked down.

Held his breath.

At first he couldn't tell; there were so many wires, all pulled taut and looking . . . well, looking like the inside of a piano. But then he began to notice a few wires spaced farther apart than others. He propped the lid and bent in low, examining.

God.

He *wasn't* imagining it.

He blinked, wiped some sweat off his face, counted again.

No mistake. He stared into nothingness as his mind shuddered.

Four wires were missing.

Have yourself an interesting evening.

"Lose something?"

Her voice startled him; he pulled up on reflex and cracked his head into the piano lid.

Susan laughed as she pulled him in toward her. "Oh, hon, I'm sorry. Want me to kiss it and make it feel better?"

He doubted anything would make him feel better until he found Chris.

"Hey," said Susan, "you okay? You look . . . a little wired."

"I just . . . I just remembered something I didn't do at work. I'm gonna have to run over there for a little while."

She looked at him, then the piano. "You leave your tuning fork there or something?"

He forced out a laugh, quickly put the lid down before she noticed anything. "Nah, I was just . . . hell, I don't know."

"I understand. You musicians."

"I'm not a musician," he said weakly.

"The hell you're not! You're the best damned pianist I've ever heard, and I've heard plenty." She put her arms around his neck, played with his hair. "Of course, I *am* a bit biased now." Despite the terror in his chest he smiled at this. Then she kissed him. "Dinner tonight?" she said. "I'll cook. Then maybe we can rent a movie or something?"

He stared at her, still mystified. "You could go out with any guy you want."

She considered this for a moment, gave a nod. "You know, you're right. I *could* go out with any guy I want. But you're the only one I'd care to stay in with." She turned and saw her dryer lying on the chair. "Oh, there it is."

He hoped she didn't suspect anything.

She gathered up her dryer and started out the door. "You better show up at eight or I'll be heartbroken." She stopped in the doorway and looked at him; so radiant, so serious. "You're not gonna break my heart, are you, Andy?"

"Oh, God, no! No."

"Good," she said, smiling. "I think we've both had enough of that." Then she was gone.

Three minutes later Andy was running toward the downtown square. He had to find Chris, and soon. The ring, the damned ring had done it all. It had made him play and . . . and . . .

He couldn't imagine it made him kill, but it had. He'd played so beautifully and Susan heard him and—

—he stopped, short of breath—

—*and then she kissed him.* Ohgod.

He stared at the ring on his finger. What if the ring caused her to feel the way she did? What if it wasn't him at all, but the ring?

It's got magic powers.

He walked slowly then, lost in thought and worry. Then he heard an echo. The sweetest of all echoes. Chris was singing. Someplace near. He stood immobile amid the milling bodies and tried to find where her voice was coming from. His left hand felt on fire. It seemed to be pushing him to go east, so he did, following the fire until it led him to a corner far from where he'd met her.

She stood there, unnoticing of him, pouring out Margarita's tortured soul to anyone who would listen. In her voice was the rage of love unfulfilled, the anguish of a passion so strong it could no longer be contained. Andy had never before heard such a sound. Even now people were slowing as they walked, many of them looking at her with respect and surprise, even awe. She reached the crescendo of the aria's final stanza, and when she finished there were shouts of admiration and loud applause from the small crowd gathered round. There was money this time, green money, not coins. She folded her hands over her chest and curtsied with splendid grace. Soon the crowd was off to their worlds of work and worry, leaving her to sing for others.

"I knew this would be a better corner," she shouted to a woman who'd given her a five. Then she sat on her wooden crate, dipped into her hat, began counting the money. She was still counting when Andy walked over to her.

When she looked up a small shriek escaped her; she quickly covered her mouth, eyes wide with horror, and looked away. "I'm sorry, Erik . . . please, my love, please, I beg your forgive—" Her words cut off when she glanced back. The terror left her face. After a moment she even smiled, but it was strained. Her body shook with the aftersurge of fear. "Andy, I—"

"Who's Erik?"

"An old . . . I knew him once. Long ago." Her face pleaded with him not to press her for further details, but the lingering memory of the blood on his hands fueled his confusion into something akin to rage.

"The ring," he said. "Why can't I remove it?"

"Ah, yes," she said. "The ring. You put it on, after all?"

"Yes, I did. And you know what happened then, don't you?"

"Erik," she whispered. "Will you never be free? Will I?" She began gathering up her belongings and money. "Come. We must go somewhere and speak of this privately."

Andy snapped his gaze up to meet hers. Her voice was different now; it sounded the same, but the inflections were sharper, the vocabulary more formal.

As if she knew it was no longer necessary to put on an act.

He followed her until they found a small coffee shop where he bought them hot rolls and tea. As she ate her meager breakfast he told her everything; about the face, the playing, the strangulations and missing wires from the piano, about Susan and how she'd come to him after he played, all of it. Spoken in near-panic.

"What do you know of the ring?" she asked. "You know something. I can tell by your eyes."

He told her about his visit to the jeweler's and all he found there. "Who is Christine? Was she your great-grandmother or someone like that?"

"No. *I* am Christine."

He stared at her, unbelieving. "You can't be. That'd make you—"

"Exactly one hundred and twenty-eight years old, yes. Believe it. My name is Christine Daaé and I disappeared after a performance at the Grand Opera in Paris in 1891. Because of me many innocent people lost their lives. Sit back, my dear Andy. I have a story I wish to tell you."

Andy sat back, but he couldn't relax. Not at all.

"The weapon used to kill those people," she said, "is called a Punjab lasso. It was used by only the most skilled assassins of Persia, long before that country was called Iran. Some credit the Gypsies with inventing the lasso, but its true inventor was never known. However, the one who was most lethal in the ways of its use . . . he was quite famous, but not for that."

"Raoul?" asked Andy.

"No, not at all." She stared long and hard at him before speaking again. Something like terror mixed with pity crossed her face as she said: "Erik. But you would know him better by the name history gave him. 'Le Fantome de l'Opera.' "

Andy felt his stomach drop as he remembered the terrible death's head mask in his mirror. "My God, I thought that was all—"

"A fiction?" she said. "Such was the intention, for Leroux knew well that none would believe so outlandish a tale. But the Opera Ghost, as he was known then, really existed. He was born in the small village of Rouen to simple but good parents, a carpenter and his wife. However, at birth his face and much of his body were hideously deformed. His mother and father, believing the child a punishment from God, gave him no love whatsoever. He ran away at a very young age and made his living as a freak in a sideshow. During this time he learned many things: how to sing, which he did with stunning beauty and power; how to use the Punjab lasso, with which he became quite skilled at strangulation; how to compose the glorious music that exploded from his very soul; and he learned the art of designing and building great palaces. He was widely acclaimed to be the most original mind on the Continent, and his reputation earned him an invitation from the Shah-in-Shah to come to the palace at Mazenderan, where the little sultana was becoming bored and unruly.

"It was in this way that the Shah came to acquire Erik's talents for his own use. He quickly encouraged Erik's musical talents as well as his skills in assassination. He even coaxed Erik into building a series of torture chambers for the little sultana to amuse herself by slowly killing friends fallen out of favor or the wretches who awaited execution under the Shah's unjust regime.''

She swallowed hard before going on, obviously pained. ''You must understand that during this time Erik's contempt for himself and humanity worsened. Here was a young man whose heart could have held up the empires of the world. He had the greatest of musical gifts to offer, but those remarkable talents had been placed in a form so loathsome even the strongest of people shrank away in fear at the sight of him. Here was a man who should have walked with kings, danced with princesses, and inspired poets; instead he ended up scuttling through cellars with rats, afraid to show his horrid form or reveal any capacity for human love. Such pity hearts should have had for him.''

She took another breath, wiped away a tear, and continued her sad tale. ''The Shah quickly lost interest in Erik and ordered him executed, but before that could be done Erik escaped to Paris, where he fashioned a false face to wear in public and found employment helping to build the new Grand Opera House. While working he fashioned for himself a series of chambers underneath where he made his home. These chambers were so low and dark that not even the rats would venture down so far. He lived there like a dog for many years. A dog. But he was a man. A man in pain, in torment. A man who was nearly mad from loneliness, anger, unused love, and a thirst for revenge against a world that shunned his gifts because of the way he looked.

''And then he found me.'' She looked at Andy and tried to smile, couldn't do it. ''He said that my voice awakened his love and romantic passion, for I had true greatness when I sang, though it needed training. So he trained me. It is because of him that I sing as I do. But he fell in love with me . . . obsessively in love. The details are long and sordid; suffice to say that, in the end, he knew he could not win my heart and agreed to let me leave with Raoul—the man I truly loved. Erik even arranged our disappearance that night. He was most kind to me. He killed many people that night to ensure our escape, but the atrocities were committed out of love for me. I know now that his was a true love. So very true.''

She pointed to the ring on Andy's finger. ''That ring was a gift from him. He placed it on my finger. He told me he'd blessed it with powers, magical powers. Erik had a great but secret interest in the ways of the occult. I believe that he made a pact with . . . whatever or whomever that his soul be transferred into that ring upon his death.''

''How?'' said Andy. ''If the ring was with you?''

''After Erik died I returned to Paris and placed the ring on his finger, as he'd instructed me to do the night I left. I then waited one week and hired grave-robbers to steal his body from the pauper's cemetery so I could take back the ring. And, just as Erik said, it contains all the powers and gifts that were once his. Even the echo of his image. That is why I cringed upon seeing you. For a moment you were him in every way.''

''What about Raoul?''

''He died many years ago from drink. The last few years of my life with him were a nightmare of beatings and . . . things worse. I do not wish to talk about it.''

Chastened, he pointed to the ring. ''Why did you give it to me?'' His voice was tight and strained.

''At first you reminded me of Raoul when he was younger. But when I looked into your eyes I saw a pure soul, a good and loving soul, a soul that very much wanted a talent but had none. I saw the loneliness in your eyes. You so very much deserved a talent, how could I not give it to you? You are so kind.'' A tear escaped her eye and slid down her cheek.

Andy once again felt the tight ball of pressure pull up in his chest. ''But . . . the killings . . .''

''I know,'' she said. ''I had believed that Erik transferred only his musical talents, his *creative* talents, to the ring. Now I see that his anger and thirst for revenge

live on in it, also.'' She began to reach across and take
the ring back. Andy saw the pain and terror in her eyes.
His mind reached over all she'd told him, and then—

—*holygod*—

—and then he *knew*. The look on her face told him,
and he knew. ''He tricked you somehow, didn't he?''

''No. It was not a deception. I believe, in the end, he
wanted to give everything that was good in himself to the
ring, but by that time so much of his spirit had blackened
he could not control the transfer. I know what he was
like toward the end, how sad and lonely and repentant,
and I cannot easily believe that he passed on his murderous skill purposefully.''

''I'm not talking about that,'' said Andy. ''He died,
Raoul died, yet you didn't. He tricked you into—''

''No,'' she said, raising a hand. ''It was my choice. I
knew that I would not be able to die until I passed the
ring on to one who was *willing* to accept its powers. I
just didn't . . . didn't think it would take so long.''

''I understand,'' said Andy. ''You know I can't remove
it now.''

''Only *I* can remove that ring from your finger.''

He blinked, took a deep breath. ''God, how can I let
you now?''

''It was cruel and stupid, what I did, giving you the
ring without knowing the extent of its power! Until I met
you and saw what was in your eyes, I had never encountered a soul worthy of Erik's musical gifts! Please, Andy,
I like you so very much and you must believe that if I'd
known the ring held his ability and desire to kill, I *never*
would have given it to you.''

''What . . . what am I supposed to do now?'' he said.
''If I give it back to you, you can't die, and if I keep it
. . .'' His words trailed off. There was no need to say
more. After a while he was able to say: ''Did the ring
cause Susan to . . . to . . .''

''I don't know,'' said Christine. ''Perhaps it just allowed for your true feelings to surface and she responded

to them. She may have fallen under the spell of the music. I just don't know.''

Andy turned and looked out the window. Couples young and old were walking past, holding hands, laughing, lost in the wonderful silliness of love and romance. He tried to picture himself and Susan at sixty-five, walking past a coffee shop window and holding hands while some lonely-looking young man followed them with his eyes and wondered: *Will I ever be that happy?* "Why does it have to be this way?" he said. "Why does love always have to carry a knife with it? Why is it that no measure of happiness can be without an equal measure of misery? I'll never understand how human beings can allow something as worthless and destructive as loneliness to go on existing. Look what it's done to you.''

"And you,'' she said.

He wiped his eyes and rose. "How long would I have to wear it?''

Christine wrinkled her brow in confusion. "I don't . . . don't . . .''

"Until you die? How long?''

She swallowed. Her sad eyes glistened in the noonday sun. "One week. The same as when Erik wore it.''

He reached out and took her hand. "Will I get caught?''

"No. Impossible. He knew too well how to avoid it, how to hide. You'll carry that with you.''

He thought long before speaking again. "I suppose that, in a way, it's not really me, is it?''

"No. It's Erik, but that still will not—''

"—make it any easier, I know!'' He lowered his voice, calmed himself. "Sorry. I didn't mean to shout at you like that. I'm just not . . . not sure.'' And he thought: *murder.*

All of it was murder. His hands had taken four lives last night and now were cursed to take more.

He looked down at Christine's aged and saddened face.

What about *her* curse? Would it really be that bad, being immortal? To never face the fear of death?

Yes, came the answer.

It would be. To fall in love over and over again and watch as your loved ones died while you lived on. It was unthinkable. It was too cruel.

But to *kill!*

He watched as the waiters and waitresses served their other patrons. He noticed the color of their hair, the looks in their eyes, the Band-Aids a few of them wore because of cuts in the kitchen, and he wondered about the value of commonplace dreams dreamt by commonplace people. Would any of them be willing to kill in order to possess a talent others would respect and admire?

Perhaps they would.

But he couldn't. And he could not allow Christine to go on as she had been, now that he knew the pain she must endure, the sorrow that clung to her.

Loneliness and its effects. You could only measure life by loneliness and its effects. Why did it have to be this way?

He looked at another waitress. Saw her, a Band-Aid, the tiredness.

He made his decision. "You got it," he said.

Christine's face collapsed under the sudden weight of relief. She pulled his hand to her lips and kissed it with more affection than he'd ever known. "I do not believe that I have ever loved any man half as much as I love you right now," she said. "You have freed me." She rose and touched a gentle hand to his face. "I have one last favor to ask of you."

"Name it."

"Once during a lesson, Erik sang with me. I have not since sung as well or with as much passion and skill. His voice, you see, is within you now. Will you . . . could you . . ."

"It would be an honor." And so they left the coffee shop and returned to Christine's special corner where they sang together. Andy did not know where the words and notes came from, he only knew that they created the most glorious sounds, sounds of love and anguish, longing and glory. Between their breaths he could feel her pain and isolation die away.

Perhaps the memory of this time would comfort him later. Perhaps.

So they sang.

And in some Elsewhere, angels wept at the beauty of the sound.

IV

On the seventh day he returned to her corner and found the ambulance there. A small crowd had gathered round to watch as the attendants lifted her into the back.

She was still alive. She called his name.

He went to her.

"It is done," she whispered to him. "I . . . shall always be so grate—'

She was dead.

He made his way quickly from the scene, trying to hide his tears. He ran blindly for what seemed miles, until he could run no more. He fell on a bench and sat there trying to breathe.

Eventually he calmed himself and rose, remembering his small steel lockbox. He walked until he came to the harbor, then heaved the box—which was weighted down with stones—over the fence. He smiled as he watched it sink.

"Rest," he whispered to the ripples. "It's all over now. I promise."

Sometime later—he wasn't sure how long, time had meant nothing to him the last several days—he found himself in front of Susan's door. He knocked. When she answered, there were no words for a few moments.

Her face pulled in on itself as she threw her arms around him. "Ooooh, you little shit. I've been trying to find you all week. When you didn't show up for dinner, I knew something was wrong."

"It was just a damn silly accident," he said. "Some of the equipment is a little tricky."

She pulled him inside and sat next to him on the sofa, holding onto him as if she never intended to let go. "When I heard about it I got so scared. God, it must've been terrible."

"I've had better . . . times. I'm just grateful it was only *a part* of my hand." She reached down and touched the bandaged stump. He winced. God! Was it ever going to stop hurting? If his aim had been better, it would have been just the ring finger, but . . .

"You know my piano playing days are over?"

"I don't care about that," she said. "I'm just glad it wasn't . . . well, you know . . . something even worse." She stroked the back of his head. "What am I gonna do with you?"

"Not break my heart?"

"That's a given, dummy."

"Then how about something to eat?" She kissed him and went to the kitchen to make some lunch.

Andy sat in the living room, staring at her upright piano a few feet away from him. His left hand felt on fire, but that couldn't be, especially where it was the worst— his last two fingers. They weren't there anymore.

He laughed to himself.

Phantom pains, he thought.

He crossed to the piano and sat on the bench.

Lifted the cover.

Okay, Erik, he thought. *Let's see if you're finally at peace, too.*

He placed his hands on the keys.

DAW

Welcome to DAW's Gallery of Ghoulish Delights!

HOUSE SHUDDERS
Martin H. Greenberg and Charles G. Waugh, editors
  Fiendish tales about haunted houses!
☐ UE2223 $3.50

HUNGER FOR HORROR
Robert H. Adams, Martin H. Greenberg, and Pamela Crippen
Adams, editors
  A devilish stew of horror from the master terror chefs!
☐ UE2266 $3.50

RED JACK
Martin H. Greenberg, Charles G. Waugh, and Frank D.
McSherry, Jr., editors
  The 100th anniversary collection of Jack the Ripper tales!
☐ UE2315 $3.95

VAMPS
Martin H. Greenberg and Charles G. Waugh, editors
  A spine-tingling collection featuring those long-toothed ladies
  of the night—female vampires!
☐ UE2190 $3.50

THE YEAR'S BEST HORROR STORIES
Karl Edward Wagner, editor
  ☐ Series IX   UE2159—$2.95
  ☐ Series X   UE2160—$2.95
  ☐ Series XI   UE2161—$2.95
  ☐ Series XIV   UE2156—$3.50
  ☐ Series XV   UE2226—$3.50
  ☐ Series XVI   UE2300—$3.95